ROOTS OF THE ANCESTORS

BURDEN OF FATE

R.A. SISCO

Published in the United States of America by Sisco Publications
First originally published by Page Publishing 2022

ISBN 979-8-9901470-0-3 (paperback)
ISBN 979-8-9901470-1-0 (digital)
ISBN 979-8-9901470-2-7 (hardcover)

CHAPTER 1

Moisture gathers on the inside of an old Chevy as it rolls down the highway. Rain pouring down by the bucket full as its wipers move so fast that it seems they could snap off. The driver squints through the deluge, barely able to make out the road as his free hand reaches up and wipes away some of the fog forming on the window. The driver is a gruff man, more than rough around the edges, sporting a three-day beard and a two-day hangover. Dark brown hair juts out from under his old trucker cap down past his ears, framing in angry brown eyes that belie the playful smirk on his face. His complexion is dark from long hours spent working under a hot sun, making it hard to hammer down a distinct ethnicity although his fashion sense can only be defined as redneck.

His name is Richard Dunn. He is larger than most men, standing well over six feet tall. Broad shoulders and a solid frame fill the seat, his right leg rests against the center console, foot switching back and forth from gas to brake while his left foot lazily toys with the high beam plunger behind the clutch. A weathered brown flannel wards off the cold, the barely legible tag attached to the neck pokes out above the collar. His button-up blue denim work shirt is stained and tattered, threadbare in several places. Discount jeans that were better off as cotton with a pair of high-quality work boots finish off the ensemble.

As he hurdles down the road, he clicks on the radio and tunes to the nearest station. The local news is on.

"A wave of burglaries targeting morgues and funeral homes has the local sheriff baffled and disturbed. Evidence suggests doors and windows were forced open from *inside* the buildings. Authorities say that the purpose of these larcenies is as of yet, unclear, and declined further comment. Details at the top of the hour." Outro music plays as the station shifts to commercials.

"Bunch of sick fuckers…," Rich mumbles to himself.

To his right, a female voice speaks up.

"Yeah. No doubt. I bet ya they are stealing organs or something. Some kind of black market stuff."

A pile of fabric rustles next to Rich, a head slowly emerges from near the top. Two soft hazel eyes gently open and take in their surroundings. Slowly, the head rises to reveal a neck hued in a lovely cocoa brown with a shoulder following. Her curly hair is worn short but still long enough that a rouge coil falls from her hood and lands in her eyes. She raises her arms over her head as she stretches then reaches out toward the dash resembling a cat roused from napping. Well-manicured nails reflect the light of oncoming traffic, casting little sparkles onto the roof of the truck. Her toned long arms retract and wrap around her chest as she shivers off the cold. Her build comes off delicate at first until she is observed closely, then one can see her capable frame is coated in a defined muscle that constricts and bulges as she jockeys for a more comfortable position in her seat.

Long legs twist around themselves as they stretch the sleep out. Her skin was taut and flawless as though she were carved from ebony. Her muscles writhe under her fitted sportswear as she vigorously rubs her shoulders in a vain attempt to generate heat. She is adorned in high-end athletic clothing. Her name-brand running shoes were covered in a multicolored menagerie of neon reminiscent of the 1980s. Black tight-fitting capris sat above them. Twin bright orange stripes go up the left leg. Her top was of the same brand, but its stripes ran the length of the right sleeve. She shakes her black hoody loose from behind her and draws it close as she zips it up. She shivers as she wraps her thick blanket around her again. She looks at Rich and with a terrible country accent says, "Nah, guys, let's take muh truck. It's much better-er fer huntin'."

Rich rolls his eyes and grunts with laughter. "Perhaps we should have taken your hybrid then? I'm sure there would have been room for an elk in the back…"

"Yeah, *sure, whatever.* At least my *hybrid* has a working *heater,*" she replies as she rolls toward the passenger side door. Her thoughts drift toward her workout routine and how she's committing one of the most heinous sins of the gym—she's skipping leg day to spend time with her friends. "Might as well be doin' curls in the squat rack…," she whispers under her breath.

From the back, she hears,

"Sonya Sheppard, what will we do with you? The gym will be there when you get back."

Sonya turns her head around to face the source of the voice and smiles.

The voice in the back seat takes form and lifts upright. His name is Evan Faust. He is silhouetted from the headlights behind them until an oncoming semi reveals his features. His hair is red as fire with skin white as milk. Pale blue eyes squint hard against the illuminating assault. With his wispy form momentarily revealed, were it not for the presence of epidermis, one would think a skeleton had just sat up from its grave. His hands reach forward and grasp the top of the seat, he leans in, crosses his arms, and rests his chin on them. His sunken cheeks and bulging eyes make him appear jester like in low light. As he perches there, his comically long spindly arms fall over the seat and into the front.

A long neck and narrow shoulders lean in as his head slowly worms its way into the front half of the cab. He is wearing a ghastly mustard brown baggy sweater that is at least three sizes too big. It is so oversize that it slips over one shoulder, forcing him to pull it back up every so often. The design and color insinuate that his sweater is likely as old as the truck he is riding in. To make matters worse, he is wearing large pajama pants, sporting a print of an avocado wearing sunglasses that is assuming various sexual positions with a slice of toast. His feet are bare, but on the floor of the truck, there are a pair of open-toed sandals and some socks with more than an allowable number of holes. If it weren't for the fact that he's wearing top-of-the-line Bluetooth headphones and holding an equally high-tech cell phone, one may think he is a transient hitching a ride to the next town.

The old diesel pickup careens down the highway, its passengers all lost in thought. They have been driving for nearly three hours now. It was well before dawn when Rich picked them all up. Evan had decided to crash at Sonya's house to make logistics easier, and were it not for the trio having known one another for over three decades, Evan would have been more resistant to this adventure. So given their extensive relationship and Sonya's threats of violence, he decided his attempts at becoming a professional streamer could take a spot on the back burner for a weekend. He honestly wasn't sure how long it had been since he was this far from home. As they draw further away from civilization, his signal grows weaker and weaker. He painfully watches as his bars drop faster than a new hit single. With a groan of discontent, he turns off his phone, then his headphones and places both gently in an equally expensive backpack. With a crack of his knuckles and a healthy yawn, he rouses from his cybernetic coma.

"Hey, Rich…," mumbles Evan, "what kind of stereo do you have in this old beast?"

Rich laughs under his breath. "This 'old beast' is equipped with the finest quality audio equipment money could buy you… In 1980…"

"Okay, *Rich*. What would that be, and does it actually work?" chides Sonya.

"Well, *Sonya*, what we have here"—Rich leans over and opens the glove box—"is a gen-u-ine, one-of-a-kind, Ohh Eee Emm, 8-Track." He pulls out a large plastic brick from the cavernous expanse of his truck's jockey box.

"Holy shit, Rich, are you serious? Maybe if you spent less money on all these 'muddin' tires,' you could afford something from this century," interjects Evan.

Rich rolls his eyes as he holds up the 8-track, "Ladies and, well, Evan, this is a copy of George Straits 1987 hit, Ocean Front Property." He ceremoniously blows off the business end of the tape and gently inserts it into the player. With a slight twist of a knob and the press of a button, the ancient piece of technology grinds to life. A song starts to play from the doors of the truck, its quality rough and gritty. Evan actually appears to be in physical pain for a moment, and Sonya's brows raise then furrow at the audible distortion of the old player. The first few notes of the song come gliding out of the stereo's speakers, Rich's fingers drum on the steering wheel in nostalgic excitement.

He takes a deep breath as the intro closes in on the first verse, and as he goes to belt out the lyrics, he is met with a harsh grating sound that permeates the cab and forces those with free hands to cover their ears for fear of being deafened. Rich hastily lunges for the volume knob to shut off the auditory assault. While attempting to both steer and end the chaos, the knob snaps clean off the deck. The noise persists, slightly louder now. The occupants are screaming out in protest as Rich fumbles with the machine in a vain attempt to shut it off. In a fit of rage, he snaps the 8-track out of the player and then reaches under the dash. He begins swerving sharply, causing Sonya to panic and grab the steering wheel. Rich blindly tries to find the back of the stereo, and once located, he rips the wiring from the connector, the screeching stops, allowing a stillness to overtake the cab until it gets shattered again by Evan.

"Wow, Dick, that was an amazing song. Thanks for sharing that with the class. Best…song…ever," says Evan in a dramatically sarcastic tone.

"Fuck off, Evan. Even the noise of my 8-track dying is better than that whiny emo bullshit you listen to." Rich huffs in mourning. "I'll have you both know that cartridge was worth money. It was a collector's item."

"Yeah. Like your truck?" Evan quips.

"Kiss the fattest part of my ass, Evan," Rich replies.

"I'm sorry," whines Evan, "you're going to have to be more specific than that. It's hard to tell exactly where you mean."

"Okay, ladies," says Sonya, as she throws her hands up in a mock attempt to break up their catfight.

"Rich, your truck is old. Older than your granddaddies buckskin condoms. Evan, your taste in electronics is posh AF. Wish the same could be said for your clothes. We are all tired from the excruciating lack of sleep since we just *had* to be in the woods before daylight. An' frankly, if y'all don't chill the fuck out, I just may Dick Cheney your asses once we hit some dirt roads…"

Rich and Evan are both silent for a moment. Evan is the first to make comment. "Uhhhmmm…what does a Dutch-Jewish diarist have to do with the forty-sixth vice president?"

"What?" Sonya says as she kicks her head slightly to one side, glaring at Evan.

"You said Anne Frankly," whispers Rich.

"And Dick Cheney," adds Evan.

"I did not say Anne Frankly. I said, 'And frankly.' Get your shit straight, George," Sonya retorts with a venomous tone.

"*Hey*, don't you *dare* use his name in vain. That man is a legend. Hell, you were both probably conceived to one of his songs. I know I certainly was."

"Rich…what road were you looking for, again?"

"Nehalem Highway, Mr. Evan, sir."

Evan laughs. "Well, you just passed it, homie…"

Rich sighs deeply as he slows the truck and eases it to the shoulder. "Guess I better turn around then…" He sighs.

He holds the clutch in while throttling the engine, the turbo starts to spool, its whistle growing louder. With a reckless grin on his face, he slips his toe off the clutch, forcing the back wheels to spin and scream against the pavement. He cranks the wheel sharply to the left, slinging the ass end of his truck around the front until they are facing the way they came.

"Let's see your hybrid do *that*!" mocks Rich.

Sonya smirks and then frowns at Rich. She slowly raises her hand, extending her middle finger proudly. "At least I actually care about the environment, Dick…"

The party travels in silence for a while. Pavement turns to old concrete, which then gives way to hard-packed gravel. The homes become scarcer as the crew winds further and further into the wilderness. Daylight has begun to pierce through the dark sky, dimly illuminating the dense foliage in a murky gray hue. Evan powers up his phone, hoping that maybe there is a slight shred of signal. Sonya is busy taking selfies with the forest as her backdrop. Rich is focused on the coming hunt. It's been a while since he took time off work for anything. He feels somewhat out of place, uneasy that he isn't on the clock, keeping his hands busy and mind distracted. He begins to reminisce about days gone, but his thoughts turn to an unpleasant place, and he forces himself to speak, "So, guys, we're almost there. I know we wanted to be there before daylight, but it's just now dawn, so I think we should be okay."

"Who's 'we'? You got a turd in your pocket?" Evan asks.

"What the fuck is that supposed to mean, exactly?" Rich replies. "I'll have you know that was a royal 'we' because your opinion matters naught. Peasant."

Evan laughs. Rich smiles and looks on down the road, glad to have broken the silence and given his mind something to digest. Sonya stares out the window as they push on, lost in the landscape of the forest as Rich cruises slowly down the gravel road. As she studies the flora, a deep chill concentrates in the back of her neck. Her eyes are drawn to something ahead protruding from the brush, but as her eyes focus on it, she can see what appears to be a person. As they draw closer, she can see it's a male form wrapped in a thick gray cloak, hunched forward slightly as he leans on a walking stick. Sonya's eyes catch the figure and are fixated. Their travel seems to slow as they pass the wanderer. Sonya can't look away. Something about this figure has her so entranced, so incredibly intrigued that she rapidly rolls the window down and leans her head out to get a clear view.

"What the hell, Sonya!" objects Evan to the sudden blast of bitterly cold air.

Sonya is undisturbed by his protest. She wants only to gaze upon this stranger. She drinks him in as they approach, her body begins to tingle with exhilaration.

They are nearly next to him now, her eyes straining from the intensity of her stare. His hooded visage is almost tangible. As the brim of his cloak passes, his face is now visible. First, she sees a beard, long and white with not a single hair following along with another. Then the tip of his nose, red and chapped from the cold air. His cheeks follow suit. Then his eyes come into view, closed lids with a furrowed brow. She gazes inquisitively, drinking in his peculiar but strangely familiar profile. As they pass by, she looks back after him, and without any motion, his eyes snap open to reveal a deep red iris. A gaze razor-sharp pierces right through Sonya. She inhales hard as she is clutched by his stare. A rush of sensation flies through her mind as if a thousand voices echo inside her all at once. The stranger turns away, releasing her from his enchantment. She bats her eyes several times, unsure of what just happened. She looks back only to see a withered old tree stump that had snapped off about a man's height from the ground. With the ferocity of his image still plaguing her, she sits back in her seat and gently rolls up the window.

Evan asks, "Are you okay? You gonna barf or something?"

"Didn't you see him?" she responds.

"Uhhhhhhhh…no… Rich, do you know what she's talking about?" says Evan.

"I didn't see shit, man. Just focused on the road," he replies.

"My eyes are just tired. It must have been the light playing tricks on me or something. Forget it."

Sonya's not sure if what she thinks she saw was real or just some ocular fantasy brought on from sleep deprivation. She brushes it off and tries to act cool.

"I totally thought I saw a Bigfoot or maybe just one of Rich's relatives?" she jests, attempting to play off her odd behavior.

Rich scoffs with indignation. "I will have you know, we Dunn's revere and respect the Bigfeet of the forest. Have for centuries."

Rich sees the old dirt logging road up ahead. "Here we are, fellas!" Sonya smacks him in the ribs and says, "I'm a *girl*. Be *inclusive!*"

Rich feigns grave injury as he slowly pulls over to a wide turn out alongside the road. He sets the parking brake on his old truck and places the transmission into first gear then shuts the engine off. He energetically leaps from the driver seat and heads to the tailgate. Evan groans and looks at Sonya. "Do we really have to, Sonya…?"

"He needs us right now. The anniversary is next week. I'm just glad he's sober. For now. So just get your shit together, play along, we will be done soon enough and back home in no time," she says.

"All right. Fine. I guess. Let's get this done with." Evan moans as he sits up and opens his door. He eases himself into his sandals as he steps out of the truck.

Sonya sighs quietly to herself and gathers her things into their bag. The image of the old man creeps back into her mind's eye. She is still disturbed by how it felt when she looked him in the eyes and how she felt like for that split second someone was living in her head with her. She shakes it off and opens her door, stepping out into the forest. Breathing in the crisp air, feeling the oxygen-rich atmosphere fill her lungs. It brings her a small wave of calm, easing her nerves. She smiles and walks around to the rear of the truck where her friends are.

From just a few yards away, those same red eyes watch her quietly as she walks toward her friends. A smile cracks his wrinkled face as he turns and heads deeper into the woods. He hums quietly to himself as he goes, his walking stick poking into the brush as he goes.

"They are coming," he whispers aloud as his shape fades to a silhouette, then disappears into the forest completely.

CHAPTER 2

Rich tries to lower the tailgate of his truck, the handle sticks a bit at first, but after a few attempts at manipulation, he grunts with a mild rage and smashes his fist into the area next to the handle, causing an audible *clank* to resonate from inside the tailgate. It slams open as though the truck was in pain from its state of disrepair. One corner hangs lower than the other thanks in part to a broken steel cable that is no longer supporting its side.

"Dude, is there anything on this truck that actually does what it's supposed to do? Or was it busted from the factory?" Evan mocks.

"Evan, I know it's an ugly bitch at first glance… But it's not the looks that matter. I have spent thousands on the engine and transmission alone. This truck is far beyond anything else on the road right now."

"How exactly is this better than a newer truck?" Evan asks.

"Well, I am very glad you asked." Rich grins. "It all starts with the engine, you see. It's a—"

Sonya cuts him off, "It's an ugly truck that runs great but has no heater and a stereo that tries to kill you with sound. 'Nuff said."

Rich, looking slightly off-put at losing his chance to talk shop with Evan, lifts the hatch of the truck's canopy and grabs three packs from just inside the bed along with a large shopping bag. Rich opens the sack and grabs prearranged bundles of clothing from within it, handing one to each of his friends. They dress in silence with the tension of the long and unpleasant car ride still weighing on them.

Rich had taken the liberty of purchasing old surplus camo for his friends, and he guessed their sizes pretty well. Sonya was unhappy with the unflattering fit of her pants, and Evan was still too thin to fill in his shirt, which was sized "extra medium" according to Rich. Evan reaches into the bed, pulling out two of the three hiking bags.

He hands one to Sonya and leaves the other on the tailgate for Rich. After a few brief moments, they are all fully assembled and ready for their excursion.

"What kind of sniper rifle did you bring? .308? .7 mm? .338 Lapua?" Evan asks.

With a rather cross expression on his face, Rich states, "There is no such thing, Evan. A 'sniper' is the man behind the rifle. The rifle is the tool."

Rich continues to elegantly lecture Evan on the disciplines involved in long-distance shooting while Sonya opens her issued bag and starts examining its contents. There are some light provisions, a couple of bottles of water, a small first aid kit, a thermal blanket, and under that, a large silver handgun in a black holster.

"Uhhh, Rich, I think I got the wrong bag. There's a bazooka in mine."

Rich laughs as he takes the bag from her. "Sorry, Sony. That was supposed to be my bag."

"Wait a sec, you're going to have *both* guns?" Evan objects. "That's a tactically foolish idea. If we need to defend ourselves and you get taken out, both weapons go with you. I think you should—"

"Here you go, Sonya," Rich says as he hands her back the bag.

Evan's mouth hangs partially agape. Sonya shrugs as Rich removes the handgun from the bag and clips it to her belt. Evan mumbles his protest, but his words go unnoticed. Rich pulls a large rifle out of a soft case. His hands caress the maple stock as they inspect it for any damage that may have been sustained during travel. He pulls the bolt back to inspect the chamber then begins loading it.

"All right, men!" he says. Sonya glares at him, and he hastily adds, "And women! And furries and troglodytes and whatever gender-fluid you choose to identify as!" She smiles and shakes her head. "What? I'm trying to be *inclusive!*" he wails mockingly while he walks into the woods. Sonya follows behind him with Evan bringing up the rear. "I should have some kind of weapon too…" he whimpers. Rich looks back at him, whistles, and tosses him a small pocketknife.

They wander deep into the woods. The trees around them are close together, most branchless for several feet, with a thick layer of duff coating the forest floor. Each footfall brings the soft crunch of needles and old twigs breaking through the silence of the woods around them. Chilled early morning air meets their breath and turns it into a thick fog as they exhale. Through the brush and trees, the babble of water coursing over rocks takes precedent in their immediate scenery.

"All right, we're going to move upstream from here for a couple of miles. It will be uphill for a bit, but then we will cross this creek, and right on the other side of it, there will be a game trail that will lead us north to a small clearing. I marked it with some hi-viz ribbon last time I was here, so we know where to cross," Rich whispers as he points in the general direction of their next destination.

"What's hi-viz ribbon?" Evan inquires.

Rich slings his pack across his chest and reaches into a pocket. He pulls out a roll of neon pink plastic ribbon and hands it to Evan.

"This'd be it," Rich answers. "Make sure to tie a length of it on a tree every hundred steps or so. Make sure it's obvious so we can follow it back." He removes a compass from the same pocket and flips it open to verify the direction they are moving.

"All righty, let's keep going," Rich adds as he places the compass back in its pocket. He slings the pouch onto his back and clips it together in the front.

The glowing yellow corona of the morning sun is not long from cresting a mountain range to their east. The forest is starting to rouse from its slumber as the temperature gradually warms with the increasing light. Chirps and squeaks from a menagerie of woodland critters can be heard all around them. Sonya can see ahead fairly well now as the trees spread out. The ground underfoot is changing as well, transforming from soft and loamy to more barren as the vegetation grows sparse. Her breathing has become labored, and she can feel perspiration growing on her back. She notices that the grade of their terrain has steepened in the last few minutes of travel. She is right behind Rich, who is maintaining a decent pace. She looks back to see Evan trailing further behind. His bright red hair matted to his forehead with sweat.

Sonya grabs Rich's arm and tugs on him. "Rich, let's hold up for a minute. Evan is looking pretty ragged back there." Rich turns to look and sees the state his friend is in.

"Yeah. I think you're right. I don't feel like carrying his boney ass out of here." Rich stops and sets his pack on the ground. Cool air hits his back where the pack rode and sends a chill up his spine as he stretches. Evan catches up to them and with an exhausted sigh flops onto a clear patch of dirt and falls backward onto his pack. Rich walks over to him and offers a canteen of water. Evan reaches for it greedily and drinks deep from the contents. Rich snatches it away from his lips after a few seconds and scolds him for being wasteful. "Quit chuggin' all my damn water! You got your own in the bag, jackass!"

"Well, I had some, but it's gone," mutters Evan.

"Gone? What do you mean gone? I put two liters of water in each bag. You mean to say that you drank it all in the last forty minutes?" demands Rich.

Evan says nothing. He simply shrugs his shoulders and looks to Sonya for backup, only to find that she isn't paying either of them attention. She is busy snapping pictures of the rolling forested hills still glistening from the early morning rains.

"Break's over anyways. Now get back on your feet. We're only like fifteen minutes away—hey, where did that ribbon go I gave you?" demands Rich.

"Oh, I ran out. I tied some on a tree every like hundred steps or so like you said to. See?" Evan points at the last ribbon he had hung just a stone's throw from where he now stands. About shoulder high is the ribbon, tied in a neat bow around the trunk of the tree.

"You used like eight feet of ribbon on that tree! And why the fuck did you tie it in *a bow*?" Rich lets out a heavy sigh. "Well, I guess that's my fault for not being more specific," Rich says as he starts heading further uphill.

Sonya steps next to Evan, raises her cellphone, snaps a picture of the ribbon, and laughs. Slipping the phone back in her pocket, she gives Evan a pat on the shoulder and follows Rich.

"I should have stayed home," whines Evan. He pushes himself to his feet, brushes off his legs and butt, then stomps after his friends, grumbling quietly to himself.

The uphill climb makes its presence known to the group. Their thighs and calves burn with anger at the constant effort as the hill grows steeper underfoot. The stream's soft babble has grown into a dull roar to match the grade, but it is not enough to drown out the repetitive thump of heavy boots pounding the dirt. Evan has lost any sense of time and space. He just blindly follows behind Sonya, his eyes staring holes into the ground. His mind is so lost that does not acknowledge his travel companions have stopped. His head bumps into Sonya's back, causing her to stumble forward.

Sonya attempts to regain her footing on some rocks near the stream's edge, but they dislodge from the impact, sending her entire foot plunging into the icy cold water. She inhales sharply from the shock of her warm boot being infiltrated by the offensive chill. Evan, reacting to his own blunder, grabs her arm and helps her find stable ground. "Evan! What the *eff*, dude!" scolds Sonya, her tone momentarily as cold as the water in her shoe.

"Sorry, Sony! I was lost in thought at how much fun I'm having and didn't notice you had stopped." Evan's sarcastic tone only helps him catch an elbow from Sonya.

Rich is standing near a narrow section of the stream. Large rocks break the surface in a formation close enough to allow passage over the water. "Here's the crossing. It's kinda precarious, so watch your step, especially you Sonya, don't want to get both boots wet!" teases Rich.

Sonya slaps him in the arm and shoves him toward the water. "Age before beauty!" she says with a gesture, encouraging Rich to go first.

"Think you meant 'pearls before swine'!" replies Rich.

Sonya takes another swing at him, but he leaps partway across the stream, passing over several stones and landing near the middle. With another leap, he is now almost across. Rich turns to his cohorts and takes a self-satisfied bow. As he learns forward, his weight-bearing foot shifts on the slime-coated creek boulder and slides from its perch. Rich overcompensates and throws his weight backward in an attempt to catch himself, but he only succeeds in losing all balance and landing flat on his seat in the water.

Evan and Sonya are silent, anticipating Rich to start raging at his situation, but his reaction is much humbler than expected. Rich is on his feet and out of the water in almost one movement. He stands on the other side of the creek, staring at his friends.

"I, uh, I probably deserved that," mutters Rich.

"You absolutely deserved that," Sonya says as she and Evan burst into laughter.

Cautiously, Sonya makes her way over the rocks, followed by Evan. A very soggy Rich takes the lead. He points at a slightly weathered pink ribbon tied to the top of a short piece of brush. "This is what it's supposed to look like, Evan. In case you were wondering," offers Rich.

Evan just shakes his head and follows along, eager to end the day so he can hurry up and get home again. Only a few moments have passed when Rich stops them just short of a large clearing filled with inviting warm light reflecting off the grass, making the ground glow with a soft green hue.

"This is the spot," whispers Rich. "There is a game trail on the north side that filters right into the meadow. Last time I was up here, the place was just lousy with elk sign. Let's set up here and wait." Rich draws a knife from the sheath on his hip and begins hacking into a bramble of huckleberry to hollow out a space wide enough for the three of them to cram into. "It's going to be shoulder to shoulder in here so we can keep some heat between us. It's pretty chilly still, and once we stop moving, we will get cold pretty fast. So pile in and get cozy, who knows how long it will be before the elk show up. You're in first, cinnamon stick."

Evan scoffs at Rich as he scrambles in and makes space in the musty underbrush. Rich hands his rifle to Sonya briefly as he takes position to the right of Evan. Sonya hands the rifle back to Rich as she hesitantly sits down next to him.

Evan draws in the dirt between his feet. Sonya is busy editing her selfies on her phone. Rich is quietly watching the opposite tree line. He slips his hand inside his jacket and pulls out a flask. He pops the cap and takes a nip. He offers it to Evan next who takes it and places it under his nose.

"What is this? Smells like a fermented campfire," he says.

"This is a fine scotch. Cost like tree-hunnid a bottle," Rich gloats.

"Tree-hunnid? Gross. You're not cool, Rich," Sonya says.

Rich pushes up on the bottom of the flask, urging Evan to drink. He takes a sip and immediately gags on it but manages to swallow it down. Rich takes it back from him then offers it to Sonya. She hesitates but then takes it and drinks.

"This tastes like a drunk hobo pissed out a burning shoe," she says dryly.

"It's an acquired taste. Probably a little too sophisticated for you, common folk." Rich takes a second nip before placing it back in his jacket. Seconds later, he spies movement in the brush across the meadow. "Shhhhhh...," he whispers.

A large dark brown head emerges first followed by a tan body, but no horns, a cow. After a dozen more enter the meadow, a rustling can be heard drawing nearer. The antlers are first to emerge, wide and imposing. Rich counts the tines under his breath, "Eight? That's an eight-pointer! No way!" He hisses, trying hard to be as quiet as he can. He draws his rifle up to his shoulder and smoothly opens the action to chamber a round. He pushes the bolt forward carefully, moving imperceptibly slow. The latch closes over, and he thumbs the safety off. He places his eye behind the scope and draws aim.

In between slow, steady breaths, he whispers, "Cover...your...ears..."

Sonya, already aware of what was happening, was braced. Evan is still gawking in awe at the majesty of the creatures before him. He slowly starts to put his fingers in his ears, elbows resting upon his knees. Rich takes a deep breath and slowly begins to exhale. His finger rests on the trigger, pressure increasing as he reaches the bottom of his breath. A cool breeze comes from behind them, blowing their scent directly toward the bull elk who picks it up immediately. His head turns to look in the direction of the wind. That same breeze snakes around Evan's collar and caresses his neck, bringing with it a soft whisper that's just loud enough to catch his attention. His head cocks slightly to the side, causing his elbow to lose purchase on his knee. It slips off and hits Rich in the thigh. The rifle fires. The bull elk leaps in the air as the bullet pierces his torso. The herd rushes into the forest from where they came. Rich's face is red with rage as he turns his head and glares at Evan.

"What the *fuck*, man?" he says through clenched teeth. "What is your goddamn problem? *Huh*? You fuck! I had that shot! Now we gotta spend god knows how long tracking that bastard through the brush. I am *not* losing that animal. That's a trophy right there. Maybe even a state record! And you fucked me! Little ginger bitch."

"I... I'm sorry... I heard someone talking and I... I got distracted. I didn't mean to fuck it up, man. You have to believe me." Evan looks at the dirt, even more disappointed with himself than Rich was.

"It's okay, Evan." Rich sighs. "It won't get far. That was a gut shot, but it may have hit the liver. If so, there should be a nice and dark blood trail to follow. Let's go." He jumps up and grabs his gear, slinging his rifle over his shoulder as he starts walking in the direction the herd went.

Sonya pitifully eyes Evan. "Pretty sure he was close to killing you for a second there." She gets up and follows Rich.

Evan sighs aloud and heads off behind them.

Thick blots of dark crimson blood are scattered across the forest floor. It's easy to follow, and they are making good time. Rich kneels and wipes some blood off a fern with two fingers. It's still warm to the touch. The animal is near.

"Blood can be smelled from a mile away if the wind is right. Could draw in all sorts of predators. Keep your eyes open and stay alert," Rich says softly.

As the trio pushes on, ragged breathing can be heard coming from somewhere in front of them. Rich puts his hand up, gesturing his friends to stop. Chambering another round in his rifle, he walks closer to the sound. Just ahead of him is an uprooted tree. The moss-covered and rotted trunk lays in a dense thicket of brush. The exposed root wad creates a fan of wooden tentacles reaching skyward in an arc, and right in front of it, he can see the tips of the elk's antlers protruding from behind the log. Rich gestures for Sonya to come close to him. He engages the rifle's safety and hands it to her. He then unsnaps the holster on her hip and draws the silver revolver. Rich circles slowly behind the roots of the tree, his weapon raised and cocked. As he passes the root wad, the elk slowly comes into view. A large swath of brush had been smashed down as the animal collapsed. Its hind legs lay limp against the dirt, too weak to carry it further. Its forelegs stamp and scratch at the ground as it desperately tries to flee. The elk's eyes widen with fear when Rich comes into view. It grunts and shakes its head in a feeble act of aggression. Rich aims just behind its shoulder and fires, piercing its heart. The elk's legs give out it crashes to the ground. Its eyelids flutter, then close. It inhales sharply then releases its final breath. Its muscles relax, and a peace washes over its body.

Rich's hands are shaking from the adrenaline. He lowers his handgun and places his pack on the ground in front of him. From behind, Evan and Sonya approach slowly, completely unsure of how to behave in this situation. Rich trades weapons with Sonya. After holstering the handgun, he takes his rifle and leans it against the root wad.

Rich pulls a small curved knife from his belt, then says to Sonya, "Open up the front of that bag and hand me the folding saw, please. We have to clean and prep this animal fast. Evan, you've got game bags in yours. Whip 'em out for me."

His friends busy themselves in their bags in search of the requested items. As Rich moves toward the elk, he freezes in his tracks.

"Did you hear that?" he whispers.

His blood turns to ice. A rush of adrenaline hits him as his eyes catch a brief shudder of brush when from the other side of the thicket erupts the head of a massive bear. No, not massive—*gigantic!* It effortlessly clears the downed tree and stands tall over the elk. Rich looks down in horror as he sees the font paw is bigger than the entire chest of the deceased game. Rich's eyes lock with the bears as he crouches in place, knife in hand. His mind frantically trying to think of an escape route. He looks back at his rifle, judging if he would be able to get to it and fire off a shot in time, then looks back at the bear. It looks him in the eyes, then looks at his rifle and grunts disapprovingly. It rears up on its hind legs and lets out a roar so deafening that all three of them become disoriented, unaware of what they were just doing or why they were even there to begin with. With a rumbling chortle, almost like a laugh, the freakishly large bear picks up the entire elk in its maw and begins to rush past them, casually stepping over Rich. Sonya leaps out of the way. Evan is caught in the chest by its elbow and launched to the ground. Rich doesn't say a word. He grabs his rifle and chases after it. Sonya and Evan stare after him, still disoriented.

"We gotta…," Evan begins, but Sonya was already sprinting after Rich.

The beast is far ahead of Rich and gaining distance, but its wake of destruction makes it easy to follow. He would be able to drive his truck through it and not hit either side. This monster of a bear was knocking down entire trees, snapping them clean off at the ground! His lungs are burning. His stomach aches from exertion, but the thought of losing his trophy drives him forward. Sonya is next to him, keeping pace easily.

She looks at him. "Still…got…the gun?" he gasps between breaths. She nods. He looks back and sees Evan struggling to keep up.

They must have chased the bear for over a mile. It's not even visible anymore. They just hear it smashing through trees and brush, grunting in a tone that makes Rich feel like he's being mocked. Fatigue forces them to slow their pace so they stop and wait for Evan to catch up. Once he's rejoined, they can't help but notice that his face is whiter than usual, and his entire front half is soaked with sweat. They give him a minute to recover, then keep moving. The trail is not easy to miss. They follow it until a large cave comes into view with the signs left by the rampaging carnivore heading straight into it. The group stops a few yards from the cave entrance, unsure of the situation before them.

"It's totally in there, isn't it?" Sonya asks.

"Definitely," Rich replies.

"And w-we're going in there?" squeaks Evan.

"I am. You guys don't have to, but after this crazy shit, I am not leaving empty-handed," Rich proclaims.

"Okay. Let's go," says Sonya as she draws the pistol from its holster.

With an abundance of caution and a resolute will, Rich leads them into the gaping maw of the cave. The entrance is unusually clean, just well-worn stone. There are no random loose rocks or scattered leaves and twigs. The only real sign of dirt is the enormous paw prints left by the bear and the odd drop of blood from the elk it carried in its mouth. The only vegetation to be seen are a few ferns peppering the outer rim of the floor and a small section of wall covered with honeysuckle.

"Guys," Sonya whispers, but the resonance of the cave defeats her attempts. "There is something off about these plants. They feel too decorative."

Rich and Evan both look at her, their eyebrows a matching tone of intrigue. Neither responds to her. Rich simply puts a finger to his lips and keeps moving forward. Their path catches enough ambient light that most of their immediate surroundings are clearly visible and well-lit for the first dozen yards or so, but as they venture deeper, the light dies off exponentially. The cave becomes dank. The air gets thick and pungent and so heavy it feels difficult to draw breath. What little light they had is gone entirely now. Rich pulls a small flashlight from the side of his pack.

"Get your lights out," he whispers.

Rich's light probes the darkness ahead of them. It sweeps along the floor and stops when something catches Rich's attention. On the floor of the cave is a small tuft of tan fur damp with blood. Rich kneels down, grabs the fur, and rolls it in his fingers. The metallic tang of blood hangs in the air. The path curves enough that he cannot get a clear view of what lies ahead of them. Anxiety burns his nerves as he creeps forward, his weapon held at the ready, finger just a hair's breadth from the trigger.

As they maneuver through the bend, the hind portion of the elk comes into view, its body battered and bloody, chunks of flesh missing from being smashed against trees as the bear ran through the forest, with large teeth marks clearly visible in the abdomen of the elk. Evan kneels next to it for a closer look as Rich stands over him and observes the bite.

"Those canines are at least twenty inches apart. That's fucking unreal," Rich says under his breath. As Rich studies the body, his light makes its way to the head. "No way, no fuckin' way," he murmurs as he illuminates a pool of blood on the cave floor. "It took the head."

"What? What do you mean, Rich?" asks Evan.

"That means this fucking bear removed the head and took it deeper into the cave," Rich replies in disbelief.

Sonya looks around, her light traces across the floor to the wall, then the wall to the ceiling. She looks up at the ceiling, then the realization hits her. "Rich, how tall was that bear?"

"Fuckin' tall. Like taller than a house," he says.

"And how tall would you say this cave is right now?" she asks.

Rich looks up, and his eyes bulge as he sees what she is talking about. The ceiling of the cave hangs above them out of reach but not by much.

"I don't understand…," he wonders out loud. "There is no way in hell that thing could have made it this far!" His eyes shoot back to the elk. He looks closer at the neck, his eyes narrow as his focus sharpens. "These are cuts… These are fucking cuts. The head was *cut* off."

Rich raises his rifle, finger on the trigger and flashlight in his supporting hand. He walks deeper in. Sonya is right behind him with Evan close behind her, his folding knife in his hand and opened. Rich pushes further in. The corridor starts to constrict around them as they progress. His senses are heightened so intensely that it's almost overwhelming. His heart pounds in his chest so hard he can barely hear over it. They come to an opening in the tunnel. Ahead, there is a large cavern. He can hear movement echoing around the chamber. He readies himself for whatever might come. As he enters the cavern, a large shadowy form appears on his right. He spins around to meet it, but a mighty swat knocks the rifle from his hands with ease. The flashlight skitters across the floor, briefly illuminating their assailant. Sonya is right behind Rich. She shouts his name in fear and aims at the mass attacking her friend.

Right before Sonya can fire a shot, a booming voice fills their ears, and a flash of light blinds them.

"ENOUGH!" it shouts.

Rich is thrown to the ground. The air forced out of him from the impact, his head bounces off the hard stone floor. Sonya's firearm is ripped from her hands. A dull red glow penetrates the darkness as her handgun heats up. The shine it casts illuminates a palm so large the gun she once needed two hands for now seems like a child's toy. The weapon glows brighter then melts into a puddle of liquid metal. The palm tilts, allowing the molten steel to pour onto the floor. From the dark, a tremendous force grips her by the neck and shoulder, tossing her easily to the ground on top of Rich. Evan cowers against the wall, overcome with fear.

"LIGHT!" the voice booms again.

Torches spring to life all around the room. The figure becomes more visible as the light grows. Sonya blinks through the pain of being tossed to the ground as she tries to focus on what she's seeing. Before them stands no bear but a man.

CHAPTER 3

As Rich came to his senses, he gazed around the room in a state of dreamlike stupor. Lights line the walls, and a small table with two stools can be seen near the mouth of another tunnel. Through the mental haze, he can make out a body standing near the wall in between. They are tall and lean, wearing a dark brown cloak with the hood up. Rich's eyes track a second form emerging from the hallway next to the first. This one is roughly the same height as the first but broader with a similar brown cloak, hood drawn over their head. His senses scream at him as he remembers that there was still a third stranger in the room with them. His head snaps back to his original assailant. His heart beats hard in his chest he can feel fear biting at him as he glimpses over Sonya's shoulder at what stands motionless looming over him. Staring at him with eyes that are cold as the floor he lays on, a glare so intense it's tangible.

The third stranger is not cloaked, or even clothed, but standing before them fully nude! His head is bald, clean-shaven, but he has a full thick beard that hangs down to his chest and is littered with colorful beads. His dark skin is almost completely black. Broad cheekbones sit above a chiseled jaw, his nostrils flaring as he breathes deeply. This man stands at least nine feet tall with a head as large as Rich's chest! His shoulders resemble two boulders set on either side of him, and his arm is easily the size of a normal man's torso with thick veins pulsating in time with his heartbeat. Sonya is lying partially across Rich's chest and blocking his view. He rolls her off him, exposing all the man before them. His feet are as long as Rich's thigh but half again as wide. His calves and quadriceps contain enough meat to form four good-sized men on their own. Then Rich lays eyes on his manhood.

With that same booming voice, the stranger commands them, "Stop staring at my penis."

"Right. I could leave the room and still see it waving goodbye to me," Rich says as he begins to lift himself off the ground. He could swear he heard a snicker come from the direction of the other two cloaked figures, but he wasn't bothering to look right now. He reaches in his coat and pulls out his flask. He raises it to his lips, only to have it snatched away from him. Sonya drinks deeply from it then hands it back. Rich looks away from the naked monster in front of him and shifts his gaze to the other two near the wall, "Well, I guess that bear belongs to y'all then?"

"It was not a bear, and it is not our pet," says the thinner of the two in a distinctly female voice.

"It was *him*," she says, motioning with one hand back toward the mountain of flesh.

Rich looks back and sees him attempting to put pants on now. His intimidating presence somewhat lessened as Rich compares what he is seeing before him to a toddler attempting to dress themselves as the man struggles to fit his bulk into a pair of handmade trousers.

"You guys got some of that good shit, don't ya? I don't know if you noticed or not, but that's just a really, *really* large man. More like a sasquatch than a bear, honestly," Rich says.

"Please demonstrate," the other cloaked figure says. This one is a male with an interesting accent, something exotic with a little more flare to it.

"I just put my pants back on," the large man says, his voice constantly booming but totally monotone and devoid of any emotion, almost robotic.

"Then choose something small," the cloaked female says.

With a mighty sigh, the large man closes his eyes, places his hands outstretched in front of him, palms facing away, and begins chanting. His words fill the room, echoing off the walls and through the heads of the trio. Sonya covers her ears while Rich just stares, unable to look away as he watches him *shrinking*! His frame compresses down smaller and smaller, fine white fur begins to spring from the top of his head, coating his face. His ears point and begin moving up the sides of his cranium, coming to rest just at the top. His arms become furry as well, his fingers retracting into paws, his nails shaping into claws. He continues to shrink down until his pants consume him and he is lost from sight completely. A fluffy white tail pops out from the mass of wool on the ground, then the creature fully emerges.

"He's a fuckin cat," Evan mutters as his eyes flutter and roll into the back of his head. He falls over and lays still on the floor.

"Did that one just pass out?" says the male figure.

"I believe he did…," replies the female.

"Oh my *god!*" Sonya cries. "Look how *cute* it is!"

The cat midway through licking its back paw growls in protest, but that only furthers her adoration. With a loud "awwweee," she reaches down to pet it. Before she can close the distance, the cat stands up on its hind legs and begins enlarging, rapidly returning to its former shape of a man. This time, he was able to bring his pants up with him.

"So that just happened, right?" Rich wonders out loud. "And why the *fuck* did you try to pet it, Sonya?"

Sonya shrugs and dryly states, "I like cats."

"I am not a cat," the large man booms.

"No shit!" snarks Rich.

Sonya walks over to Evan and shakes him, pulling him upright and gently smacking him around as he came to.

"Enough parlor tricks. This is not a time for merrymaking and amusement. We have a business to attend to," the female says. "I am Vitra Shadowbane."

She lowers her hood and removes her cloak. She wore clothes made from the same rough-hewn wool that the large male was still struggling to fasten, a wool vest, and some crude trousers. Her undershirt is sleeveless, exposing arms that are ghostly white and totally free of imperfections. Long jet-black hair parted down the middle frames her angular profile. Her neck is eerily thin and long. Her shoulders and arms were wiry, but her frame was very lithe, tight, and capable. On her waist, she wore a leather belt with several pouches.

She casually drapes her cloak across the corner of the table she stands near and says, "This man next to me is Ral O'Talon."

Ral steps forward and bows gracefully, then with a flourish throws his own cloak across the room, landing on one of the torches and extinguishing it. He proudly stands before them, dressed in similar garb as the others, only dyed black. Wavy brown hair is lazily swept back from his forehead with a single rebellious lock dangling just next to his eye. He is a road map of scars that crisscross his face and neck. He wears a defiant smile, but his eyes are a familiar warm hazel color. Powerful large shoulders sharply cut down to a narrow waist. Sonya notices that the skin all over his body is scarred. Every inch of exposed flesh has an old wound. Were they more symmetrical, one may think he was masquerading as a tiger. He continues to hold his pose before them until it becomes obvious that the initial intrigue has passed. He steps back with a last flare of showmanship, bowing politely as he returns to his original position near Vitra. Rich looks at Sonya and raises his eyebrows sarcastically while mouthing "wow." She looks back at Evan. He is now standing and slowly moving behind his friends.

"The large man behind you is Gaian Rootward."

They all look back at him. Gaian stands motionless, glaring, an insincere "Greetings" is the only thing that escapes his tight-closed lips.

"I'm sure you're all curious about why we led you here," she begins,

Rich interrupts her, "*Curious*? That's a bit of an understatement. I am absolutely flummoxed. Tripod back there turns into a big-ass bear and takes off with my elk, leading us here to your fuckin' hippy drug cave. You look like Wednesday Adams after she found crossfit, and the third sorry bastard is acting like I'm supposed to be impressed with him."

"Your words are sharp, boy. Have some respect," Ral offers calmly. "We understand this is a…shock to you. We apologize for the theatrics, but if we just walked up and asked you to follow us back here, would you? No."

"He has a point, Rich," Sonya adds.

"Please, follow us. We have food and drink. We will explain every-thing," Ral says as he reaches out a hand toward the group while motion-ing down the dark hallway he and Vitra came from with his other.

Evan is beginning to look whiter than normal once more. His eyes dart around the room hastily, searching for a way out.

"Fuck this…," whispers Evan.

He turns and looks back at the way they came from. Gaian casts a sideways glance at him, sensing his intent to run. Evan hesitates for a moment as he considers his next move. Then with a surprising speed, he makes a break for the exit. Gaian was waiting for it and swings his large arm down to catch Evan. He grabs him by his coat and begins to lift his feet off the ground. Evan throws his arms over his head and slips out. He lands on one knee and quickly has his feet under him, running at full tilt.

"Wait," booms Gaian.

Vitra shakes her head, and Ral laughs gently.

"Please wait here." Ral sighs.

With an unnatural speed, he takes off after Evan, catching up to him in the blink of an eye.

"Please come back, my boy. You won't like what's about to hap-pen," he says.

Evan is running on instinct. His eyes wide with fear as he looks at Ral. Evan can see light ahead, faint but clear. His heart fills with hope as he uses what strength remains to push for the opening. As he rounds a bend in the tunnel, his body comes to a very, very violent stop. His arms smash into an unseen barrier, then his face makes con-tact with a sickening thud. He is unconscious before he even hits the ground. Ral effortlessly catches him in his arms and lifts him onto a scarred shoulder while walking back.

Once Ral rejoined the others, he places Evan on an empty stool and holds him up to get a better look at his face. His nose was badly broken with a large laceration on his forehead from where it met the wall.

"He is likely concussed. He hit the barrier at full speed. For being so scrawny, he was surprisingly fast," Ral states as he examines Evan.

"Vitra, I think this one may need your touch," he adds.

Vitra walks up to Evan, tilts his head back, and looks into his eyes. She reaches into her nearby cloak and pulls out a small vial of dark green liquid. She pours a single drop in his mouth. As soon as it hit his tongue, a plume of smoke rises from where it landed. It floats in his mouth for a moment until he inhales it. With a sharp cry, he sits up straight. His eyes move around rapidly under closed lids. His nose cracks and shifts as it returns to its original position. The jagged cut on his forehead closes itself shut and fades, as do some of the small cuts and scrapes he suffered while chasing the bear that was Gaian. Ral is supporting him as his body relaxes. When his eyes open, he sees his friends looking on with concern and wonder. Ral comes into view, and he pulls away.

"This fuck attacked me!" he screeches.

"I promise you, I did no such thing," Ral offers calmly. "Allow me to demonstrate. Please, follow me."

He turns to walk away. Rich follows Sonya as she chases after him. Evan looks on as his friends trail behind Ral. He stands up. His body feels light. He is no longer sore from running through the woods. He quietly tries to understand why as he walks in the direction of the others.

When Evan finally catches up to them, he sees Rich standing there with his hand firmly pressed against a solid wall of empty space. Rich slaps his hand hard against the barrier as his brain processes what he is feeling. Sonya is squatting down a few feet away, tossing small rocks at it, watching carefully as they bounce back at her. Ral is standing off to one side with his arms folded, allowing them to experiment. Evan reaches out and touches it. There is a sensation of smooth glass under his fingertips. It is also bitterly cold he can only touch it for a few seconds before the bite is too much for him.

Ral walks over to them and says, "What you are experiencing is a barrier that was put in place as you all entered the cave. It is condensed energy. It is only a finger's width thick, but it is quite impenetrable."

Rich looks on in sustained disbelief while Sonya continues to toss things at it. Evan begins to get upset. "Well, undo it. Let me leave. I don't want to be here anymore. I want to go home. I should never have gone on this stupid fucking trip anyways."

Sonya turns and glares at him. Rich lets his hands hang at his side, his head slowly lowers.

"Evan, stop it. You're just scared. So are we," Rich says. "I am aware that I brought us out here. For that, I am sorry. At this point, I have no clue what's happening. I can't decide if I'm tripping balls, in a coma, or dead. I assume I'm not dead because I'm not surrounded by fire and little pricks with pointy tails. So we can either freak out more or listen to what they have to say. I'm heading back. I want to know what they want."

"Yeah, me too," Sonya adds. "This shit is not normal, and I am *really* curious about what else they can do."

Evan clenches his fists as his eyes swell with tears. "What about what *I* want? *Huh?* Do either of you give a shit? Because I know *he* doesn't." Evan motions toward Ral.

"I know you are scared. I can feel it," Ral says calmly. "I feel your anxiety, your anger, your sadness. There is a lot of it. More than what you let on. It grows anytime yo—" Evan cuts Ral off. The look in his eyes turns from mad to nervous.

"Fine, let's just fucking go then. When they skin us alive and wear our faces, don't say I didn't warn you."

The party walks back in silence, Ral leading the way, and Evan trailing to the rear. They enter the room where Gaian and Vitra await them. Ral motions for them to lead the way. Gaian walks behind Vitra as they wind through a narrow passageway. Rich eyes Gaian as they go, watching the giant carefully filter past protrusions as he makes his way through the tunnel.

After what could not have been more than a minute or so, they enter a great stone hall filled with basically anything one would need to live day to day. A large rectangular table with six chairs, one of them comically large, sits in the middle of the floor. Behind that, a wood-fired stove and a sink next to a small stream of water that flows naturally from a crack in the wall. On the counter next to the sink sits six hand-carved wooden plates, with six wooden mugs sealed with wax. On one side of the room, there are six beds laid side by side, one of them significantly larger than the rest. Sonya looks around, examining everything carefully. She watches the water flow from the wall and down into a natural drain with a man-made grate placed over it. Her hands run across the tabletop, feeling the grain of the wood. Vitra asks them to have a seat. Ral volunteers to make some tea. Gaian takes his seat at the far end and stares straight ahead. Rich sits at the other end of the table, Vitra to his left, and Sonya and Evan to his right. Vitra looks at them one at a time.

"This is going to be hard to swallow, and I need you all to be more open-minded than you have been. I will explain everything to you, as promised."

Rich leans in closely, locking eyes with Vitra, and says, "Well, go on then. Let's hear it."

CHAPTER 4

"A long time ago, there were a group of beings created for the task of maintaining the balance of this planet. Nine of us to be precise. Every one of us with our own domain to oversee, air, earth, day, night, water, fire, electricity, life, and death. Mine is the darkness, night itself. Ral was given the realm of air, the circulation of Our Creator's breath." Ral smiled and snapped his fingers, a gush of wind hit Evan in the face and startled him. "Gaian was given governance over rock, root, and earth. Our Creator tried to name us in a fashion that represented our purpose. You could say it was just her way of being quaint."

"*Her?*" Rich interrupts.

Vitra holds up her hand, gesturing for Rich to hold his questions.

She continues, "Things were quite peaceful for many centuries until one of us grew discontent with their position. Erra was his name. He was the watcher of death. It was his duty to ensure life was passed from its conscious form, back to its source, so it could then be returned to existence in some other form as Our Creator dictated. He became restless, lost focus on his work, and began experimenting with something more sinister. He would piece together all varieties of dead creatures. Starting with small animals, mice and bats and what have you, he soon found a way to skim life energy from the dying. He saved it and was able to manipulate it so that it could reanimate his creations. His monstrosities became more and more grotesque as he moved on to larger and larger corpses. They started off mindless and barely alive, but he soon was able to give them some basic intelligence, and as time went on, he honed his craft until they actually became *sentient*."

Ral walks over to the table and pours a fragrant tea into their cups. Sonya takes a sip and exhales with satisfaction. Ral puts a hand on her shoulder and smiles, then serves Rich and Evan.

"When Our Creator learned of this, she immediately commanded he stop his work and destroy all that he had made. Erra pleaded with her, trying to justify his work. He said he had found a new form of life, one which required little food and was totally subservient. A workforce that could take over day-to-day chores and eventually handle complex orders without tiring. She accused him of perverting the natural order of things. He defended his actions, citing how others were engaged in mastering studies not related to their purpose, how I had my potions, Gaian had his forge, so on and so on. She refused to hear his argument and gave him the ultimatum of either obeying her wishes or leaving her paradise. So he left. He left everything behind and disappeared. He was gone many years, no signs of his existence ever seen. Until that fateful day, when Our Creator grew ill. Her flesh was cracked and dry, her body too weak to even stand on her own. Her only words after the sickness took her were 'Find Erra.' So Ral and Gaian volunteered to hunt him down while I began working to heal Our Creator."

Sonya is looking down into her drink. She can make out little particulates curiously zipping around her cup. Like bubbles in a soda, only moving back and forth instead of rising to the surface. She stares at them as Vitra continues her story.

"They returned almost two weeks later. Ral was nearly dead. His body was covered in deep wounds. When they began their journey, Gaian took the form of a great eagle, soaring through the sky while Ral rode on his back, creating a tailwind to drive them on faster. They had found Erra's new home after only a few days. They landed nearby on a hillside to observe. It was a large walled fortress nestled in a deep draw with only one doorway. They saw no activity and decided to venture in. As they came closer, they saw that the walls were made of bodies held together by iron straps that flowed almost organically across the surface of corpses. Large bone spikes driven through holes in the iron held the mass in place. They passed through the front gate, which was left open as though guests were expected. The main building was carved from the mountainside itself. One solid piece of granite turned into a palace of death."

Rich drinks deeply from his tea. He feels a wave of ease wash over his senses as he listens to Vitra's story.

"Erra showed himself once they were well inside the walls. They demanded that he explain himself and tell them what hand he had in the Creator's illness. He told them how he found a way inside her. How he found a way to use her existence to empower his own and using this new strength enhance the abilities of his legions. He offered them a chance to join him. He said they would be put to good use and made generals in his army. Ral struck him across the face as Erra's betrayal proved too much for him to tolerate. Then the walls of corpses began to writhe and moan. Arms and legs popping out, then entire bodies falling to the ground. Soon the entire edifice collapsed, leaving a ring of living dead surrounding them. Erra raised his hands, sending forth a blast of energy. It passed through Ral and Gaian harmlessly, but when it hit the bodies around them, they sprang to life, rising and turning to look directly at them. Erra simply smiled as his horde charged. They were grossly outnumbered and not expecting a fight. Gaian and Ral were quickly overcome."

Evan is stirring his drink, taking in everything she is saying. His thoughts keep wandering away from here, back to his home and his computer. He takes a sip and feels his discomfort lessen.

"Ral was swarmed almost immediately," Vitra says. "Had it not been for Gaian's quick reaction, neither of them would have made it out alive. He made himself into a great bull and began plowing and bucking his way through them all, trying to draw attention. Once he had the opening, he leaped into the air, returning to his human form, and slammed into the ground, sending shockwaves through the earth and knocking most of the horde to the ground. Ral summoned his strength and sent a whirlwind blasting through them, clearing a path for their escape. Ral began to fall, unable to stand under his own power, Gaian rushed to his side and held him under one arm, sprinting for the nearest way out. Erra screamed with a deep rage, sending his horde into a frenzy. Gaian was barely able to take the form of an eagle again before they were on him. He had several clinging to him as he flew away with Ral barely conscious on his back. After shaking them loose and gaining some distance, he knew he had to stop to tend to Ral's injuries."

Rich had finished his tea at this point. His body was becoming somewhat numb, comfortably so. He looks at his friends and sees that they are beginning to doze off.

Vitra sees his focus has shifted and begins speaking again, directly at him. "It took Gaian three days of care to keep Ral from dying. Erra had sent winged devils after them, forcing Gaian to travel by foot. They moved only at night, maneuvering around the hordes of ghastly fiends that swarmed the mountains and plains, constantly trying to evade whatever evil was hunting them. If he hadn't made his way back to us when he did, Ral would have been lost forever."

"I did die, Vitra," Ral says. "I died that day and was reborn. I chose to rename myself, O'Talon. Of Talon. To represent all the scars I now carry with me. To remind myself of Erra's betrayal."

Vitra nods then says, "Our Creator remained ill for some time. Her physical form succumbed to the sickness that Erra had poisoned her with. We who were still loyal convened and decided that one of us must visit her in the aether. I volunteered. After venturing into her realm, I found her. She had black tendrils penetrating her body, entering *every* orifice. I went mad with hate and began ripping at them, trying to tear them off her. As fast as I removed them, they replaced themselves. Finding any way into her they could. She told me to stop. Said that she had devised a plan to imprison Erra. She explained it all to me in detail, and I left immediately to carry it out."

She pauses and looks at the trio of friends. She notes their tired expressions, with a look toward Ral, and a confirming nod from him, she continues.

"I gathered the remaining loyal together and explained to them the final steps and that one of us had to give our life to prevent him from being able to escape, their physical sacrifice would harden the shell. Enki, the guardian of life, volunteered. Once we were ready, we circled Erra under cover of darkness. Each of us took our designated position around his encampment. We placed our talismans at our feet and began chanting the incantation she gave us. He retaliated by sending his hordes, but the earth under their feet split apart, sending them all hurdling into oblivion. Our barrier, similar to the one your friend ran into, began to close in around him. As he realized his folly, his anger and rage began turning the earth around him black. He cast balls of concentrated evil at the walls of his new prison. They shook the ground with their impact, but the barrier held. I started the incantation as Our Creator instructed, the others standing guard. Erra was not without his tricks. Several legions of his creations had been hidden around the outskirts of his fortress, outside the barrier. These were different, faster, and far more ruthless. Ral was the first to be attacked. His sword was a cyclone of razor-sharp air. Gaian was right next to him. The ground under his feet rolling up his body and forming itself to him then hardening into armor, filling his hands and becoming weapons."

Sonya is in a haze. Her head is spinning. She can't focus her eyes, but she can hear Vitra loud and clear, her voice echoing inside her head.

"The other three were engaged as well, fire raining from the sky, jets of water crashing down, bolts of lightning striking the enemy and scattering them across the ground. Erra was more skilled than we had realized. Ral and Gaian fought side by side, fueled by fury. Lost so deep in battle trance that they wanted only for violence. I used their bloodlust to my advantage and began the ritual. As Enki's life drained from his eyes, Erra began to weaken. He fell to his knees, clutching his chest as though the air had left him. When he lay still, his horrors fell as well. Erra was put into a state of suspended existence. Our Creator recognized that he would still be powerful in death, so her grand idea was not to destroy him but to contain him for a long time, a very long time, until she was able to prepare, *things*, for what would eventually come."

Evan is asleep. Rich is almost there himself. Vitra looks at Sonya and speaks one last sentence before she falls asleep with her friends. "This is why you are here, girl. Everything is ready."

Sonya blacks out. Gaian carefully picks up all three of them and lays them in the beds he prepared. They sleep soundly, physically exhausted after the day's events.

Ral looks at Vitra and asks, "Do you think they will manage to finish this?"

"They have to," she replies. "There is no other option."

Rich awakens, his brain slowly putting things together again. For a brief moment, he imagines it was all a dream. The elk, the bear, the people who were living in that cave. Then his eyes open. The dim light of the cave illuminates all before him. He sees Sonya and Evan still sleeping. He sees Ral sitting at the table, alone, presumably left to guard them as they slept. He sits up and swings his legs over the edge of the bed. He stares at his feet for a moment, remembering everything that Vitra had told him before he passed out, wondering what any of that had to do with him and his friends, wondering why he was here, wondering if anyone was missing him right now back at work.

Ral looks over at him and says, "Good morning or afternoon or evening. It's hard to tell time in this cave. What would you and your friends like for what we shall pretend is breakfast?"

"How about a glass of whiskey?" Rich asks.

"Well, we have plenty of spirits here, but you should not indulge so early. You have work to do today. How about…some biscuits and sausage gravy with caramelized onions and fried eggs?" Ral says with a smile.

Rich looks at him for a moment, then says, "That's my favorite food, ever. How did you know that?"

"Easy enough, my boy. You were basically shouting it!" Ral laughs as he stands up and walks toward the stove. He tosses some wood in its belly and grabs a pan from the wall. "Come, have a seat. I made coffee. Your friends will wake soon. There is still much to discuss, and the others will be here in a moment."

Rich walks over to the table and takes a seat. He notices his clothes have been changed. He is now dressed in robes like the cave dwellers. He looks back at his friends and notices that they are dressed similarly. "So did y'all drug us? Because that tea was dank," he says.

"No, it was not what you would consider drugs. Just herbs to help you all sleep," says Ral as he cracks an egg into the pan. "You feel rested, yes?"

"Yeah, actually. Now that you mention it, I feel great." Rich kicks back into the chair and puts his feet up on the table. He looks around again, letting the details soak in. From what he can tell of the place, they have lived here for some time. The floor around the table has smooth grooves made around the feet of three of the chairs. The cast-iron skillet Ral is using to cook is well used also, caked in soot around its bottom.

"How long have you guys been in this cave?" Rich asks.

"That is a hard question to answer. You would make me define something that had no definition," Ral responds.

Rich shakes his head and goes to speak again when he sees Sonya sit down across from him.

"I feel amazing," she says. "Like I don't remember the last time I slept like that. Oh em gee! What smells so good? Is he cooking?"

"Yeah, my favoritest food ever," Rich adds.

Vitra walks in with Gaian, her pale figure diminutive compared to the giant behind her. She looks around and sees two of the three are awake. She points to Evan and Gaian silently walks over to his bed, grabs the side of it with one hand, and lifts it up, dumping Evan on the hard floor.

"What the fuck, dude!" Evan cries in protest.

"You have been awake for some time," Gaian states calmly. "It is rude to eavesdrop."

Evan stands up and adjusts himself, straightening his clothes. He walks over to the table and sits next to Sonya.

Vitra looks at them, taking them in, examining their dispositions. "Well, you all remember my story, yes?" They all nod, Gaian included. "I wasn't talking to you, dear," she says, laughing. "So the reason you are here is to finalize the Creator's plans to eliminate the threat Erra poses to the world."

"Yeah…about that," begins Evan, "what you're telling me is that you're really old, yeah? Because clearly none of this has happened in recent history, yes? So how old are you? And why aren't you all dead?"

"Well, I explained the barrier keeping you in here, but what I didn't tell you is that there is a spell of sorts on the cave itself. Basically, time is almost stopped entirely inside the cave. Well, not stopped, but it slips around us, like water around a rock in the stream," Vitra says.

"Well, that was actually a really good explanation…," Evan whispered.

"Right. Me, Sonya, and *Evan*. Stopping a dude that can make zombies and shit. Clearly, you drank too much of that tea." Rich chuckles as he takes a sip of his coffee. "How are we supposed to make that happen, eh?"

"Let me begin by explaining something to you all. You are not just average people. You are, in fact, direct descendants of our bloodline. Our power flows in your veins, in your very DNA," Vitra explains. "Our Creator allowed us to merge with humanity, knowing that one day our progeny will be required to take up the mantle and bring an ultimate end to Erra and his evil."

Evan is staring in disbelief, his mouth open and eyes wide. Sonya is leaning on her elbows, listening intently. Rich is still reclined casually, as though he heard nothing at all. Hands behind his head, smile on his face.

Evan looks at him and asks, "Hey, man, did you hear any of that, or is your head too far up your ass?"

Rich just keeps smiling and says, "I heard every word of it, Evan. I'm just enjoying the experience. This is fun, yeah? Magical necromancers, a tripod that turns into a pussycat." Gaian grunts in annoyed protest. "Emo patient zero, and what did I say last time? Buff Wednesday Adams? Something like that. I'm afraid she might catch a sunburn from a flashlight."

Vitra looks at him and says, "I do not know who this Wednesday Adams is, but I'm assuming your analogy is derogatory. I understand you may be upset due to the current situation, *but every word was true*." Her anger got the better of her. The lights in the room dimmed as though they were being smothered. Her skin glowed softly then began to darken with the room until she was almost invisible, and in a second, the lights flared back to life, and she returned to her standard self.

Rich is sitting up straight at this point. He leans in and says to Vitra, "Will you just get to the fucking point already?"

"Fine." She huffs. "The drink that helped you all rest last night was a special herbal mixture that will help the latent energy in your body intensify to manipulatable levels."

"Sooo…superheroes? You're making us into superheroes?" squeaks Evan with a hint of glee in his tone.

"No, not superheroes. Just reawakening your genetic ability to use the powers bestowed to us by Our Creator," Vitra replies.

"And we're the only people with these powers…yes? No one else has these abilities besides yourselves and this bad guy?" Evan says.

Vitra looks at him, "Yes, Evan. This is accurate."

"Yeah. We're totally superheroes," he says as he stands up and walks away from the table. He heads back to his bed and lays down, throwing the cover over his head.

Ral sets down several large platters of food in the center of the table followed shortly by a stack of plates and silverware. Rich and Sonya do not engage in any further conversation. They are overcome with an intense hunger at the sight of the fresh food before them. Rich and Sonya immediately dig in. Evan, hearing the scraping of forks on plates, leaps out of his bed and quickly joins them at the table. Vitra stands by, watching them feast, while Ral sips gently from a steaming cup of coffee. The three friends devour the food in minutes, leaving behind nothing but a couple of crumbs and empty dishes.

"Okay…so we've had our 'powers' turned on. What next?" Sonya asks.

"That should be obvious, my dear. We begin training," says Ral. "Each of us will take one of you, our descendant, and teach you how to use what you have been given. Rich, you are with Vitra. Sonya, you will come with me, leaving Gaian with Evan."

Gaian is standing over Evan, leering at him while Evan sheepishly looks back. Gaian says, "I believe you have mine, Ral. This one is puny and pale. Perhaps it's yours, Vitra?" For a brief moment, Gaian's brow furrowed as he exhibited emotion in the form of discontent.

"I'm sorry, my friend, but these are the correct pairings. *He* is your kin.

With a heavy sigh, Gaian slumps his shoulders and begins walking out of the room. "*Come to my quarters, boy,*" he bellows. Evan sits up and looks at his friends. Rich raises his hand and waves with palpable sarcasm, flapping his hand at the wrist. Sonya stands up. Ral offers her his elbow. She smiles and loops her arm through his, and he leads her off. Rich looks at Vitra, with a half grin, says, "All right. Let's get started then."

CHAPTER 5

Gaian enters his cavern. The roof is tall and domed. It smells of dank musky earth. It's easily sixty yards long and forty across. Immediately to the left of the doorway is a large desk and chair surrounded by stacks of books as high as Gaian himself. In the corner of the room was a massive forge complete with enormous tools and an anvil bigger than Evan. Gaian walks over to his desk and opens drawers as he searches for something. With a deep grunt, he pulls out a small bottle from one of the drawers and examines it.

"Boy," he says flatly.

Evan looks at him and sees him standing there with the bottle carefully pinched between two fingers. He hesitates for a moment then slowly begins walking toward Gaian.

"What is that?" he asks as he eyes the shimmering green liquid contained in the bottle.

"This is what you will need to reach your full potential. The mixture of herbs you drank earlier needed time to take effect. Now you must consume this to finish the transformation." Gaian's voice booms through the cavernous room, reverberating from the walls like a chorus.

"What's, uh, what's in it?" Evan asks.

"What is in it is irrelevant. You only need to know that it's necessary to moving forward," Gaian says sternly. "Now drink it."

He thrusts the bottle toward Evan who takes it from his fingers. He looks concerned as he pops the cork from its neck and slowly raises it to his nostrils. He takes a whiff of its contents and finds the aroma rather sweet. He presses it to his lips and takes a sip. The flavor is similar to the smoothies he used to get from the organic grocery store, sweet but with a flavor that always tasted very "green." He drinks the bottle down and hands the empty vessel back to Gaian. They stand there, looking at one another for several moments. Evan looks around the room, trying to avoid making eye contact with the giant. He begins feeling more and more anxious as time goes on. Then Gaian sighs heavily.

"This should have worked by now," he says. "I don't understand why it is ineffective." He walks back to his desk and opens the same drawer he got the bottle from and pulls out another. He hands it to Evan and motions for him to drink again.

"Are you sure I should drink another already?" Evan asks nervously.

"Wait, not yet," the big man says.

He turns to his desk again and flips through pages of a book. He tosses it down and grabs another, repeating the process. He does this several times until he finds the page he had been looking for. He kneels on the ground and grabs a piece of chalk from his pocket and begins drawing. First a circle, then seven intersecting lines placed equidistant around it going from edge to edge, joining in the center. He draws characters in the spaces between the lines. They seem oddly familiar to Evan, like he's seen them somewhere before but can't recall exactly where.

"Place your left foot here and your right foot here," says Gaian. Evan complies. "Now drink the potion."

Evan lifts it to his lips again, subtly tremoring with uncertainty. As he drinks the second vial, he hears Gaian chanting in the strange tongue he used when he turned into the fluffy cat. As the last drop falls from the bottle and lands on his tongue, he feels his stomach twist. Afraid of vomiting, he tries to move away from Gaian, but his feet are held fast in place. Looking down, he sees roots growing from the ground, encircling his ankles. The reality of his situation strikes him in the chest like a meteorite. Perspiration dews on his forehead and palms while his mouth dries up as the fear inside intensifies. An immense dread is making itself known, looming over its victim like a predator closing in for the killing blow. Nothing that had happened up to now really felt that dangerous, almost like he was playing a game or watching a movie. He wants so badly to undo everything and return home to the safety of his room, his entire being is trying to force this all to just stop and disappear. He closes his eyes hard against the stark truth that is slowly pressing down on him as the stress burns away at nerve endings.

His breathing quickens as his heart races. He clutches his chest, feeling like his heart is about to fly from his ribs. He feels like the room is getting smaller. The roof is closing in on him. A sharp sting flies up his legs all the way to the back of his neck, taking his breath away. He looks down as he gasps for air, trying to find its source. He can't believe what he's seeing. His legs are longer now, thick and muscular. His entire body is growing, elongating. Then the pain hits. It feels like joints are being simultaneously ripped and twisted apart, from fingertips to toes, mind-numbing, excruciating pain. He arches back then rolls forward as core muscles convulse from the unrelenting misery.

He looks at his hands. They are three times the size they were, but the fingers are gangly and crooked like those of an old witch, bones jutting out in different directions, twitching and snapping as they grow. He gets hit with another wave of searing pain. It flies up to his spine. He can feel vertebrae grinding and popping as they enlarge and stretch. His breath is gone now, his face a twisted expression of agony. His jaw and cranium shift and crunch, bringing with it a sickening metallic taste in the back of his throat building into pressure so intense it feels like his eyes are about to erupt from his skull. With a final sickening snap, his bones are still. His body slumps backward to the floor. His massive shoulders and frame make a wet slap as he connects with the ground. The roots binding his feet retract into the earth. Gaian stands over him, examining the outcome. Evan is now at least four times his former size. Muscular and large, similar to Gaian, but smaller. His red hair matted flat from sweat. After a moment, Gaian checks his heartbeat, making sure he still lives. He feels a pulse and sees Evan's chest heave gently as he takes a breath into his lungs. Gaian stands up and looks at the empty bottle on the ground.

"The second vial was too much, but at least the boy didn't die," he booms out loud.

Ral leads Sonya into a room filled with tall pillars. Chains and ropes connect to them randomly. Platforms hang from the ceiling and walls. This room is so long Sonya cannot even see the other side. As she stands there, taking it in, Ral walks over to a large carpeted area just near the doorway. There are two chairs on either side of a small table. On this table sits a small chest adorned with gold filigree. He opens the chest and pulls from it a vial of clear liquid with a faint opalescent hue.

"Drink this, please," he says as he walks toward her. "You will feel the effects immediately. It will be intense but not painful."

"What is it? What does it do?" Sonya asks.

"Well then," Ral begins, "the tea you drank before you went to sleep had a specific mixture of herbs and extracts in it, right?"

"Yeah…?" she replies.

"Well, this is like the medication that does the work, whereas that tea you had first is like the catalyst that will allow this new tincture to smoothly alter your body's DNA to effectively implement a new metabolic process."

"That sounds really complicated," Sonya replies.

"I could give you a more detailed explanation to help you better understand, if you like," Ral says.

"No thanks. I'll just drink it…" Sonya downs it with a fast gulp. She stands still for a moment, waiting for something to happen, her stomach lurches slightly, her chest tightens, and she places her hands on her abdomen, unsure what is coming. She feels a pressure rising in her throat as if something is forcing its way out. With a sudden gasp, she opens her mouth, and a large belch escapes. She looks at Ral, whose eyes reflect both disgust and surprise.

"Excuse me," she says sheepishly.

Ral looks at her and replies, "You are excused. It's hard to say exactly how this was going to affect you, so if that was the worst of it, then I suppose we sh—" Ral is cut off by Sonya abruptly falling to the ground. She desperately gasps as she struggles to draw breath, her hands clawing and grasping at her throat. Ral is instantly kneeling beside her. "Calm your mind, child. Focus your thoughts. Picture the air coming into your lungs and filling them!

"Do as I say!"

Her eyes are looking more desperate now, the whites are turning bloodshot from the strain. She begins to feel consciousness slipping away from her, her lips and fingernails turning a deep blue.

"*Hear me, girl!* Focus! *Focus!*" Ral shouts at her. Her eyes flutter. Her head rolls back, and as Ral begins to feel dread creep over him, Sonya suddenly inhales a deep breath. Her lungs consume the air with ravenous hunger. The color returns to her lips. Her eyes begin to move around, keying in on the look of terror on Ral's face.

"That…was terrifying," she wheezes. "But I think I got it."

"Excellent," Ral says with a heavy sigh. "Can you feel the air in your body? Can you sense its presence? It should feel like a warm humming inside your lungs and limbs."

"Yes. I can feel it," she says. It's strange but somewhat pleasant. With every breath, she can feel it build, like a pressure inside her. As she exhales, it diminishes, losing its bite.

Rich walks behind Vitra, gently whistling an old country song as he follows her. They soon come to a solid door made of oak, banded together with iron and rivets. Vitra pulls a key from her waist and places it in the lock. With a deep rumble and a heavy creak, the door begins to swing open.

"Please come in," she says.

As they cross the threshold, Rich can't help but notice the total lack of light inside the room. It's pitch black save for one small oil lantern on a table in the middle of the floor directly in front of them. Alongside the lamp was a single vial of a strange green-hued liquid that was gently flickering in the low light. Rich approaches it and examines its contents. Vitra closes the heavy door behind them, latching the deadbolt into the jamb.

"Let me guess. I'm supposed to drink this, right? Why is it so damn dark in here? You guys forget to pay the power bill?" Rich nags as he picks up the vial and holds it closer to his face.

"Hello. My name is Vitra Shadowbane. Welcome to my secret lair." Vitra rolls her eyes as she walks up to Rich's side. "Yes. I need you to drink this. Your keen skills of observation are astonishing."

"Whoa. Easy on the sarcasm, Grandma. I'm the smart-ass here," Rich boasts. He picks up the vial, examining it briefly as he rolls it in his fingers. "So what's going to happen?" he asks.

"It will amplify your current ability to manipulate darkness," she answers.

"I see. So I drink the Kool-Aid and become a ninja," Rich says to himself. "Sure, why not?" He pops the cork out and downs the bottle in one gulp. "So what's next?" he says as he walks away from the table, edging closer to the darkness beyond the light of the dim lantern.

"Next will be a brief, yet a severe moment of intense pain as the potion you drank alters the very fabric of your humanity," Vitra says with a sneer.

"What? Now *that* is some dark shit!" Rich laughs. "Get it? *Dark* shit?" He turns to look at Vitra, but she is gone—vanished without a sound. Rich looks to the door, wondering if maybe she slipped out, but it is shut tight. The room goes black. The lantern extinguished as his back was turned. His eyes adjust slowly to the change.

"I stopped being afraid of the dark some time ago, Granny. What's the next step? Eh?"

Rich's words are chased by a low growl of discontent. He shuffles his way through the blackness back to the table, as he reaches around for the lantern his eyes begin to ache. He reaches one hand up and rubs them, but the ache intensifies into a burn, then a searing fire. His knees buckle as he catches himself on the table. A scream rips past his lips as the pain feeds his rage. His fist slams down, cracking the wood under it. His body burns as though it is on fire, muscles so tense that they feel like they are ripping away from the joints. With a wave of sudden relief, his body relaxes. The pain is gone. His chest heaves violently as he calms himself, slowly returning to normal. His eyes open cautiously, trying to brace for more pain, but it has gone entirely. As he blinks a few times, he notices his new surroundings.

Everything is a dark blue color with traces of ultraviolet streams coming and going through the air and crawling on the ground. He reaches out to grab one as it glides by his head. As he closes his hand around it, the tendril of violet wraps around his fingers. It's smooth and cold to the touch like he's holding a snake made from ice. It floats and dances in his grip as if it were waiting for something. He could feel its anticipation as though it were a living thing.

Vitra's voice drifts to him from far away. "I see you're becoming acquainted already. Excellent. Take a look around the room now. Do you see what's before you?"

Rich looks up and sees a single opening in the wall behind the table. There is a long corridor that goes on for several yards. A single torch on the wall at the end of the corridor ignites itself. The purple tendrils retract violently. Rich winces, sharing their pain momentarily. As he gathers himself, he hears Vitra again.

"Look at you," she says dryly. "Quite like the proverbial duck to water. I dare say I may be genuinely excited for the first time in millennia. Are you ready to begin your training, my boy?"

Rich clenches his hands into fists. A bold wave of determination sweeps through him. He raises his head and replies, "I am."

CHAPTER 6

Evan slowly wakes on the floor of the large domed room. A few aftershocks roll through his body, a lingering side effect from the trauma it just endured. Everything running through his mind right now seemed so unreal, so insanely preposterous that it just could not have been, but as his eyes adjusted to the presence of light, reality bared its fangs. He had hoped that he would wake up in his bed, in his apartment, in his town, not here, not in this damned musky cave of anguish.

Evan sits up and rubs a hand over his face but feels something is not right. He pulls his hand away and stares at it. In place of the thin, lanky fingers that once were now sit thick long digits attached to a palm that resembles a slab of meat. The fingers wiggle around in disbelief, flexing and extending as their owner twists the hand around in examination. Quizzical eyes move down the palm to the forearm, thick cords of muscle contract and bulge under the skin down to the elbow. Evan's eyes light up further as they proceed up the arm. Mountainous biceps that are at least the size his head used to be now take up the majority of his upper arm. The shoulder responsible for carrying the new appendage is of equal measure with heavy mounds of brawn adorning both sides of the neck. A set of pecs that would make even pro bodybuilders jealous are rigidly mounted to a powerful chest. Evan eagerly leaps to his feet and looks down to see two legs extending to the ground that are more like tree trunks than actual legs. He is almost built the same as Gaian, just a bit shorter and ginger. He looks around, making sure he is alone, then pulls his pants open. "Oh, fuck yeah!" he whispers to himself. This mutation did indeed make everything larger.

Heavy footsteps approach from the distance. Evan quickly lets go of his pants and turns to look in their direction. Gaian, coming through the doorway, says, "Good, you have awakened. We are behind schedule due to your nap."

"I wasn't napping. I was blacked out from the pain of your shitty voodoo potion," Evan says.

"It worked, though," Gaian replies.

"Yeah. It sure fuckin did. I'm gigantic. Hurt like a mofo," Evan says.

"Pain is a small price to pay for what you have gained," Gaian says as he walks toward Evan. "It is time for you to learn the extent of your capabilities, boy."

"Sure. Where do we start? You gonna teach me how to be a blacksmith or something? That would be cool," Evan says as he heads for the forge.

"No. You will have no need for smithing once you have grasped your powers." Gaian walks toward him and places his hand on his shoulder. "Your power comes from within you. Your body is now at one with the earth. She will do as you ask so long as you know what you want. You must believe that it will happen. You must feel it in your heart, or else you will be left wanting." Gaian takes his hand away from Evan and raises it above his head. He doesn't say a word, just looks Evan in the eye. Evan can hear a low rumble. He feels it in his toes. He looks down and sees the earth writhing around Gaian's feet, moving like a liquid. In the blink of an eye, the teeming mass of earth flies up Gaian's leg and into his hand. Roots and rock roll over one another, taking the form of a handle, then elongating into a blade. The root catches fire, and the rock begins to melt, smelting itself into obsidian. Gaian twirls the blade easily through the air, tossing it up with one hand, catching it with the other. Then he presents it handle first to Evan. Evan takes it from him, and it crumbles in his hands, falling back to the earth as sand.

Gaian steps back and puts his arms straight out to his sides. The earth swirls at his feet again. This time, it rolls up his body, molding to every muscle and joint, shaping itself into a suit of armor made from solid, yet fluid, granite, moving with him as he begins to walk around Evan.

"All you have to do is will it to happen, and as long as your feet are on the ground, the earth will listen."

"So. I like, just think it? And it happens?" asks Evan.

Gaian nods. Evan closes his eyes and thinks about what to conjure. The first thing that comes to mind is a high-level axe from one of the RPGs he used to play a lot of. With an outstretched arm, palm open in anticipation, Evan focuses on the image, imagining the rock climbing up his back and out to his hand, then taking shape of the legendary Orcish battle axe. He opens his eyes to find nothing: no axe, no bits of rocks climbing over him, just an empty hand clutching only air.

"Hmmm," grumbles Gaian. "Try summoning some armor."

Evan takes a deep breath, trying to collect himself, but the pressure of the situation starts coming down on him. His mind empties but fills back up again. He squeezes his eyes hard against the negativity, but fighting it only makes it worse. A brief montage of his biggest regrets flashes through his mind's eye, forcing him to lose all concentration.

Evan hangs his head. "I can't do it," he says. "I'm not like you. I'm not meant to do any of this. It's just not who I am."

Gaian grows angry. His voice rumbles throughout the room. "*Boy,* I told you how to make it happen. You need only will it into existence. If you do not hold belief in your own ability, you will not be able to accomplish anything."

"What the fuck do you know? Huh? I *tried.* It didn't work. Maybe you're just wrong? Did you ever think about *that?*" Evan lashes out at Gaian.

Gaian remains stoic and emotionless, impossible to read. "The diamond does not form on its own. It requires pressure," Gaian says. He walks over to the desk full of books, picking up one wrapped in hand-sewn leather. He opens the book and begins reading. He kneels again and draws more strange symbols in chalk on the ground. He forms a small dagger from rock in his right hand and cuts his left palm, dripping blood onto several of the purposefully arranged images. He stands back from the effigy, looking directly at Evan, and raises his bloody palm toward him.

The ground under Evan's feet shakes and shifts. At first, he thinks that he's finally using his magic, but he soon realizes that is not the case. Something is climbing out of the dirt. A hand bursts from the ground, its flesh gray and rotted. Then an arm reaches out and slams into the surface, pulling an upper body out of the earth, followed by hips and legs. Four more of them erupt in a similar fashion.

"What the fuck is this, Gaian! What are these things?" Evan looks around in a panic. He sees Gaian walking to the doorway. "WAIT!" he yells.

Gaian turns to look at him, a rock wall begins to fill the hole that was the only way out. "Those are draugr. I told you what must be done, boy. Choose to live."

The wall closes up entirely. Evan turns to see the group of draugr shambling closer. He exhales a panicked wheeze as the terror takes control of his body. He backpedals and slams into the wall. On the outside of the room, Gaian raises the earth up to an observation window. He stands on the platform, watching as the draugr close in on Evan.

"So where do we start, Ral? What's a first? You gonna teach me how to fly or something?" asks Sonya, the fear of what had just occurred totally gone from her mind already.

"No, my dear. No flying. I have a simple first task for you." Ral walks over to the base of one of the closest pillars and places a candle on the ground in front of it. "Blow out this candle."

Sonya takes a step toward it. Ral holds up a hand and says, "No, from where you are. Blow it out from there."

The candle is too far away, at least fifteen feet or so. Sonya looks at Ral and says, "How am I supposed to blow it out from *here*? That's impossible."

Ral walks over to her side, turns to face the candle, and looks her in the eyes as he puckers his lips and blows. He sends a sharp burst of wind from his lips and extinguishes the candle. She gawks at him as he walks back to the candle and reignites it.

He returns to her side and folds his arms.

"You can do this as well. You only need to understand that air, wind, your very breath, is now an extension of your physical being. You can accelerate the molecules leaving your body to such a speed that it can penetrate a living creature, a tree, even stone. All you have to do is will it. Don't think about it as something magical or supernatural. Only think of it as something your body does, like pumping blood or digesting food."

"Autonomic is the word you're looking for," Sonya offers.

Ral looks slightly impressed. "I did not expect you to have that kind of vocabulary. I must not underestimate you."

"Well, before all *this* happened," she says while waving a hand over her head, "I had been going to school to be a nurse. I mean, I was trying to be an influencer, but I realistically needed a backup plan because I was pretty sure it wouldn't work out."

Ral nods his head and says, "Yes, the world of social media is a fickle one indeed."

"You've lived in a cave for, for I don't know how long. How do you know what social media is?" Sonya asks, one of her eyebrows raises from intrigue.

"We are not as closed off here as you may assume. There are many ways for us to learn what goes on outside this lonely cave." Ral sighs slightly as he finishes his sentence.

"You're full of surprises, aren't ya?" she replies. "So blowing out a candle, from across the room. All I have to do is believe it's a part of my body?"

Ral nods. "Yes. That's it. Don't think it. *Feel* it." He turns to walk away. As he nears the door, he turns to look at Sonya, feeling her gaze as he left. "I will return soon. I need to check in on Gaian for a moment. I feel my presence is required."

"Okay," Sonya replies. As Ral leaves the room, she aims her focus on the candle. Everything that Ral told her is rolling through her mind. She thinks about how it felt once she regained control of her breath—the feeling that pulsed inside her body. She tries to reign it in, drawing it to her again. She puckers her lips and looks at the candle. Then exhales sharply. She feels her eyes bulging with the effort, but all she accomplishes is spitting a large stream of drool out of her mouth down her chin.

"Gross," she says as she wipes it away.

She tries again, focusing as she was told to do, willing it to happen. Her eyes find the flame. She stares it down and releases the wind in her lungs.

The flame flickers and dances for a moment. Then straightens out and returns to normal. Sonya's excitement builds, and she jumps in place, letting out a squeal.

"Yaassss!" she says to herself. She shakes her hands out, trying to find her center again. "Okay, Sonya. You got this," she says to herself with a confident smile.

Rich is idly playing with the wine-colored wisps of night that swirl and wind around him. He watches how it flows and moves like it's alive, like it's sentient. He traces his finger through it and observes as it follows. Vitra's disembodied voice comes to him again. "Your training will be simple enough once you grasp the new reality of your existence. Those trails of smoke circling around you are a physical concentration of darkness. They may seem like they are alive, but they are not. They are simply responding to you. Your body is a conduit. The darkness around you can flow from you—through you, into you. You are now a creature of night."

"Like a vampire or something?" Rich asks.

"No, not like a vampire. I said you are a creature of night. Meaning that you are made from it. It is now a part of your very genetic material. It is a part of you. You are a part of it. You can manipulate it, manifest it into physical objects. Open your palm and look at it," Vitra commands.

Rich opens his hand and looks at his palm. As he stares at it, a small cyclone of darkness whips around in his hand. He leans in closer to it, examining its actions. It begins taking shape, little particles of night swirl and dance in his palm, forming into a solid object. It grows heavier as it gains substance. Its shape gradually becomes recognizable. It's a key, a simple key. He fiddles with it for a moment after it solidifies, rolling it around in his fingers, feeling its weight in his hand.

"Neat trick," Rich says with an unusually serious tone in his voice. "So how can I do that?"

"All you need to do is feel it in your heart. Will it into existence. Think about what you want and command your body to manifest it. Don't doubt yourself. Just command it." As Vitra finished, the key in Rich's hand returned to purple vapor and vanished. "Go ahead. Give it a try. Make anything at all. Whatever comes to mind."

Rich looks into his hand. He tries to force something into existence, but nothing happens. After several breaths, he tries again, this time hovering his other hand over top in an attempt to help but to no avail. "Goddamn it!" he groans through clenched teeth. The dark around him spins and twists, circling around his head, forming into a cloud of black rage.

Vitra's voice comes to him again. "We need to discuss something, Rich."

"Hell yeah, we do! I'm all out of fuckin whiskey, and it's bullshit," Rich says angrily.

"*That* is part of your problem. You have no need for alcohol. It clouds your mind and weakens your judgment. I know why you drink so much. I can feel it. You miss them very much, don't you?" Vitra says as she walks closer to him.

"Please don't," Rich begs. "Stay the fuck out of my head…"

"They aren't gone, you know. They are still here," Vitra offers quietly.

Rich looks at her, his eyes burning with fury. "Don't patronize me with some touchy-feely hippy bullshit. I've heard it a lot over the years, and I'm sick of it." Rich is glaring at Vitra, anger building in his veins.

"Rich, you misinterpret my words. They are *here*, with us, your wife and child. They did not cease to exist." Vitra raises a hand, an image takes form in the dark mist swirling around her: two people—a woman and a child. Rich falls to his knees. Tears stream down his face as he reaches out with both hands, his body yearning to draw them in for one last embrace. His eyes study their faces, the bittersweet feeling of old memories washes over him.

"Margaret… Suzanne… I miss you both so much." Rich is on his hands and knees, tears pouring from his eyes. He sobs uncontrollably as he looks upon the face of his wife and child. "Susie would be thirteen now. Her mother and I loved her so much. She wanted to be a lawyer, can you believe that? A seven-year-old that wanted to be a lawyer." He barely manages to get words out between sobs.

Vitra kneels beside him, placing an arm around his shoulders. "I can feel the pain inside you, Rich. I understand. Your spirit is suffering, and that's what is making it hard for you to think clearly. You rely on alcohol to dull your senses to a tolerable level. Otherwise, you would not be able to function."

Through his tears, Rich says, "Is there some kind of potion you can give me? Something that will make the pain go away?"

Vitra shakes her head gently. "No. There is nothing that I can do about this. The wounds are there. They cannot be healed." Rich rolls back onto his shins, his arms folded across his chest. "I do have some information for you that may help."

Vitra's words hit him like a hammer. He snaps his eyes to hers. "What? What is it? Tell me!" he begs.

"The energy that creates life is not our own. It is borrowed," Vitra says. "When we die, it returns to Our Creator, but it's different at that point. It carries with it the essence of what makes a person who they are, their soul, if you will."

"What are you drivin' at?" Rich asks.

Vitra huffs at his impatience, then says, "They are here, but they have simply returned to the Creator, waiting for you."

"Waiting for me!" Rich shouts.

"Yes, Richard, they are waiting for you. You will see them again once you and your friends accomplish what's being asked of you, but before that, you have to learn to control the darkness within you. Now stand up. We have work to do." Vitra reaches down, offering her hand to Rich. He looks her in the eyes and takes grabs it, pulling himself onto his feet.

CHAPTER 7

Evan runs for his life from the undead that are pursuing him. Their rotted flesh drops to the floor in chunks as they give chase. Evan looks back, his eyes soaking in every detail of these abominations, their faces empty of expression, mouths agape, searching for sustenance. Thin arms swing violently as their legs carry them onward with awkward agility.

As Gaian watches his progeny, Ral appears at his side, peering into the room with him. "Do you see what he does? He runs. All the might of the earth at his disposal and he runs like a scared child," Gaian says with disgust in his voice.

"He is not experienced with any of this, Gaian. Having him be chased by the undead will not help either," Ral says.

"I know his kind. This is the only way. He is weak of mind and spirit. His body is much more capable now. He just needs to realize it." Gaian flicks his wrist, and a single root lifts from the ground. Evan, who is too preoccupied with the draugr, does not see it. It catches his foot, sending him toppling to the ground.

The draugr are tearing and biting at him as soon as he hits the ground. He lashes out, sending them flying back with every hit, but their hunger has given them frenetic energy. They quickly regain their footing and lunge at him again. Evan screams for help, tears pouring from his eyes, begging Gaian to stop them. His arms and chest are covered in blood from the lacerations caused by tooth and nail. Their teeth rip into his skin as they begin to consume him. Ral moves to help, but Gaian grabs him by the shoulder with one mighty hand. "Not yet," he says. "Watch."

As Evan is devoured, he feels the fear of death gripping his chest. His eyes close as he flails in vain to protect himself. He starts to shout at them, "Stop it, goddamn it! Get the fuck off me! Stop it! STOP!"

With his last words, a rush of power washes through his body. His anger blasts through his fear and doubt. As a wave of cold washes over him, the sound of tearing flesh is replaced by the scraping of teeth on stone. Evan is still huddled on the floor, arms over his face, but the pain is gone now. He opens his eyes and looks down, his skin is coated in rough stone. The draugr are now gnawing on solid granite, their teeth cracking and chipping. His right hand reaches down and grabs one of his assailants by the throat. He easily lifts it off the ground and crushes its neck with one powerful hand. He throws aside the lifeless body and targets a new victim. This one's head is smashed between his two mighty fists. Brain matter and chunks of cranium splatter his face. He grabs another by the leg and throws it across the room. He casually slaps the others away as he laughs maniacally. Their bodies hurdle through the air as he makes toys of them.

Remembering what Gaian wanted him to do, he reaches out and looks on as rock begins to crawl up his legs, his torso, and into his hand. A massive hammer takes shape in his palm. He reaches it to the sky and swings it down with all his might. It plows through a draugr's cranium down into its chest cavity. Vulgarly cleaving it in two. He kicks it in the chest and sends the body smashing into the wall. Its entrails exploded out of the hole where the hammer was. He grabs the next one by the hips and the shoulder and rips it in half like a piece of paper, slamming its upper body into the ground. He stomps on its face, flattening its head into a pile of unidentifiable mash.

There is one draugr remaining, dragging its limp lower half as it crawls toward him. He had thrown it across the room with such force its pelvis exploded on impact. He walks up to it and kicks it onto its back. He holds it down with one foot as it struggles to grab him. Its nails peel back and snap off on his stone skin. With slow, deliberate pressure, he caves in its chest, forcing blood and other bodily fluids out of its cranial orifices.

The rocks barring the exit recede into the earth again as Gaian enters the room. He looks around at the carnage Evan left in his wake and nods gently, approving of what he sees. "Good work. I knew that you would be able to control it, just needed the proper motivation." Evan looks at Gaian, anger courses through him.

"You could have killed me, you fucking psycho!" Evan fumes. "Could have just given me a few more tries or some shit, but nooo, let's just jump straight to attempted murder! Thank God you live in a cave far away from other people."

"Stop your incessant whining. You actually accomplished something today. When was the last time you could say that?" Gaian says as he walks toward Evan.

In a fit of rage, Evan swings his hammer above his head and sends it soaring at Gaian. Smiling, Gaian catches it smoothly in one hand and throws it back at Evan, catching him in the abdomen. It sends him careening back into Gaian's desk, scattering books around the room.

Gaian lets out an irritated grunt and says, "Given the circumstances, I will not be mad at you for destroying my library. I am pleased with your newfound aggression. You need to harness that. Make it work for you. I have no real fighting technique. I simply rely on my sheer might and rage."

Evan lifts himself out of the pile of books and broken desk. His outer skin crumbles away, revealing his normal condition. He looks at his body and sees that his wounds are still there, but they are mostly healed. "Gaian, I'm sorry for trying to smite you. I don't know what came over me. I think I'm hangry. I've never been this hungry in my entire life. Can we get some food?"

"Yes. One thing you need to be aware of though, your new body requires a massive amount of caloric energy for both normal function and earth manipulation. You will need to eat, often, and a lot, as do I. We must go now." Gaian turns to walk through the door. Evan dusts himself off and looks back at the carnage he left.

With a snicker, he says, "Sweet. I'm a total badass now." He moves for the door with his head held high.

After giving up on trying to reason with Gaian, Ral returns to his chamber to check on Sonya. He enters the hall sees the candle is still lit and unmoved, but Sonya is nowhere to be seen. A low hum becomes audible from the distance, rapidly closing in. Unsure of what to expect, Ral takes a defensive stance. With a gust of wind so sharp he was forced to blink, Sonya is standing in front of him, smiling ear to ear.

"This is like having sex when you're camping!" Sonya exclaims happily.

"I don't understand the expression," Ral says with an eyebrow raised.

"It's fucking *in tents*!" she shouts as she takes off again.

Ral smiles as the joke settles in. With a gust of wind, he is gone, chasing after her. She is hardly touching the ground as she runs, her body taking readily to the change. Ral examines her form, taking note of small mistakes and areas for improvement. With ease, he overtakes her then throws his hands out in front of him, stopping almost immediately. Anticipating his actions, Sonya reacts swiftly by leaping over the top of him, flipping her feet overhead and bringing her face close to Ral's. His eyes lock with hers for a split second, and he sees her mocking glare all too clearly. Ral feels a tingle of exhilaration run down his spine. He hasn't had a reason to put much effort into anything for some time. He decides her next lesson will be in humility.

Sonya is zipping through the chamber, pillars flying by her so fast they look like a solid wall. She looks behind her and sees Ral gaining ground. She accelerates, wanting to show him how quickly she has taken to her power. When she looks behind her again, he is almost right on top of her. She blinks, and he is gone, vanished entirely. She scans her surroundings. To her left, Ral appears for a split second only to instantly vanish. Her eyes are darting every-where, trying to find him. He reappears on her right, then in front of her, then to her left again. Sonya tries to lose him. She is pushing herself harder than she has yet dared. Ral is behind her. He reaches out and taps her shoulder. As she turns to look, he is gone again. Her concentration broken. She is careening straight for the wall of pillars on her left. She looks ahead and sees she is about to make contact. She panics and attempts to correct herself, but she failed to compen-sate for her speed and overcorrects.

She stumbles, one foot hitting the ground and violently ripping back tearing tendons in her ankle. The pain is blinding. As she falls to the ground, her arms instinctively raise to shield her from the impact.

Her eyes are closed tightly in anticipation. As she is about to make contact with the floor, Ral is there again. He grabs her shirt with one hand and slows them both to a standstill. He lets her fall the rest of the way. She grunts as she crumples to the ground, immediately rolling onto her back and grabbing her ankle. The pain is so intense she can hardly breathe. Ral leans over her and examines her injury.

"It would seem you have done serious damage to your ankle. We should go see Vitra. You're lucky I was here to catch you. Do you have any idea how fast you were going?" Ral looks at Sonya, waiting for her to respond, but she is suffering too greatly. "I am impressed with you. I haven't moved that quick for some time. You made me break a sweat."

Ral lifts her into his arms and carries her off. "I really am impressed, you know. I asked you earlier if you knew how fast you were going, would you like to know?" Ral asks her.

Sonya, ignoring the pain, nods her head.

"Well, when I first gave chase, you were doing about forty miles an hour or so. When you ran away from me, you pushed it to nearly sixty-five. Right at the end there, when you nearly tore your foot off, care to guess?" Ral says as he looks down at her, but she shakes her head. "Fine. I'll just tell you. It's hard to tell exactly, but it felt close to one hundred miles per hour. If my math is right. Current units of measure for speed are different from what we used in our time."

Sonya's eyes widen a bit as she weighs the information. "How do you know what speed I was going?" she says.

"That's the easy part," Ral begins. "All I had to do was see how many feet you were moving per second, using the pillars as a physical reference."

"Ral, so how exactly was I moving so quick?" she asks.

"I'm glad you want to know. Basically, your body reacts with the molecular energy contained in the oxygen around you. The more oxygen, the more you can manipulate. The way you move through the air like that, your body pushes the air around you down. It hits the ground and creates a cushion under you. You occasionally will have to propel yourself upward again. You're not flying, just floating for a bit, at high speed. The faster you go, the more oxygen you have access to, the faster you can go. That's a rather advanced skill to be able to run like that. Tell me, how quickly did you blow out the candle?" Ral looks down at her.

She looks up at him and then looks away. Then replies, "I, uh… I didn't actually blow it out. Couldn't quite figure it out. I got flustered and wanted to go for a quick jog so I could try to calm down. I just started running. I pushed myself really hard and ran faster and faster. Soon, I started like, floating? I thought I was jumping, but then it just started getting further and further. Then I didn't even need to put my feet on the ground."

Ral's eyebrow raises slightly. He says, "Wait, you didn't put your feet on the ground at all? That entire time?"

"No. Didn't think I was supposed to," Sonya mutters timidly.

Ral looks at her and says, "Sonya, not even I can stay afloat for more than a few seconds."

Sonya's cheeks flush with blood from the acknowledgment of her achievements.

"But as soon as your foot's better, you're going to blow out that candle before I let you take another step," Ral says sternly.

*****

Vitra walks in circles around Rich, her eyes studying him. "Our first lesson will be simple. I created a key and placed it in your hand, correct? So you must do the same, with a twist."

Rich cocks his head to the side and says, "A twist, eh? Go on."

"I am going to vanish deep inside the catacombs that lie at the end of this hallway. You must find me and place the key in my hand," she says.

"So hide-and-seek, Vitra? That's it?" Rich says.

"No, that's not it at all. You must also stand within this circle." She waves a finger, and a circle of darkness whirls into existence around his feet. "If you step outside of it, I will know it. There will be consequences should you step out of bounds. Try it now."

Rich looks at the circle of mist around him. It is roughly three feet across, not leaving him much room for movement. He hesitantly reaches a hand out across the threshold. As his fingertip breaches the border, a single needle of concentrated night lunges out from it and pricks him sharply in his index finger. A drop of crimson quickly forms from the wound. It begins to drip steadily. Rich looks at it in quizzical horror. For such a small injury, it is bleeding profusely.

"When flesh is rived by darkness, it does not heal. It will not stop bleeding. That little pinprick you have will eventually cause you to lose consciousness and black out. Then you will die from exsanguination." Vitra looks at him, waiting for his response.

"Uhh, what's exsanguination?" Rich asks, his eyes absently searching the floor.

Vitra rolls her eyes and says "That means you will bleed to death, Richard."

"Oh. I mean, I knew that. I just wasn't certain." His hand reaches to the back of his head nervously. As he brings his arm down, he forgets about his confines and swings his forearm past the circle. A larger spike shoots out and punctures his arm just below the elbow. Blood starts slowly pouring from the second wound.

"Well, fuck me, that was an accident. Can I get a mulligan?" he asks.

"No. You cannot. There are no second chances outside this cave. Therefore, there will be none inside this cave. Find me, and I will share with you the secret of how to stop the bleeding." With her last words, she began to vanish. Her entire body turns into the purple mist that swirls around him. Vitra's disembodied voice echoes through Rich's head. "Judging from the current rate of blood loss, you have about fifty minutes before you lose consciousness. Perhaps eighty before your death. You need to focus. Use the night as an extension of your own senses. *Feel* where I am. Nothing of solid matter can hide from you when the light is gone."

Her voice leaves him. He is standing there alone, blood running down his arm and hand slowly pooling around his feet.

"Okay. You got this, man. Don't be a bitch. Just feel it." Rich looks at all the tendrils of dark flowing around him. He closes his eyes and tries to focus. His mind wanders again to his wife and child and how it felt to see their faces again after so long, as his heart aches for them, causing his mind to cloud. Through the storm, a voice comes to him, a female voice, but not Vitra. It's Margaret. Her voice is clear as though she were standing beside him.

"Richie, honey, I'm so happy to get to talk to you again. I miss you more than I can explain." Rich closes his eyes hard against the swelling emotions. He wants to speak, but he can't force the words out. Margaret continues on, "I know you're in pain, honey. I'm so sorry that you're suffering. I can't help you with that, but I can promise you that when this is all over, you will be with me again. I know it's hard to comprehend, but it will happen. There is a lot that you don't know. Everything will make sense once this is over, but you have to live up to this new potential, or it's never going to happen. So you need to do your best, okay?" Rich simply nods, tears pouring from his eyes and snot running from his nose. Blood still leaking from his arm. "I love you, Richard. Find me when you're done! We miss you!"

His mind is blank. His heart aches so hard he feels like he's about to die. Margaret's words are still weighing heavy on him. His emotions are shot. His body is numb. He starts to feel a cold chill around his left bicep. He looks down and sees a strand of darkness coiling around his arm. It swirls around his bicep, slowly meandering its way to his palm. Rich glares at the crimson wisp and wishes that it would just leave him alone, his patience all but gone at this point. Without hesitation, the tendril dissipates, taking the chill with it. Rich blinks away the disbelief as the tumblers of the lock on the barriers of his mind fall into place. He finds the feeling in his chest that made the shadow vanish, this time urging it to return to him. As fast as it left, it reappeared, entwined around his fingers and palm.

Realization of the new connection sets in. He makes it spin in his palm. A tiny little tornado forms and whirls around and around as he pokes it with his fingers. He wills it to stop, and it stands still, frozen in place with statuesque precision. His imagination takes flight. His mind runs wild at the sudden understanding of what he is experiencing. He focuses on the key, closing his eyes and forcing the image to manifest in his mind's eye, remembering its weight and feel in his hand. He senses something moving in his palm and looks down. There sits a small key, identical to the one Vitra made earlier.

He closes his fist around it, commanding it to dissolve. The heft of the night in his hand gradually diminishes. Dark mist pours out from between his fingers, landing in a pool on the ground that swirls and writhes at his feet.

He recalls what Vitra said, how everything was connected to him in the absence of light. He looks down the hallway behind the table to the single burning torch on the wall. He starts by looking at the ground, not just seeing but feeling the cobblestone floor. He can sense its texture, warm but rough. Every minuscule dimple in the face of the rock feels like a crater. Even the tiny cracks between the stones are like canyons. As he feels his way down the corridor, his reach is cut painfully short by the radiant glow of the torch. There is no way around it—its light is just bright enough to make further probing impossible.

With every second he spends manipulating the night, he grows more adept at controlling it. He expands his perception, closing his eyes to feel the whole hallway at once. The entirety of its presence is visible in his mind's eye. The torch is just a bright void, a glowing hole in the veil of darkness. He considers his options while the thought of his blood steadily flowing from his body weighs on him, but he is able to stifle it. An idea springs to mind. Just outside the halo of the light, he begins to form a needle of solid dark. He aims it at the brightest point of the burning void and hurls it forward. It flies true but begins to disintegrate as it nears the lit torch. He forms a second, this one longer and thicker than the first. He sends it at its target. It fades like the first did, but there is just enough of it to strike the torch, rocking it loose from its sconce. The torch falls to the ground and rolls a few feet away from the wall. The wooden handle casts enough of a gap for darkness to creep through. In a flash, he is feeling his way down the hallway, the full image of his progress forming in his mind.

He has searched out at least a hundred yards of this grotto and has yet to discover Vitra. Unease washes over him with the recognition that his time is growing short. Vitra's words replay in his mind. Everything the dark touches, touches him. He is connected to everything that is bathed in darkness. His senses slow, an idea is coming to him. Gradually, he stops rushing his way through the maze of hallways. Instead of looking for her, he just listens.

At first, there is silence—no noise at all. Through the dark, a steady beat can be heard, soft and slow but rhythmic and constant. It's a heartbeat, Vitra's heartbeat. He sharpens his ear, focusing on the sound. The darkness begins to pulsate in time with the beat of her heart. Like ripples from a stone tossed in a pond, waves of sound emanate from the source. The image builds itself in his head as he feels his way through the endless corridors.

The pulse from Vitra is strong now. He is close. She must be just ahead. As he senses his way around the next corner, he is brought to a painful halt, a burning void of light is blinding the image. Her heartbeat is strong and clear. She must be just at the end of this hall under whatever light source is blinding him.

Her voice comes to him in his mind again, "Good job. You found me. You're learning fast. You're almost done. Just put that key in my hand and you'll be ready to advance."

Rich focuses on the brightest point in the void and hurls a massive spear of blackness at it. A sharp reverberation rattles his senses. He landed a strong hit, but there is something in the way, preventing him from coming in contact with whatever source the light is coming from.

Again, he hears Vitra through the night, laughing, openly mocking him. "Foolish, boy. Brute force will not help you here. You're going to have to try harder than that. I'd suggest you hurry though. As you sense my heart, I do yours as well. It's growing weak and rapid. You've lost a fair amount of blood. I'd wager at least a quart. Too much more, and you'll faint."

Rich's mind is raging. He's so angry with her for mocking him. For putting him in this entire situation, he can't concentrate enough to examine the hallway. Veins in his forehead bulge as his eyes press closed so hard he sees stars. He wants so badly to calm himself, but the more he tries, the more he fails, making him angrier. His ire is beyond containment. A deep growl grows in his throat and erupts into an outright scream. Vitra hears it echoing down the hall, her eyes open. Her concern is evident on her face as she listens to Rich's agony.

From under her hood, she sees the darkness in front of her manifesting into something. She can discern a head and shoulders emerging from the mist. As it continues to take form, it becomes unmistakable, its Rich's visage, but in shadow form. It walks toward Vitra, the light burning it more intensely with every encroaching step. Rich's shadow is looking directly in her eyes, unmistakable rage displayed on its face. Its gaze shifts to the source of the light. From above her, there is a piece of convex steel hanging on the wall. Its surface has been polished to a fine mirrored finish. The shade looks up to the ceiling, a cavity is dug out from the rock hiding a single lantern with a large lens that is projecting concentrated candlelight directly onto the steel. The shadow's face contorts horrifically. Slowly, its draws back its left hand while forming a fist. With a single powerful movement, its arm fires forward. It extends out as it launches at the reflective surface of the steel shell.

The light burns and crackles the outer layers of the arm while it launches toward the source of the light. The appendage elongates and morphs into a single long shaft with a large boulder-like obtrusion at the end of it. The force with which it impacts the mirror is so intense that it makes Vitra shudder with surprise. The mirrored steel falls to the ground behind her. The immediate area is enveloped in night. Vitra is frozen in place. She has never seen anything like this before. The effort required to penetrate the light in such a manner must have been massive. The shade closes the ground between them until it is standing over her, its glare intense and filled with hate. It extends a hand and points its finger. Vitra feels pressure build in her palm. She looks down and sees the end of a key protruding from her closed fist. The shadow lowers its arm and crumbles. The look of rage fades to a blank expression. Rich's shadow falls into nothing. The hall is quiet and still.

Vitra's fists are clenched from fear. As she relaxes, she feels the key still sitting in her palm, even after Rich's shade had vanished. The same one she placed in Rich's hand at the beginning of their exercise. She smiles through her anxiety and stands up. She reaches out to hear Rich but can't find him. She listens for his heart and finds nothing but silence. After a few steps, she is in total blackness. she disappears into the shadows and apparates instantly in front of Rich. His body lies still on the ground. Half of him outside the circle with large spikes of dark piercing his torso. Vitra dismisses the ring with a wave of her hand and looks at his still figure on the floor. Dread fills her heart as the severity of his situation sets in.

She is quick at his side, her hand searching her waist for a vial of liquid. She places her ear to his chest and can barely make out a faint heartbeat. Her fingers find the square bottle. She quickly pulls it from her belt and rips the cork out with her teeth. She dumps the entire bottle into Rich's mouth then places her hands over his heart and begins whispering to herself. She reaches into a pouch on her hip and produces a fine powder. She coats her hand in it and slams it into the ground. It ignites, covering her hand in a dull blue flame. She presses it to his open wounds, cauterizing them and stropping the blood flow.

Her words are growing more rapid as her desperation intensifies. The incantation isn't working. She raises her right hand into the air, a cloud of black smoke forms around it. She plunges it into his chest, the smoke filling his heart, forcing it to pump what little blood was left. The mixture she dumped in his throat is beginning to take effect, reviving his body and restoring the life that had drained from him. He sputters and coughs, spewing blood and bile as his body is forcibly reanimated.

His eyes open up. They are bloodshot from the strain he has endured. He looks at Vitra and asks her bluntly, "Did you get your fucking key?" He smiles defiantly before his eyes roll back into his head as he blacks out.

CHAPTER 8

When Evan and Gaian reach the main hall, Evan sits down at the table, anxious to eat. His new body is amazing, but its demand for food is unbelievable. He used to only need to eat once a day, maybe twice if he went out with friends. Now he's starving like he's never felt before. If his stomach had a mouth of its own, it would be screaming at him. He watches Gaian as he hastily prepares a meal.

Evan is poking at his healed wounds, amazed at how fast they closed up when he hears steps approaching the main hall. Ral appears in the doorway, carrying Sonya. Evan leaps to his feet and rushes to help. He takes her from Ral.

"This way, Evan. Lay her on the table." Ral directs him while he begins to rummage through a cabinet on the far side of the room. "Gaian, do you know where Vitra is?" he asks.

Gaian shakes his head. "I have not seen her. She should be back soon."

While Ral searches the cabinetry, Evan is tending to Sonya. His eyes are immediately drawn to her foot. It hangs limp and turned almost backward. Her ankle is swollen bigger than her leg. She puts up a strong face, but the pain in her eyes is evident.

"Sonya, what did you do?" Evan asks as he stares at her leg.

"I, uh, tripped, while running, sort of," she says while looking away.

"*Tripped?*" Evan says in shock. "On what? A bear trap?"

"No, I was just running really, really fast. Ral said it was around one hundred miles an hour or so." She smiles as surprise washes over Evan's face.

"No way, although I am a giant, and I beat five zombies to death, well, to undeath I guess. So I suppose you running super fast isn't that far-fetched."

"Zombies…? Are you kidding me?" Sonya says with a quiet shock.

As Evan's chest swells with self-satisfaction, Vitra bursts into the room, Rich's limp body suspended in a mass of black fog, following right behind her as she runs.

"Ral! Move away!" Vitra shouts as she enters the room. She is in the cabinet before he realized what happened. Vitra reaches into the back of the top shelf and pulls out a bottle of black liquid. The mist places Rich on the other end of the table, then fades away into the ground, his body absolutely motionless. Vitra is by his side seconds after he was laid on the table. The black fluid in one hand, she opens his mouth with the other and pops the cap, pouring a large amount into his mouth. As it works its way into his body he begins to convulse, his limbs thrashing and flailing violently. Ral rushes to help, holding down his arms at the shoulder. Evan leans over the table and lays on his hips. Rich's body is shaking so violently Ral almost can't hold on to him.

Sonya momentarily forgets about her own injuries as she crawls across the table to get a clearer look at Rich. His body is covered in blood, clothes soaked in a dark crimson. His skin is pale, almost white. His body is still shaking on the table, the intensity has diminished greatly, and it seems they are slowing down.

Rich lies motionless on the table. Vitra stands by, staring intently at his figure, waiting for some sign of life to return to his body. Ral and Sonya are huddled together near his head. Evan is standing over his feet. Gaian has been cooking the entire time, ostensibly oblivious to the entire situation. Vitra kneels next to Rich, placing a hand on his neck, searching for a pulse. His body is cool to the touch. Her eyes close, hoping for something to happen.

A dull throb hits her fingertips, her eyes open and look at Rich. His lungs fill with air. His eyes fly open as life shoots through his nervous system. He looks at Vitra and with considerable effort raises his hand off the table and using one finger motions for her to come closer.

"That juice you gave me tastes like ass," he whispers. "Can I have something to drink? Like right now?"

Gaian appears next to him, glass of water in hand. Rich takes it from him and brings it to his lips, but he is still weak from his endeavor. His strength fails him, and the glass slips from his fingers. A spiral of darkness manifests itself from the shadow of the table and catches the glass, slowly lifting it back up. Vitra takes it, and the mist vanishes back under the table. She hands it to Rich.

"Thanks for catching that. Quick reflexes," Rich says to her.

"I did nothing, Rich," Vitra says.

Rich stops for a second, looks around the room at his friends, and drops the glass again. That same spiral of night shoots up and catches the glass. It again lifts the cup slowly toward Rich. He reaches for it, taking it from the mist that retracts back under the table once more.

Rich looks at Vitra, the question readable on his face. She beats him to the punch. "I don't know what that is, Rich. I don't know why it is reacting that way. It's not sentient. It's like water or dirt. No intelligence. This is very exhilarating."

Rich takes a sip of water, clears his throat, then takes a longer drink. He sets the glass down and swings his legs over the table, trying to put some weight on them. He reaches out to steady himself and misses. Vitra grabs his arm and holds him up. Ral sets a chair down nearby so Vitra can guide him to it.

"All right. So I'm pretty sure I almost died. Yeah?" Rich asks.

Vitra nods. "Yes. You were mostly dead."

"Okay. So how did you stop the bleeding? I missed that part," he replies.

Vitra looks at him. "It should have been obvious to you. I was counting on you to figure it out and stop the bleeding yourself. The only way to make it stop is with light. That's the only thing that can seal the wound. The only thing that can defeat darkness is light."

Rich's expression is blank. "Well, fuck. That was obvious, wasn't it?"

Vitra nods. "Yes. Yes, it was."

Ral steps forward. "Vitra, Sonya needs some attention as well. Her ankle is broken."

Vitra checks her foot and ankle for a moment, examining the swelling.

"Can you feel your toes?" Vitra asks.

"Not the piggy toe. That one is totally numb," Sonya replies.

"I will have this fixed in no time, my dear. Broken bones are easier to mend than a dead body." Vitra looks back at Rich.

"Hey, go big or go home! Now if any of y'all try to one-up me, you're gonna have to actually die!" Rich laughs at himself as he leans back in the chair.

Vitra looks at Evan, eyeing his almost healed wounds. "Do you need anything from me?" she asks him.

"Nope. I'm fine. I am totally starving, though," he says.

From the back, Gaian booms out, "Food will be ready in a moment. It would be helpful if all people could get off the table."

Evan helps Sonya into a chair so Vitra can continue tending to her ankle. Then he grabs a rag and wipes the blood off the table with Ral's help.

Rich sits in his chair, staring under the table in the dark, watching it circle and flow in the low light of the hall. He reaches down to it, extending a finger. It moves closer, a shapeless mass at first, then silently shifts into a single oblong protrusion. Its tendril elongates and contacts his fingertip. For a brief second, he felt something strange, like his head is a radio that is picking up two stations at the same time. Only one of them was garbled and staticky. The connection was severed as Sonya's shriek of pain broke through, jarring him back to reality.

He looks over and sees Vitra physically setting Sonya's ankle back in place. She rubs a red poultice on the joint and wraps it tightly with a cloth. A fine haze can be seen emanating from the bandage, bringing with it a harsh odor of sulfur mixed with wet earth. Vitra stands up and walks to the sink. She rinses her hands in the spring then returns to Sonya. She offers her a drink of another potion.

"What's that one do?" Sonya asks.

"Just a little something to ease the pain, all natural. Just like all our medicines." Vitra offers it to her, but Sonya turns it down.

"I'm okay. Thank you, though," Sonya says. "I heard someone mention something about food a few minutes ago? I don't think I've ever been so hungry in my life."

Vitra smiles. "The medicine I have given you speeds up your metabolism significantly. That's why you're all able to heal so fast. I'm just aiding your body's natural abilities. But yes, as a side effect, you all need food, a lot of it."

As her words leave her mouth, Gaian sets down a huge platter filled with several varieties of food: sandwiches, slices of cooked meat, grapes, cooked veggies, entire turkey legs, and huge steamed buns filled with steak. Evan is the first to it. He pulls the entire plate to him and tucks in. Sonya scoffs at him and snatches a chunk of meat. Gaian reappears in seconds with another platter. This time, he sets it in front of Sonya.

"This one is yours," he booms.

Sonya's eyes light up as she pulls the platter close, taking in all the food before her. She throws the chunk of meat back to Evan who catches it in midair and tosses it down his throat. She tears into her meal like she hasn't eaten in years. Gaian places another platter in front of Rich, then sets a small cup down next to it. Rich looks up at the giant, but Gaian offers no word or expression, just walks away. He picks up the cup, expecting another funky concoction of some sort, but to his surprise, it was scotch. He takes a sip, letting the spice sit on his tongue. It was smooth with pronounced flavor, like someone took fire and removed the burn but left all the warmth. He relaxes for a brief second, letting himself release a small amount of tension that had been riding on his shoulders. He turns his eyes to his meal and begins to eat. Every bite he takes is like it's filling holes in his soul. He looks around and sees his friends engorging themselves and feels somewhat satisfied, glad that for this fleeting moment, they are happy.

Vitra walks away from the table, closer to Gaian who is busy washing dishes. She discreetly waves over Ral. He approaches, seeing that Vitra was eager to say something.

"I assume this is about his manipulation of the dark?" Ral asks.

"Yes, it is," Vitra states quietly. "I've never seen that before. I didn't think it was even possible. The level of this one's ability is, is, just horrifying. When I was testing him, he actually manifested himself as a shade and proceeded to sustain the image as he neared me. I was sitting under a mirror reflecting a white light, a very *bright* white light. I would have had a hard time projecting even the simplest objects if I were three meters *behind* him or, rather, his shade." She looks concerned, but her eyes are filled with excitement. She looks at Ral, then says, "I think this will work. If he is this powerful, I can only imagine how the others are. Speaking of which, Ral, Gaian, how did yours do?"

Ral lifts his chin proudly. "I can say that Sonya is exceeding my expectations by leaps and bounds…" Ral chuckles softly to himself, pleased with his word play.

"I don't understand why you laugh," Gaian booms.

"Gaian! Shout more quietly," Vitra scolds as she elbows him in the hip.

"I am not shouting. This is my normal speaking voice." Gaian, clearly oblivious to Vitra's sarcasm, continues to wash the dishes.

"Sonya is doing well, then, Ral?" she asks.

Ral nods. "The girl would surpass me with a few months of intense training if we had the time."

"Agreed," Vitra replies then looks to Gaian. "What of Evan? How is he? Clearly, he's tripled in size, but how is his grasp of things?"

"Currently, the boy is a giant coward." Gaian's blank face studies the pots and pans in the sink. "But he enjoys killing, which is good. He is slowly learning how to control himself. His power will follow, and he seems to have an affinity for blunt weaponry."

"So you're satisfied?" she asks.

Gaian hesitates, then grunts his affirmation.

"Now that they have their legs under them, shall we move to combat training?" Ral has a hint of giddiness behind his words.

"I suppose so," Vitra says as she looks at Rich. "I am anxious to see what he can do. Are you ready to move on as well, Gaian?"

"Yes," Gaian offers dryly.

"All right then. After they eat, I will replenish their vitality. Then back to work."

Vitra walks away from Ral and Gaian. She rummages through the cabinets from which she retrieves three empty glasses and several other vials of mysterious liquids that she then mixes together. Gaian is finishing his chores. He collects the used plates from the table and sets them on the counter next to the sink. He grabs Evan from the table and puts him to work, washing dishes. Ral leans against the counter, trying to decide where to begin with Sonya once they pick up steel. Sonya is playing with the candles in the chandelier above her, making them shake and shimmer with tiny gusts of wind she sends out with a flick off her finger. Rich sits quietly, eyes closed, hands clasped together behind his head. He is thinking of the brief moment he had with his wife. He quickly changes his focus to something else, anything else besides her. His attempts are futile as she comes crashing back into his thoughts, reminding him of the night he lost it all.

They had been arguing all day long, about his drinking as usual. He couldn't take anymore, so he threw his cell phone on the counter and left the house and headed straight for the bar. It was three o'clock on a Saturday afternoon, but he didn't care. He was a grown man, and he could do as he pleased.

When he finally made it home, it was almost eleven at night. He saw her car was gone. He heads inside and checks his bedroom first. Her drawers were all open, and most of the clothes were missing. A lot of them were scattered on the floor. He went to Suzie's room to find it in a similar state. He stumbles his way to the kitchen and grabs a couple of beers from the fridge. He walks past the counter and stops when his cell phone's screen lights up. He grabs it, bringing it close to his face and squinting through his drunken haze so he can make out what it said. There were dozens of texts and missed calls. He unlocks it with his thumb and navigates to the voice mail. He has one from his mother, two from his dad, two more from his in-law's home phone, and one number he did not recognize. He opens that one first and puts the phone to his ear.

"Hello, Mr. Dunn, this is Deputy Staubach with the Sheriff's Department. I regret to inform you that your wife and child have been in a car accident. Initial examination of the scene suggested that she lost control while trying to negotiate a curve. The vehicle left the road and struck a tree, impacting behind the driver's seat. I need you to call me back as soon as you can and head directly to County General."

The beers hit the ground and shatter as cold sobriety slams him in the guts. He sprints out the door to his truck, leaving the house sideways as he speeds off to the hospital.

His truck screeches into the emergency room driveway, slamming the parking brake down to the floor, leaving the truck running with the door open in the middle of the entrance. The hard shot of adrenaline has worn off, causing the alcohol to take control again. He sprints and stumbles his way inside the building and starts screaming at the staff to take him to his wife. They are trying to calm him down, but it's useless. His mind is swimming. He can't even form coherent sentences. A security guard, drawn by the commotion, comes running in and takes him down to the ground. He struggles until a second guard appears and slaps some cuffs on him. He lays on the ground long enough to calm himself. He apologizes to the staff between sobs and begs them to take him to his wife and daughter. He gives their names and waits in a puddle of his own spit and sweat as someone searches the hospital's database.

A group of nurses gather near the desk and talk quietly among themselves, exchanging stern glances under tight-knit brows. Rich strains to hear, but he cannot discern any of it. One of the nurses waves a guard over. She whispers something in his ear. He nods and walks back to Rich. The guards grab him by the arms and lift him to his feet. Both men keep a hold on an arm as they escort him down the hall. A nurse ahead of them is waiting by the door of an exam room toward the back of the ER. The nurse leaves after the guards seat him on the table. The room is dead quiet. The guards exchange an uneasy glance like they are expecting things to turn bad. Rich is getting nervous. His heart is pounding in his chest. Sweat is pouring off his forehead, and he reeks of booze.

A doctor walks into the room and sits down on the rolling stool that was tucked against the wall. He looks at Rich then sighs heavily.

"Mr. Dunn, I'm sorry to tell you this, but when your wife arrived at the hospital, she had already passed. We tried to resuscitate her, but it was unsuccessful. She was already gone. Your daughter… she, uhh." The doctor passes a hand over his face. It stops at his brow and trembles slightly as he tries to contain his emotions. "She was in critical condition. She suffered massive internal trauma and a brain hemorrhage. We fought like hell to save her, but her little body just couldn't take it. She succumbed to her injuries." The doctor pauses for a moment, taking a deep breath. "I brought that child into this world, and if I could have given my life to save hers, I would have done so. Words will never express the sorrow in my heart for being the one to tell you this, Mr. Dunn."

The doctor stood up to leave when Rich, with tears pouring down his face, asks, "How long ago did this happen?"

"Your wife was pronounced dead at 18:37. Your daughter at 19:52. The officer who came with them to the hospital tried to contact you and your family. No one knew where you were." The doctor turns to the door. "But from the smell coming off you, I think we all know."

Rich launches off the table straight at the doctor, his soul full of anger. One of the guards tried to grab him but missed. The other catches him around the neck and throws him to the ground. Rich's head bounces off the floor with a sickening crack. He lays still as the men in the room look down on him in pity.

"Rich, HEY." Sonya smacks him in the back of the head.

"The fuck, woman. Can't man rest his eyes for a few minutes?" He casually rubs his face in a subtle attempt to wipe away any evidence that he may have been crying. He stands up and stretches, then reaches for his drink. He takes it down in one shot and looks over his shoulder.

"Hey, barkeep, can I get another?" Rich shakes the cup back and forth as he bores holes into the back of Gaian's head.

Gaian does not even look at him. "I assume you are speaking to me. No, you may not have more alcohol right now. The remainder is being saved for when you three are finished training."

Rich scoffs and sets the cup on the table. "Fine. Guess I'll wait." The darkness at his feet swirls and writhes in a display of solidarity.

Vitra moves to the end of the table, near Rich. "Well then, are we all satisfied?" Sonya and Evan nod in unison. Rich stands still with his arms crossed, glaring at his empty cup. "Two out of three is acceptable," Vitra says. "These weeks are going to move very quickly now that you all have a sense of your new abilities. There is going to be little time for sleep, and you all will be fed exactly as much as you physically require." Vitra sets three vials of liquid on the table. "Each of you, drink one of these. This will negate any need to rest for the next couple of days. We have a full schedule planned for you. It's going to be intense, but you will come out of this significantly more dangerous than you could have believed."

"Now *that* got my fuckin' attention!" Rich blurts out. "I believe Antonio Banderas over there said something about weapons next, yes?"

Vitra looks at Ral and asks, "Who is he talking about?"

"I believe he is referencing a Spanish American actor who was popular in the '90s and early 2000s. I find it complimentary he was a very distinguished man. Too bad he's dead now," Ral replies.

"Wait. He's dead?" Rich asks.

Vitra ignores him. "Yes. Weapons are next. Sonya will be trained in swordsmanship."

"Sword-*woman*-ship," Sonya interjects.

"Call it whatever you wish. The word is irrelevant. I will teach you the same as I would teach a man. Your skill set will be above all by the time I'm done." Ral looks directly at his pupil as he finishes his sentence. A clear intensity on his face.

Vitra continues, "Gaian will teach Evan hand-to-hand combat. He will be learned in various disciplines of martial arts and how to incorporate his mastery of the earth into his fighting technique."

Evan's face is washed with mild panic at the news. Having to stand toe to toe with Gaian is not something he looks forward to. Gaian is smiling from ear to ear, which only adds to Evan's panic.

"Richard, I will teach you advanced hand-to-hand combat emphasizing incorporating knife use into the attacks." Vitra looks around at their new pupils, the energy in the room is palpable.

"Have you all eaten your fill?" Vitra asks.

They all nod and offer their own confirmation. Evan's was not convincing.

"Excellent. Drink up then. You've already wasted too much time," Vitra says as she motions for them to drink.

CHAPTER 9

Rich picks up his bottle and pops the cork. He waves it under his nose while he looks at Vitra.

"Is there a problem?" Vitra asks.

"Every one of these we've drunk so far has tasted like Bigfoot's taint in August. I'm just trying to decide if I should plug my nose this time or not," Rich says as he cautiously sniffs his vial.

Evan sets his empty glass on the table. "It wasn't that bad, man. Kinda fruity, like, uh, like that bowl of hard candy your grandma used to have on her coffee table. Remember when I'd come over there with you to mow her lawn and shit? She would pay us five bucks and offer us some of that awful hard candy that you had to damn near hammer apart."

"Hey, man. Don't talk shit about my gam-gam," Rich says as he points a menacing finger at Evan.

Evan throws his large arms in the air and says, "I'm not. I loved that old woman… Made the best PB&J sandwiches I've ever eaten."

Sonya looks at him and laughs. "Those were made out of store-bought stuff, Evan. Prepackaged bread, jelly, and peanut butter. Bought from the grocery store. All she did was put them together."

"Incorrect, madam, she made them with *love*. That was the key," Evan says as he pokes Sonya in the arm with one gigantic finger.

"Gross. Keep your Richard-fingers away from me," Sonya says as she leans away from him.

"What the fuck do you mean by 'Richard-fingers' exactly?" Rich asks with a tone.

"I mean, every single one of the fingers on his hand looks like a *dick*. Dick," Sonya says with a coy smile.

"Whatever. He wishes his was as big as those," huffs Rich.

"Umm, my muscles aren't the only thing that's huge now, guys." Evan's smile is full of pride as he boasts to his friends.

Rich glares at Evan with pure disdain. "Well, aren't you special? Too bad you're still a whiny little girl."

"Children, that's enough," Vitra says. "We need to get to work. There is much to attend to. Rich, come with me. Gaian, Ral, get to it. Time is short. Meet back here when they need replenishing."

Gaian nods with a deep grunt. He slaps Evan on the back as he stomps by him with a large barrel and sack tucked under one arm. He hands Evan the sack as they head down the hall. Ral bows his head slightly and swiftly walks away, offering Sonya his arm as he passes.

Rich finds himself back in the room he almost died in, its walls brightly lit with torches evenly spaced around the room. He looks around, taking in the details that he couldn't make out in the dark. The walls are unnaturally smooth, like someone painstakingly carved and polished the entire cavern by hand. There are shelves sculpted into the walls on one end, several books fill the upper shelves. Peculiar instruments are scattered on the two below them. He paces around the room for a moment. As he nears the entrance to the hallway, he looks down and sees his blood still coating the stone floor. His eyes examine the dark brownish-red stain. Between the thick blots of sanguine are subtle trails gently vortexed, wider near the outside of the puddle, but narrowing as it got closer to the center. As he stares at it, Vitra steps next to him.

"Interesting shapes, aren't they?" she says.

"Yeah, but what the hell is it?" Rich asks her.

"Well, your body is a part of the night. The marks you're seeing in your blood is the darkness attempting to heal you and return itself, and your blood, to your body. It's a skill that I haven't wanted to teach you yet due to its advanced nature. It seems you have a knack for surprising me. Your body instinctively tried to do it on its own. I think." Vitra crosses her arms and looks at the floor with Rich.

"What do you mean 'I think'? Aren't you the expert here?" He lifts an eyebrow as his words hang in the air.

"There is always more to learn, my child. If anyone really knew everything, then what would be the point of living?" She looks at him and smiles. "Remember how you made that key?"

Rich nods. "Yeah, why?"

"I want you to make a knife now. Blade about six inches long, clip point, full tang handle. With a short spike on the pommel." Vitra steps back a few paces and waits.

"Little specific, but if that's what you want." He extends a hand out, palm down, and begins to will the object into existence. A dark tendril reaches up from the ground. It swirls around his palm, trying to collect and condense as he demands it to but he can't force it to manifest.

"It's not working. Maybe it's too bright?" he says.

"No, I don't think that's the issue. You manifested a detailed shade of yourself just a few hours ago when you destroyed that piece of mirrored steel. I'm quite certain the ability is there. It just needs to be coaxed out. We will touch on that again later." Vitra raises her hand and slowly closes it into a fist, dimming the lights down significantly. "Try it again," she says.

Rich puts his hand out again and stares at his palm, forcing his body to condense the night into a tangible object. Little spirals of darkness swim and dance in his hand then quickly take the shape he was holding in his mind. In his hand is a blade exactly as Vitra asked of him, only it is solid black and devoid of the shine that would usually be associated with a knife of this type. He hefts it in his hand. Its weight is much lighter than a normal blade, almost nothing at all. He grasps the handle and takes a swing, its dark blade slicing through the air without a sound. He tosses it up and catches it by the blade tip then turns to the wall and throws it with considerable force. The knife flies through the air and slaps the wall with its side, a muted whoosh can be heard as the wind chasing it makes an impact. It falls to the floor and bounces a couple of times before turning back into dark dust and drifting to the ground.

Vitra stands there watching as Rich sticks his hand out and quickly makes another knife, then sets it on the floor and watches as it too turns to powder and vanishes.

"Why does it disintegrate like that when I let it go?" Rich asks as his eyes follow the mist left from the knife.

"Your body energizes the dark, forcing it to solidify. As long as the knife is in your hand, it is constant. Once it leaves your hand, the molecules of concentrated night lose the charge given to them by your body. Ergo, they return to their original, natural state." Vitra begins to close the gap between them. She closes her hands together in front of her then pulls them apart, as she does a solid cylinder extends from her palms, growing in length as the distance increases. Her hands stop about shoulder width apart. With her left, she grasps the end of the cylinder and smacks Rich in the arm with it.

"Hey, goddamn it! That hurt," he whines.

Vitra circles around Rich. "This is the point. The two best motivators in life are pain and fear. We experience pain, and fear doing it again. This is how we learn. Mistakes become experiences. Experiences become knowledge. Knowledge becomes wisdom."

"Guess I'm one wise motherfucker then…," Rich says darkly. He puts his hands behind his back and walks parallel to Vitra. "*So is it safe to assume the combat training has begun?*"

Vitra nods in acknowledgment as she continues to pace the ground. Rich forms another knife in his hand, keeping it just out of sight. He makes his move, lunging at Vitra. His broad swing is easily anticipated. She leans back and counters him with her own attack. The cylinder she held in her hand lands a blow to Rich's side, just under his armpit. Rich swears under his breath and takes a few steps back, rolling his shoulder around trying to stretch out the injured muscle.

"You're not very sneaky, you know. I saw that attack coming before you even started moving. The goal of this exercise is to draw my blood. Once you can do that, you will be able to defeat anyone one on one. Then I'll teach you how to dispatch an entire room of your enemies. How does this sound to you?"

"Sounds fuckin' sweet!" Rich jumps forward, keeping his knife hand close to his chest this time. He stabs at Vitra's left flank. She dodges to her right. Rich swiftly follows his first attempt with a quick slash. His move worked. She isn't far enough away to dodge now. His blade nears her stomach, and just as it's about to find its target, her entire body vanishes into black smoke. His blade cleaves through the nothing that she left behind.

Rich looks around the room. He can't see her anywhere. He strains his ears, trying to listen for any signs of her. After a few seconds, he hears a rush of air moving behind him. He spins his body around in time to get smacked in the mouth by her rod. The impact lands directly on his upper lip. The pain hits him with a flash of light. He falls back onto his hands and lands on the ground, dazed and angry.

"You're going to get nowhere like that. You should get up and get serious." Vitra scoffs at him as he stands up.

His eyes are open now and filled with an all too familiar blinding rage. He forms a second knife in his off hand and widens his stance. A stream of blood trickles out of his nose and into the corner of his mouth. He licks it off his lip and takes a deep breath. With a renewed vigor, he launches himself at her again.

Sonya stands with Ral as he pulls two swords down from a shelf. He unwraps them and hands one to her. Its blade is long and thin, the grip large enough for just one hand, leaving only a small amount of handle between her pinky and the pommel. The hilt was large and ornate but functional at the same time. She steps back from Ral and turns away, giving the new weapon a couple of practice swings. It's light in her hands, almost weightless. The blade makes a subtle whistle as it cuts through the air, almost like it's singing. Ral watches her as she dances with the blade. She spins and twirls, moving the sword in tight circles around her body.

"You are most impressive already. Have you had training before?" he asks.

"No, when I was younger, I wanted to be in a band, but I couldn't play an instrument. So I joined but became a drum major. This is almost the same thing. Just sharper." She laughs at herself as she continues to twirl and dance with the blade.

"I believe you will take to this quite quickly. The real challenge will be using those skills in active combat against another person."

Ral grasps his blade, and with a gust, he is in front of her, his sword stopping hers. "Knowing how to swing a stick and knowing how to wield a sword are two *very* different skills." She lunges forward and swings her sword in an upward arc. Ral lazily sidesteps her charge and slaps her backside with the flat of his blade. Sonya lets out a sharp wail and turns to face him. "Easy, my child. You are getting ahead of yourself. We will spar soon enough, but for this moment, you need to learn how to hold your weapon before you can learn to fight with it. Show me how *you* think it should look."

Sonya thinks for a moment. She places her left leg behind her and puts her weight on it. She places her left hand square on her hip while her right hand and right foot are both extended far out in front of her, sword tip pointing straight up in the air. Ral looks her up and down, then begins to laugh. He hides his face in his hand as he chokes back his outburst. Sonya drops her sword arm and wraps the other across her chest.

"Well, how the F am I supposed to hold a sword then? Huh, mister man?"

"I'm glad you asked." Ral flicks her sword with his own, encouraging her to raise it up. "A sword is meant to be an extension of your body. Your movements with the sword should not be forced but flow naturally. Like throwing a rock, your eyes see the target and your arm sends the rock. Even this connection is not always natural. It takes practice. Some are more skilled than others, but with time and dedication, anyone can become decent at it, but not all will master it."

"So I'm going to be the world's best mediocre swordsman?" Sonya chides Ral as she listens to his speech.

"No, my dear. You are going to be the world's most skilled warrior with a sword. The fiercest blade master of all time." The room goes silent as Ral's words sink in. As his last sentence still echoes through her mind, he moves in front of her.

"Do as I do, we shall start with the basics. All movement comes from a solid foundation. When you strike, you don't strike with your arm. You strike with your entire body, starting with the legs. Whether a slash or a punch, an attack from a bad foundation is useless." Ral moves his right foot behind slightly, turning it out roughly forty-five degrees from center. His left foot moves straight ahead just a bit further than he moved his right, the toe of his left shoe pointing forward.

"This is a good foundation from which to launch an attack. You have stability, strength, and mobility. He reaches out with his left foot, moving it maybe half its distance from his body. As it finds ground, his right foot slides up the same distance, putting him in the same position he started in. "Moving from this stance is easy, but make sure to not cross your feet. That will leave you unstable and off-balance. You try it now."

Sonya does as she was instructed. Her eyes focused straight ahead as Ral walks around her.

"Your left leg is too far forward. Bring it in some. Ah, your right foot is turned too far out. Here, like this." He stands on her left and points to his own foot. "There. That's better," he says. "Now most swords are meant for two-handed use. The one you will be using later is also going to be two handed, so for the sake of practice, we will use both hands on these."

Sonya chokes up on the handle and grabs the extra with her left hand. Ral moves a couple of steps away, leaving some room between him and Sonya.

"While gripping the sword, place it out in front of you. Keep your elbows bent slightly, and don't tense up. Stay relaxed but ready. I will show you a basic downward slash, moving from right to left." Ral slowly moves his sword through the air, drawing it closer to his head. The blade begins its downward arc. As it moves, Ral steps forward with his left foot, pushing off with his right. The blade stops traveling as his left foot hits the ground. As he resets his form, he drags his right foot forward until it has come to rest in its original orientation. He relaxes his form and turns to Sonya, nodding at her to give it a try.

She takes up her stance, holding the sword in front of her like Ral did his. He walks up to her and moves her left elbow, rotating it down.

"Don't flare your elbows as such. Keep them pointed down. Your movement will be smoother this way. Continue." He steps back and watches her as she moves. She steps forward with her right foot.

Ral smacks the back of her leg with the flat of his sword.

"Owweee!" Sonya wails.

"You push off with the right, but you only move the left. Do it again."

She starts the attack over again, this time stepping forward with her left and pushing off with her right. Ral watches her as she goes, eyeing out any weak points in her form. As she finishes the motion, he begins to pace around her.

"Again," Ral says. "A little faster this time." Ral watches her repeat the movement a couple of times. As she finishes, he twirls his hand in a circle, implying he wants her to keep going. Sonya attacks, then resets, attacks, then resets, over and over again. Ral stands in front of her, watching.

"Swordplay is a dance. One that requires discipline, dedication, and, can you guess what else?" Ral looks at her, an eyebrow raised on his forehead.

"Uhh…diligence?" Sonya answers.

Ral shakes his head.

"Determination?" Sonya answers again.

"No…," Ral says with a sigh.

"You tell me then because I have no idea. There are a lot of 'D' words that could work there," Sonya says with a huff.

"Choreography!" Ral begins to laugh at her. "Discipline, dedication, and choreography!"

Sonya stops practicing and looks at Ral. "How was I supposed to know that's what it was? You had a thing with 'D' goin', so I assumed it was a trend."

"Being good with a sword is not so much a form of warfare as it is a game. Consider it like chess. You make a move. They make a move. It is this way until one of you makes a mistake. Knowing the best way to respond is as easy as having basic movements programmed into your muscle memory. Discipline, dedication, and choreography. Memorizing the moves of dance until you don't have to think about it. You just naturally react to your partner, or adversary." Ral takes up his stance again. "We will add a movement following the downward slash. Once you reach the bottom of the first swing, start another going from your left directly to the right. Like this. Downward slash to a horizontal."

Ral demonstrates the movement to Sonya. She takes up her stance and tries to copy him. The smile on Ral's face distracts from the concern in his eyes. Sonya shows much promise, but it's hard to tell if she will be able to learn everything he needs to teach her so early in her training. Ral swallows hard against his fears as he corrects Sonya's form.

Evan is lying on his back with blood streaming from his mouth and nose. He shakes his head and gets back to his feet then rushes at Gaian. The two giants clash with a herculean force. Gaian slams his right palm into the back of Evan's neck, pulling his head down. With his left, he reaches across Evan's back and grabs him by the armpit. He throws his right leg into Evan's pelvis and uses it as fulcrum, throwing Evan over his right hip with such force that Evan's body completes a full rotation in midair before landing hard on his face. Blood explodes from his nose, throwing a splatter across the ground to Gaian's feet. Evan sits up and rubs his face. As he massages his nose, he can feel the broken bones grinding against themselves under his skin. The feeling makes him cringe, but before he realizes it, his nose is mending itself back together. Cartilage realigns with bone as the blood vessels seal back up.

"That's really cool, but it hurts a lot, and it's fuckin' gross to feel the broken shards of my face in there." Evan stands up and looks at Gaian's feet. He sees a good amount of blood covering Gaian's toes on his left foot. He follows the stream back to where his face broke his fall. The puddle is large and rather concerning. His eyes begin to dart here and there to the dozen or so other splotches of his blood that decorate the hard earth floor. "Can we take a break? I'm starving."

Gaian nods. He walks over to a large sack sitting on top of the barrel that he brought with him from the kitchen, reaches in, and pulls out a fistful of small rectangular biscuits. Evan stares at the little treat as he takes them from Gaian.

"What's this?" Evan asks as he bites into one. It makes a hard snap as his teeth break through it. The consistency is similar to dry wall, but less powdery, with very subtle honey and berry flavor.

"This is something your generation knows as 'hard tac.' It is a simple baked good, but I have added several extra ingredients to aid in your stamina, healing, and speed." Gaian grabs one of the biscuits and tosses it in his mouth whole. Evan struggles to finish the ones he was given. He walks over to the barrel, grabbing the sack from on top of it and setting it on the ground.

"I assume this is something to drink?" Evan asks as he lifts the lid.

Inside the barrel is a thick white substance that smells of herbs and fermentation. Evan turns his nose away as he stifles a small gag in the back of his throat.

"It is milk. We brought it with us when we locked ourselves in this cave." Gaian moves to the barrel. He takes one massive paw and scoops up a handful of the mucus-like liquid and drinks it.

Evan's eyes are about to pop out of his head as his stomach squirms. Watching the pearl-colored goop drip around Gaian's hand then slowly roll down his beard was almost too much to deal with.

Gaian smacks his lips together then mumbles to himself, "The milk has turned." He puts his hand in and takes another helping. "It is still drinkable."

Evan is forced to turn away this time. He reaches up and nervously scratches his head. "So we got any water in here, orrr…?"

"I shall find some after we train more." Gaian wipes the remnants of the milk on his hand directly into his beard then approaches the still thirsty Evan. "Physical confrontation is inevitable. I have made you much larger than the majority of beings on the planet, but you are still weak to numbers. It is necessary for you to learn to fight against packs of enemies. You know how to use Our Mother to form weapons and how to shield yourself from attack, but you need to learn how to use the earth itself as a means of defense." Gaian raises one huge foot and slams it down into the dirt. Ripples shoot out from the impact like when a large stone is cast into water. When they reach Evan, he immediately loses his balance and falls flat on his back. Gaian squats down. The ground he is standing on bucks into the air, launching his massive frame skyward. He comes crashing down to the ground over the top of Evan, his fist barely touching the tip of Evan's nose.

"The longer your engagement with an enemy, the less likely it becomes that you will survive. When you strike, do so with the intent to kill. Nothing can withstand you. You are the earth herself, immovable and everlasting. Use this power to crush your enemies and see them driven before you." Gaian's eyes are fierce and full of hatred.

Evan snorts then begins to chuckle out loud. Gaian's expression changes to one of uncertainty as he tries to surmise why Evan is laughing. "Why do you laugh?" he demands.

"Oh, nothing, *Conan*. Tell me more about what is best in life!" Evan laughs at his own joke.

Gaian stamps on his stomach and steps over him. The air in Evan's torso is forced out of him with a large whoosh. As he sputters and gasps on the ground, Gaian leers down at him.

"We will continue training like this for now, on the ground. You will find that near the end of a real fight, it will usually be finished in the dirt. Defending yourself from a prone position will be a good skill to hone. You will find yourself there more often than you would like to imagine."

Evan begins to protest but is cut short by a series of kicks from Gaian. He blocks several, but two land in his torso. His ribs contract from the impact. He feels a sharp snap come from his side. He anticipates a rush of pain, but it was a dull ache at best. His nerves are becoming accustomed to the abuse. Gaian kicks at him again. He catches it. Then rolls away from Gaian, forcing him down to one knee. Evan leaps to his feet, dragging his right hand along the ground as he rises. Earth and rock cling to his fist, encasing it in a thick mass. He swings hard at Gaian's face as he nears the target he closes his eyes. The rubble around his hand explodes, peppering his face and chest with shrapnel.

Evan tries to pull back, but his fist is held fast in place. He opens his eyes to see that Gaian had caught his attack with one hand, stopping it dead in its tracks.

"That was excellent. You not only defended yourself, but you took me down to your level and were able to launch an almost successful attack. Let's try it again but with your eyes open this time. Before you lay back, I encourage you to get some milk. It will make you stronger." Gaian stands and motions to the barrel.

"Dude, I really do not want to drink that milk. I don't even know what kind of animal it's from." Evan gets his feet under him and brushes himself off. The pain in his side not even noticeable anymore.

"It is mastodon. I personally milked one of the best in my herd before entombing myself her*e*." Gaian lifts his chin in a show of pride.

Evan's disgust turns to intrigue. "It would be pretty dope to say I drank some mastodon milk. Will it really make me stronger?"

"I do not lie. As with the hard tac, the milk has been imbued with various elements to enhance your natural abilities," Gaian says dryly.

"All right. Fuck it." Evan walks to the barrel and takes a fist full of the milky gunk. He lifts it to his lips and lets it slide down his throat. The flavor is less offensive than the smell, and he manages to get it all down without incident.

"It was thick, but not too awful I suppose. Not bad for ancient mastodon cow milk." Evan wipes this chin and looks down into the barrel.

"Bull," Gaian mutters.

"What? Wait. You milked a *bull?* Is that what you're saying?" Evan begins to feel a rush of anxiety hitting him. He turns queasy.

"I am only joking. It is cow milk." Gaian smiles. His teeth bared, and his eyes wide with self-satisfaction at his brand of humor.

Evan recoils at the sight of the black giant's eerie display of humor. He turns to the barrel and plunges his entire face into the milk and drinks deep. He comes up for air and throws himself on his back, arms and legs raised in a defensive posture.

"Okay. Let's keep goin'…" Evan looks on as Gaian's smile remains stuck on his face. He steps closer to Evan and begins his assault again.

CHAPTER 10

Minutes grind by at a glacial pace as pain and conflict become the new normal. Hours of unforgiving training have left a stench of blood and sweat in the air of the cave. As the masters teach their pupils, they steadily increase the ferocity of their efforts. Punches stop being pulled. Strikes are deliberate and tactical. The curriculum moves away from basic instruction and becomes more visceral. No one has a current idea of how much time has passed. They are all far too busy in their affairs at hand.

Gaian and Evan have been fighting like enemies. Evan's skill in manipulating the earth in the heat of combat is almost to acceptable levels, but the giant still doubts Evan's abilities. He demands much from him and is unforgiving when Evan makes a mistake. The entire hall looks like it was the epicenter of an earthquake. The ground is uneven. Large craters mark the floor with mounds of earth scattered in between them. Evan has been able to develop a technique for ranged attacks. He hurls spears of diamond-hard obsidian at Gaian's torso. The giant easily deflects them with his granite-coated fists and arms.

Evan's breathing is becoming labored, and his wounds are not healing as fast as they once did. Gaian has been watching him slowly degrade. The giant's resolve is unwavering. He knows that there is no other option. He must forge Evan into a fearsome, unrelenting warrior. Evan moves in close for an attack to the giant's core. Gaian blocks it with one hand and sends a rock-covered fist smashing into Evan's face. Evan falls to his back and lays there for a moment. His body is reaching its limits. He brings his wits about him and rolls onto one knee, only to fall back to the ground. With a groan of discontent, Gaian lifts him from the dirt and heads back to the main hall for some food.

The sound of wind and ringing steel echoes throughout the chamber. The figures of Sonya and Ral are indiscernible, only brief silhouettes at the moment of attack, then gone again, moving almost faster than the eye can perceive. They whip back toward one another and clash again, three strikes launched and blocked in the blink of an eye. Sonya's sword feels like it is made of concrete. Her arms are shaking and weak, but she presses on, her determination resolute. She launches forward with all her body and soul, throwing herself hastily at Ral, changing directions randomly, and trying to circle around him. Ral is pleased with Sonya's tenacity. He did not expect her to come around so quickly. She clearly has been paying close attention to his instructions because her skill with a blade is vastly better than when she started. Ral ducks under a slash and blocks a surprising kick from Sonya. Her combat tactics are evolving as the hours tick by. Ral knows she will be ready soon. There is no one that will stand in her way. He knows in his heart that she will succeed—she has to. He has never trained someone with her level of grit. It is becoming obvious to him now that she is indeed his descendant. She fights with all her heart, without a hint of hesitation in her strikes.

Ral watches her intently, studying the way she moves. His keen eye is looking for flaws in form and weakness in defense. She is hurtling at him, sword raised above her head. He sees an opportunity for a teachable moment and shoots in front of her, landing a knee to her stomach. She flips over his leg and slams into the ground, rolling for several yards and coming to a stop on her belly, face down on the floor. Ral approaches, expecting her to leap to her feet any moment. He closes the ground between them, his guard dropping as his concern grows. He reaches out to check her for signs of life. As his hand nears her face, she throws herself into the air, spinning over the top of him. Before she lands, she kicks him squarely in the ass, knocking him to the ground. As Ral lay upon the floor, he cannot help but laugh at himself. Sonya stands over his head and offers a hand to help him up. He grasps it around the wrist and sticks his foot in her solar plexus and pulls her arm toward him, sending her heels over head into the ground at his feet. Sonya is quiet for a moment until she and Ral burst into laughter together.

Vitra watches Rich from within the darkness. He has not learned how to shadow step yet, and she is using that against him. She vanishes into the dark and emerges from deep shadows near him. She swings her club at his head, but an inch away from impacting his skull, Rich vanishes into the dark. Vitra is momentarily stunned, but as was his way, Rich yet again had worked out an understanding of something she had not even touched on yet. It is as though he was being fed information. She may have been shocked by his first move, but she knew what his next would be. She spins in place and brings the club down hard, catching Rich in the skull as he was halfway out of the shadow he had disappeared in to. He falls back inside it and is gone from sight again. His prowess has grown significantly in the last day or so, but his technique has begun to get sloppy. He strikes with less precision and speed than he did at first. Clearly, the tincture she gave them is beginning to wear off. Soon they will all reconvene in the kitchen for food.

As she considers the preparations necessary for the meeting, Rich emerges from the corner of the ceiling. He slowly apparates from the deep black of the room where light can't reach. He sees Vitra walking under him, completely oblivious to his next move. He forms a knife in each hand and readies himself. He leaps from the shadow, as silent as the void he was hiding in. He falls through the air, but mere inches from being within striking distance, Vitra stops and jumps backward. With a hard thud, Rich hits the ground. The air is forced from his lungs as he rolls onto his back, gasping. His knives vanish into smoke. Vitra looks down at him and shakes her head. She steps over him and heads for the door. As her foot crosses over his chest, there is a slight prick in her ankle. Vitra looks down to see a single dark needle sticking from her pale skin. It vanishes, leaving a single drop of blood forming in its place. She looks down at Rich. He is smiling back at her. With a hard stomp to his gut, she heads for the exit.

Vitra opens the door and looks back at Rich as he picks himself up from the ground. Her ankle is still seeping blood. She grabs a torch off the wall just outside the door and holds it near her leg. A small poof of black smoke leaves the wound, and it stops bleeding almost immediately. She places the torch back on the wall and walks to the kitchen. Once her back is turned to Rich, she lets a small smile crack her otherwise-stoic expression.

Gaian and Evan are in the kitchen when Ral shows up with Sonya. Gaian is cooking another huge meal for the group. Evan is helping where he can, handing Gaian whatever implements or additives he needs for the feast. Sonya sits down, folding her arms on the table and lies her head on them. She closes her eyes and drifts off while Ral begins setting the table. Vitra and Rich come bursting into the room, disturbing the peace that had settled over the current occupants.

"You're just mad that I got you. That's all. You told me all I had to do was draw your blood and my training was over. I got you. You're just being all pissy," Rich says as he trails behind Vitra.

"You were laying on the ground, defeated. I was done with you and was walking away. You didn't land a blow. you stuck a needle in my leg." Vitra's pale complexion is flushed with a slight pink hue. Ral does not look up from the table, but he is listening.

"That was not a real attack. You only made yourself look like an ass, which at this point I feel is the only thing you're profoundly good at," Vitra asserts poignantly.

"You laid down the rules. You said 'land a blow and draw my blood.' I did just that. What do you think, Ral?" Rich asks, looking on as Ral continues to set the table.

"I do not wish to get involved in your spat, but it sounds like you met the requirements set before you." Ral steals a glance at Vitra, wanting to see how his words will land with her. She is staring daggers back at him, her face calm, but her eyes seething with rage.

"Save your opinions for your own pupil, windbag." Vitra scoffs as she walks to the cabinet she keeps her potions in and removes a large bottle of brandy, taking a long pull from it.

Gaian is putting the finishing touches on their meal then handing it off to Evan who transfers it all to large serving platters. Ral scoops them up as they are prepared and sets them on the table. Sonya picks bits and pieces from the platters as they are set down around her. Evan takes a seat and starts filling his own plate. There are whole cooked potatoes, large turkey legs, thick cuts of ham, and a roast that must have come from an animal too large to fit the room in which they were gathered. Rich eases himself down with a wince and grabs a turkey leg. Vitra walks up behind him and lays the bottle of brandy on his shoulder. His eyes widen with glee as he takes it from her and pours himself a drink.

The trio and their teachers all sit down and eat together. Ral entertains them with stories from before he got stuck in this cave, telling them of adventures he and Gaian had in their days working for the Creator. Vitra quietly eats at the corner of the table. Her thoughts are lost in the coming event, their meeting with Enki. She is concerned about what this will do to the group as a whole once they learn the more brutal details surrounding the current situation. She looks at them, their faces are still full of hope and joy. She knows exactly what lies ahead and what is going to be asked of them.

As Rich, Sonya, and Evan finish their meals, Gaian leaves the room. Ral clears the table, and Vitra stands up to address them.

"Your training has gone well. Rich, Sonya, you are both excelling beyond what we expected. Evan, Gaian says you have come a long way, but he is still concerned with your overall aggression. He says you lack violence of action and that you need to understand the severity of the situation you are in. He is hopeful that this chat you're all going to have soon will speed that along."

Rich interrupts her, "Sorry, a chat with who? Is there another one of you hiding around here? This guy has control of house plants or some shit?"

"I was just getting to introductions. Perhaps I should add some lessons in patience to your curriculum." Vitra glares at Rich for a moment then continues. "There is in fact a fourth member of our little group. His name is Enki, and you are all about to meet him."

As Vitra finished her sentence, Gaian walks into the room. "It is ready. All preparations have been taken care of." He left as fast as he came, offering no further explanation.

"All right, it is time. Everyone please stand and follow me back to the main hall." Vitra leaves in the same direction.

The three friends all look at each other, exchanging an uneasy glance. Up until now, no mention had been made of any other occupants, and none of them had seen this fourth person.

"Why were there preparations required exactly? Who the hell are we meeting?" asks Sonya.

"Your guess is probably better than mine. I'm still expecting some kind of weird fuckin' sex cult shit to happen," Rich says as he shifts in his chair. He stands up and starts heading toward the door.

Evan lifts his large frame from the chair and stretches out. "Is that what you *expect* to happen? Or what you are *hoping* will happen? Eh? You seem to keep gravitating back to that."

Sonya is the last to get up. "I'm pretty sure anything at this point would be welcome for Rich. He's had a dry spell for some time. That's probably why he chased that bear to begin with. Just tryin' to get laid!"

"You're totally right. I was all about it because I thought it was your mom at first. Getting a piece of that is almost a sure thing." Rich raises his hand, giving Sonya and Evan the finger as he steps into the hall.

"I'll be sure to tell her that next time I see her, *Dick*." Sonya returns a finger back to him.

"Not if I see her first! Boom!" shouts Evan as he skips away.

The sight of Evan frolicking gayly is not something new, but the size of his new frame combined with the flamboyant movement was too much for Sonya to contain. She laughs aloud and shakes her head. Even though his form is massive and capable of so much destruction, he is still very much the Evan she loves.

Sonya moves down the dark hallway. She can hear Rich and Evan talking in excited tones at the other end. She quickens her pace, then remembers she has a new way of traveling. The air around her legs begins to move faster, accumulating at the bottom of her feet. She glides across the floor with ease, picking up speed as she goes. The feeling of being able to move so fast is liberating. She nears the end of the hall and slows herself, bringing it down to a quick walk. Entering the hall, she sees Ral on his hands and knees drawing various symbols in chalk on the floor, all around a giant circle with several intersecting lines. There are twelve points on the perimeter of the circle, each with a line drawn to the third point from it in a clockwise pattern. There is an open area in the center with three more symbols in a triangle formation. Sonya walks up behind Evan, peering around him at what's going on.

Gaian approaches them with an open hand. In his palm are three silver necklaces with dark green gems hanging from them.

"Do not smudge any of the lines. They must all be intact for the ritual to work." Gaian booms, his tone more ominous than usual.

"Did he just fucking say ritual?" Evan asks, his voice squeaks a bit from the panic rising in his throat.

Vitra offers her assurance. "Don't worry, Evan. It's very simple and totally painless. We are going to put you all into a dreamlike state. Your bodies will remain here, but your consciousness will move onto a plane of existence that is between life and death. This is where Enki waits."

Rich shrugs, grabs a necklace, and puts it around his neck.

"Did I tell you to do that?" Vitra asks sharply.

"No, but it seemed pretty obvious that you were gonna. Should I have stuffed it up my ass instead?" Rich retorts.

Ral starts to laugh but catches himself. He looks at Vitra. She is becoming quite displeased with her kin's attitude. Ral cannot help but see the similarities between the two of them, which only makes it more amusing to see Vitra get so angry when dealing with someone so like herself.

The other two take their necklaces and put them on. Evan can't get his to drape over his enormous head, and his fingers lack the dexterity needed to undo the clasp. Sonya laughs at him as she takes his necklace and puts it on for him. Rich is dramatically stepping around the lines in an immature display of rebellion. He makes his way to the center, looks at Ral, and asks, "So do I sit directly on the little drawing or…?"

"On it, but gently so as not to disturb the image itself. Make sure you are facing the center," Ral replies.

Rich makes an elaborate display as he flares his arms out for balance, then begins lowering himself to the floor.

"How much of my brandy did you have, eh?" asks Vitra. "Are you always this much of an ass when you drink?"

Rich looks up at her and says, "Not enough, and yes."

Vitra shakes her head and looks at the other two still standing near the outside of the circle. She aggressively motions for them to join their friend.

Sonya and Evan decide to not provoke Vitra's ire any more than it already has been and quietly find a place on either side of Rich. Ral, Vitra, and Gaian move around the circle, each standing behind their own descendant.

Ral speaks to them once more before they begin.

"You are about to transcend to a realm that is like nothing you've known before. It is not exactly dangerous, but you cannot stay there very long. Once you awaken, follow the signs to Enki's chamber. He will be able to answer all your questions. Now please sit with your legs crossed, palms on your knees. Eyes closed and heads tilted up to the sky." Ral raises his hands up, level with the top of his head, palms facing the ceiling. Gaian and Vitra do the same. In unison, Vitra, Ral, and Gaian begin chanting in their ancient tongue. Rich finds it vaguely familiar, but he can't place it, then he recalls hearing that same dialect as he lay dying on the floor in Vitra's hall of shadows.

The chanting gets louder and louder. Their voices combine and fill the chamber, echoing through his head. He feels an odd sensation in his chest, a cold pressure that is creeping its way up to his neck. It washes over his face, forcing his whole body to react and draw in a sharp breath. His lungs are burning with the same sensation. He wants to open his eyes, but he can't. They are held shut as if frozen in place. He can't breathe. As the panic begins to set in, he feels like his body is violently launched into the air. The force makes him feel like he is about black to out. Then it all stops. The cold is gone. His body is still. He can breathe easily again. He waits for something else to happen. After a moment, his ears adjust, and he picks up on the sound of two other people breathing.

"Guys, did you feel that?" Rich asks.

"Yes," Sonya chokes out.

"Mmmhmm," groans Evan, clearly trying to hold back the urge

to vomit.

"Can we open our eyes now, Vitra?" Rich inquires, but no one replies. "Vitra? Vitra…? Hello?"

He slowly opens one eye and looks around. He sees his friends in front of him, but no one standing behind them. Vitra, Ral, and Gaian are nowhere to be seen. He opens both eyes and takes in his surroundings. They are in the same place. Same cavern with the same furniture in the same spots, but something is terribly off about it all.

"Guys," Rich whispers, "what the fuck is this shit."

CHAPTER 11

Rich, Sonya, and Evan look around, taking in their new environment. Nothing feels right about this place. Everything around them, including themselves, looks devoid of color. The whole room looks like it's been washed in gray, like all the life was sucked out of the cave.

"Guys, I'm scared." Sonya's eyes are deep with fear. She is shivering uncontrollably. Evan crawls over and pulls her close to his chest in an attempt to comfort her. As he holds her, his large hands start running over her back as though he's searching for something.

"Evan, what are you doing?" Rich asks.

"Dude, I don't feel her, like at all. No heat. No cold. No sensation in my hands whatsoever. What the shit is this? What's going on?" Panic overtakes Evan's tone of voice. His physical might does nothing to protect his mental frailty as the fear grows in his eyes.

Rich runs his hand over the ground. He can see his hand touching the floor and hear small rocks and dirt rustling under his touch but feels nothing. He takes a deep breath, then exhales, pauses for a moment, then takes several quick breaths and smacks his lips together like he's trying to name an unknown taste. His eyebrows furrow as he tries to understand what's happening. He quickly buries his nose in his armpit and inhales.

"Okay. I can't smell my own funk. I know for a fact that I was getting pretty ripe earlier. I was actually going to ask if I could shower, then they stuck us in their voodoo circle, and now this happened." Rich states as he waves a hand at their general surroundings. Evan and Sonya stop for a moment as they test his theory.

"Okay. You're right. I can't smell and likely can't taste anything either, but I'm not going to start licking shit to find out. So what's going on? What do we do now?" Evan says as he looks at Rich for answers.

Rich thinks for a moment. As he opens his mouth to respond, he is cut short by the sudden glow of yellow light filling the room. They all look to the source and see a single torch has self-ignited near the entrance to a hallway that none of them were sure was there a few moments ago. All three stare, frozen in place, unsure of what to do now.

This way, please. We have much to discuss.

Rich looks around the room, scouring for the source of the voice. "Did y'all hear that shit? Or have I finally lost it?" Rich rubs his face in his hands for a moment, allowing the stress to work its way out.

"Yeah, I heard it, but not like, from the room, like it was in my head," Sonya says. She stands up and wraps her arms around herself, rubbing her hands against her shoulders in a vain attempt to feel warm again.

Evan says nothing. He stands up, placing himself just in front of Sonya, between her and the burning torch.

Rich gets to his feet as well. "Enki, I assume," he groans, stretching his arms overhead.

You are correct. Now please, come sit with me. We haven't much time.

Rich looks back to his friends. He shrugs, then puts his hands down. "Anyone else feels like we don't have much time?" He chuckles and starts walking to the torch. As he nears it, the next one in line ignites itself as well.

"All right. We get it. Enough of the theatrics, man. We're coming," Rich says with a gruff tone.

Very well then.

All at once, the rest of the torches come to life, their warm glow, the only source of comfort in this empty realm they have found themselves in.

They slowly make their way down the hall. The path curves gently then stop at a large wooden door with iron hinges. Rich stops in his tracks. He points to it then bends his arm at the elbow and begins rotating his hand back and forth while pointing vigorously at the door. Sonya and Evan stare at him blankly. He continues his movements for a brief moment, then throws his hands up in the air and sighs.

"What the fuck are you trying to say?" Evan says while he glares at Rich.

"Thedoorisgoingtoopenbyitself! Goddamn." Rich shakes his head and looks at the floor, rubbing his forehead with one hand. He groans softly and moves closer to the door. He slowly reaches for the handle, expecting it to shoot open. He grasps the knob and braces himself for what might be on the other side. He looks back at his friends. With his other hand, he holds up a fist. He begins counting on his fingers, mouthing each word silently. When he hits three, he turns the knob and slams his shoulder into the door.

With a loud *oofff*, Rich bounces off the door. He loses his footing and falls to the floor.

It opens toward you.

Evan begins laughing. Sonya tries to hold it back, but a snort slips out. Rich gets back on his feet and turns the knob, pulling it toward himself this time.

As the door opens, they look into a small empty room. There are a few torches on the walls and a fire burning in the hearth. In front of it sits an old man, his face so weathered that his age was quite indeterminable. He is clothed in a plain woolen robe wrapped around his body, and on his face, he wears a warm smile. His hair is silver and long. It is combed back over his head and hangs loosely behind his ears. His skin is a ghostly white, even more pale than Vitra's. He sits on the floor with his legs crossed, his hands resting on his knees. He seems small, almost skeletal—so fragile that even a small bump might shatter his bones into dust.

Rich enters the room first, with Sonya and Evan following close behind. The being before them motions to the floor.

Please sit with me.

The friends all do as requested and sit down in a half circle around the old man but exchange an uneasy glance before settling down.

Hello. My name is Enki, and I was the keeper of life.

Evan is the first to blurt out his thoughts. "Where the fuck are we, and why can't I feel anything?"

Ah, right to it then. This room around you, the hallway you walked down and the room where you started in do not actually exist. I designed it all to reflect the place you were in, so it wouldn't be such a shock when you made the transition from the world of the living to this one.

"*This* one?" The sharp inflection in Rich's tone betrays his typically cool demeanor.

Yes. This realm, this, place of existence, is one in between life and death. You are probably more familiar with referring to it as purgatory. Does that make it more clear?

Sonya is next to speak, "This whole time, your mouth has not moved once. How are you talking to us?"

Telepathy, in a way. Please, allow me to explain the situation to you, uninterrupted. I will clarify everything.

All three close their own mouths and sit quietly, eagerly waiting for explanation.

As I mentioned, this is a realm between life and death. If you came here in a conventional manner, you would be floating in infinite blackness. No walls. No floor. Nothing. Your coming here was carefully planned out. It has taken me millennia to be able to craft just what you see around you. It was quite taxing on me. The big circle you saw Ral drawing on the floor and the one you arrived here on had to be exactly the same, or else, well, we wouldn't be speaking right now.

"All right. That kinda makes sense, I guess. Like in *Star Trek*, how they needed to have exact coordinates programmed into the teleporter on the *Enterprise*," Evan says as he nods his giant head.

Yes. Like the Star Trek.

Evan's expression turns quizzical. He begins to ask how Enki knew what *Star Trek* is, but he got cut off.

We have been preparing for your arrival for quite some time. Please, tell me what you know so far, about your current situation.

Before anyone else could speak, Sonya starts explaining, "Well, we nearly got eaten by a giant bear who turned out to be a dude, then wound up in that cave and met your friends. They told us about this dude Erra that like, did some weird shit with dead bodies? Like sewing them together and stuff. He got kicked out, then Ral and Gaian went to check on him, and they got attacked, and that's how Ral got all scarred up. Nearly killed him. Then they went back with their friends and all fought then like sealed him up with their magic?"

I assume it was Vitra you spoke to. She is not one to spend time on unnecessary details. That entire ordeal was much more involved than what she made it sound. Gaian and Ral certainly did experience the horror of what Erra had created, but the resulting war was far more horrific. So it is no surprise she didn't speak of it directly. She was not the same after losing so many of her friends and family.

"Whoa, *family?* She had family! She made it sound like it was just the eight of you that were going after him. How many more were there?" Rich leans forward onto his knees as his interest grows.

There were far more than just eight of us, and the battle lasted much longer than a single day. After seeing how many creations he had at his disposal, we amassed our own army. Around one hundred thousand able-bodied men and women were a part of the attack we launched on Erra's fortress.

"Are you fuckin' serious? That's not a battle. That's a *war!*" Rich exclaims, leaning forward on his knees.

It was awful.

"You, uh, you died, right? You sacrificed yourself to seal the deal?" Rich asks.

Yes, I did. That was relatively easy. The worst part was watching people die. How they died, to be exact. Those monsters Erra sent... They were true abominations. Some were enormous, easily fifty feet tall, walking the earth on all fours and crushing anyone who was unfortunate enough to be in the way. Erra's main army was comprised of humanoid beings, people who were corrupted by his evil. Some joined willingly at the promise of power and status. They brought with them all sorts of tribute, from livestock to exotic wild animals. Regardless of what they were promised, they all ended the same. Lifeless husks, eyes empty and devoid of a soul. Their limbs twisted and contorted, elongated and tipped with razor-sharp talons. Fangs protruding from their mouth. All they desired was to destroy and consume.

When I saw what they were capable of, I was determined to give my life to stop him. They would eat our forces alive, their screams unimaginable. After they died, Erra's evil would find them and turn them into one of his hordes.

Enki's form seems to diminish, his shoulders roll forward as his memories flood back to him.

We fought. For six days straight, we fought. By the end, our ranks had been cut down to a tenth of our original number, only our most elite were left. Each of us had roughly eight hundred soldiers under our command, and the rest were guarding Our Creator in her time of weakness. Erra's monsters were relentless. They did not tire or feel pain. The only ways to stop them were with fire or total dismemberment. Our only advantage was that we could outthink them. Our Creator ordered us to draw the main body of Erra's minions toward the middle of our lines then had us begin folding the ends in, pushing their ranks closer together. As we narrowed their stance on the battlefield, Our Creator began singing, her voice lovely and calamitous. The very ground began to harmonize with her, rumbling and groaning. As she kept going, the earth began to dance to her song. We ordered our men to stand strong and have faith in our mother. The earth rose up under the opposing forces. As it came crashing back down, it split open and sent the massive horde down into the depths of the earth. As she finished her song, the earth closed, crushing all those foul beasts under its weight. Our soldiers rallied behind us, and we threw ourselves at the remaining enemies. It took only minutes but felt like hours at this point. The eight of us rushed to take up our positions. Seven of us circled his would-be grave while I walked directly to the center of it.

Their voices became as one. Their items of power are placed at their feet. I knelt on the ground as the barrier was formed between them. Erra came out of hiding at this time. He sat on the ground next to me. He told me he was sorry it had gone this far. He said that he never wanted to hurt anyone, but he couldn't allow himself to be a slave to someone who refused to see him for his potential. Right before they finished their spell, right before my body was sacrificed, he looked me in the eyes and smiled. Then I awoke here. At first, I was alone in the darkness. Then she came to me, Our Creator, not in physical form, but she was there. She was comforting me. She detailed to me what would come to be. Told me what I must do, and now we are here.

All three of them stare blankly at Enki, processing what they were just told. They shift uncomfortably in place as they look around at one another, none of them sure what to say.

"So how is he getting loose? If you died to lock him up, how come it's not working anymore?" Evan asks.

Time, Evan. Simply time. Nothing lasts forever. Not even the strongest magic. It has been over five thousand years since we locked him away.

"When did those three lock themselves away in their cave?" Rich asks.

Well, after I died, I think they had some time to prepare. Then they entombed themselves.

"So they are over five thousand years old?" asks Sonya. Her eyes widen at the sudden realization.

Yes and no. While time outside their cave has been about, five thousand two hundred and forty-one years. It's been only, roughly, ohhhh, six or seven years for them?

"So what's the math on that? Like what's the ratio?" Sonya asks as she looks at her friends.

Rich shrugs his shoulders and looks away while Evan is crunching numbers in his head.

"I could be wrong, but I think that's like eight hundred and seventysomething years passed on the outside for every year on the inside. No wonder that milk was spoiled." Evan pinches the bridge of his nose, trying to forget the taste of it.

Rich frowns as he looks at Evan. "I'm not even going to ask," he says.

"So they willingly left behind all their friends to lock themselves up and wait for this Erra dude to resurface?" Sonya asks Enki.

Yes.

"What happened with the other, uh, four of you guys? You died. Vitra, Ral, and Gaian are locked up. Erra is a douchebag. So that covers, life, death, darkness, wind, and earth. Weren't there nine of you? Water, fire, electricity, and light? What happened to those guys?" Sonya replies.

Well, I can only imagine that they have passed away. Crossed over to the afterlife while I am stuck here.

If Enki could have cried, a tear would have escaped his eye.

But that's why you are here. Your success will determine the fate of literally every living thing in the world. Your goal, the reason you have been receiving so much training, is to ultimately destroy Erra and his wicked heart.

"Fate of every living thing in the world. That sounds like a huge responsibility." Evan sighs as the words leave his mouth.

"I think that is literally *the* biggest responsibility, only thing heavier than that would be saving the entire planet," Rich says to Evan.

Should you fail, the planet will ultimately be consumed as well.

"So no pressure then. Got it." Evan folds his arms around his chest and stares at the floor.

"How long have we been here? How much time has gone by outside?" Sonya asks, the look on her face shifting into an unpleasant shade of grim.

Exactly forty-five days at this point.

Enki's words sink a dagger of fear into Evan's stomach.

"So you're telling me we've been gone from the outside world for over a *century*?" Evan growls through grated teeth, his fists tightly clenching around his elbows.

Right about there. Yes. The world as you knew it is no more. It has been ravaged by the wickedness of Erra. I know you are all very upset by this news, but there is no sense in trying to be euphemistic. The reality is that everyone you have ever known has died.

Sonya tries to weep into her hands, but nothing makes its way out. Evan is curled in a ball as tightly as his massive form will allow, gently rocking back and forth. Rich sighs then lies back on the ground, covering his face with his hands. They all remained dead silent for some time. Enki knew better than to speak. He sat motionless, allowing them to grieve. Slowly, Sonya's dry sobs began to soften. Evan stopped rocking and lifted his head up. Rich remained on the ground, his arms folded across his chest as he stares at the ceiling.

Sonya rubs her eyes and looks at Enki. "Why didn't they tell us? Why didn't Ral say something to me? They knew what was happening the whole time…" Sonya sobs softly.

Enki looks at her, his expression hard and showing a hint of anger.

Would it have made things better if they told you that seconds after entering the cave your family was dying? Would it have made your training any easier? Would it have made you more capable of focusing on the mission at hand? Clearly, the answer is no. I understand your loss, much more than you realize. I have had nothing to do for the last five thousand years except listen to the wails and moans of the dead as they pass through this realm on their way to heaven or hell.

"That shits *real?*" Rich interrupts.

Not exactly. I used those terms because it's easier for you to understand and faster than giving you a decent explanation.

"Well, now I have *more* questions!" Rich exclaims.

The point is, all of us have lost someone we love. Yet we continue on because we know that the earth and all her splendor is more important than our own meager lives. We choose to not be selfish. We choose to focus on the greater good. I can tell you that there is a silver lining to this whole thing. If you can accomplish your goal and defeat Erra, you will be reunited with your loved ones. All of them.

"How? How the fuck is *that* going to happen? Huh? You gonna set up a little visitation cave here in Nowhere land?" Evan's voice gets progressively louder as he goes on, his eyes bulging out of his face.

Enki's visage begins to brighten. The room behind him takes on a stifling white aura. His form swells and begins to lean over Evan. It is evident that Enki has lost his patience.

You need to understand that there are millions of others who did not get to spend their time safe in a cave. Literally two-thirds of the planet's population was wiped out in the first ten years of Erra's awakening. All your worlds' governments unified and unleashed their most advanced weaponry to confront their common foe, but all it did was slow the advance of Erra's forces. Their fervor leads them to destroy their own cities in a vain attempt to stop his onslaught. Nuclear weapons used on their own people.

Erra was taken by surprise, not capable of knowing what modern science had evolved into, but it ultimately was not enough. Large cities fell to him. The smaller towns and rural areas went next as the disease of Erra spread. Soon there were only fortified pockets of resistance left on the mainland. Most of the world's armies had taken to the ocean and skies for protection. They still fight, and soon you will meet up with their remaining forces as you progress on your journey. Speaking with me is the last step in your training.

"So is this where you impart some kind of magnificent wisdom upon us? Tell us the secret to defeating Erra and saving the planet?" Rich says as he sits up.

Enki's form shrinks back down to its original size.

No. This is when I tell you the last step left in your journey. Rich, you must retrieve Vitra's cloak from under the City of Filth. It is located somewhere in the sewers under the city. You will know it once you find it. Its power will dramatically enhance your own. You will need it.

"Sweet. Hunting magic pajamas in my hometown," Rich grunts with sarcasm as he rolls his eyes.

Evan, you are seeking Gaian's amulet. It is a gold chain with a large dark red ruby hanging from it. The gem is the source of the power. It is located in a forest in central Peru.

Evan doesn't speak or move. His mind is still in shock from learning how long he has been hidden away.

Sonya, you are searching for Ral's sword, specifically just the hilt. We are not certain where it is located. Last we knew, it was held in an old research facility high in the mountains of Greenland.

Rich, growing irritated, raises a hand and waves it around frantically.

Yes, Rich?

"You have neglected to tell me where this 'City of Filth' is located. Am I just supposed to ask for directions? Or what?" Rich's tone grows more annoyed with every passing moment.

My apologies. I should have mentioned that. The city sits on what was once Portland, Oregon.

"Well, *that* makes sense. At least I don't have far to drive! Right, guys? Guys…?" Rich's friends are unresponsive. They are both devastated at the realization of the loss of their friends and loved ones. He looks back to Enki.

"Well, how do we get there? I don't have too far to go, but these two have literally thousands of miles to travel. You said something about an army? Are they going to help get us where we need to go?"

Yes. The remaining human forces are going to do whatever they can to help, and yes, they will be responsible for your transportation to and from the locations we believe the relics to be at. They do not have the resources to spend on needless trips. I'm afraid it's only going to be there and back again. So we have to make sure it gets done right the first time. I wish with all my soul there was a way to fix this that didn't involve so much tumultuous heartache, but this is the only option we have left aside from allowing Erra to just run rampant and corrupt all existence.

"Yeah. Kinda obvious when you say it like that," Sonya says, her hand instinctively moves to wipe away tears that aren't there.

"Are you doin' okay?" Evan asks her, placing one massive hand on her shoulder.

Sonya nods and places a hand on his. She looks at it and laughs. "Your fingers really do look like dicks," she says.

"Can you imagine what it would look like if his hand had an orgasm?" Rich says with a smile.

Sonya removes her hand from Evan's and exhales through her teeth. Rich laughs at them both as they squirm from the image he placed in their heads.

"So why didn't Vitra, Gaian, and Ral just bring their trinkets with them into the cave? If these things are so powerful, it seems like they might be pretty important to hold on to? No?" Sonya asks.

Well, after the barrier was sealed around Erra, all their trinkets, as you say, had to be strategically placed around the planet to maintain the barrier's strength. Each one is placed at a point where the earth's energy was strongest for that particular item, adding to the efficacy of Erra's prison.

Enki stands up and unfolds himself. He is deceptively tall but very thin.

Evan, please stand before me so I may send you back.

Evan stands up and steps in front of Enki. Enki raises one spectral hand and extends a finger, touching Evan directly in the center of his forehead. Evan's body begins to glow from the inside, his form goes stiff, and with a flash of light, he was gone. Enki motions for Rich to step forward. As Rich walks by, he looks at Sonya, gives her a wink and a smile, then turns to Enki. With a stiff poke between the eyes, Rich vanishes in the same fashion as Evan.

Sonya stands up and steps closer to Enki, expecting to be sent back with her friends.

Sonya, before you go, I have something special for you. You are the most important part of this entire endeavor. I can't tell you why, but I will leave you with a gift. A special seed of knowledge that will sprout when the time is right.

"Can you at least give me a hint or something?" Sonya asks nervously.

No, my sweet child. I cannot. If I told you what you must do, the likelihood of you following through with it is very low, but I promise you, when the time comes and you realize what is happening, everything will be clear.

"No. You're not sending *me* away until you tell *me* exactly what you're hiding from *me* about what you want *me* to do!"

As Sonya finishes her sentence, Enki grabs her head with both hands, his palms glow faintly with a warm light. He locks eyes with her, freezing her in place with his gaze. Enki quietly whispers to her the final details of her mission, then seals it all away in her mind. With a final flash, he pulls his hands away from her head, still holding her gaze.

I'm sorry, Sonya. I'm so very sorry.

With a heart heavy with sorrow, he sends her away. Enki's head hangs low. He sobs quietly as he gently descends back to the floor, falling into himself. The guilt of the burden he just placed on such an innocent young girl is a weight he was unprepared to carry.

CHAPTER 12

Sonya's body lays still on the floor. Everyone is leaning over her, anxiously waiting for some sign of life. Ral paces the floor, inspecting his drawing for any imperfections or errors. Vitra stands next to Gaian as they look down on Evan and Rich, who are both kneeling at her side. Evan has her hand in his, gently rubbing her wrist and forearm, his face awash in anxiety and fear.

Sonya's body convulses violently. Rich supports her head while Evan tries to hold her still. Her eyes open, revealing solid black orbs staring blankly into space. Her mouth opens partially. Through her parted lips comes a soft, almost-inaudible whisper. Rich leans in to hear what she's saying. As he gets closer, he can hear that it's not just one voice emanating from within Sonya but several speaking all at once. It's the same language that Vitra, Ral, and Gaian have been using. With a sharp jolt, Sonya sits straight up and struggles to catch her breath for a moment, her nerves reeling from the shock of being snapped back into consciousness.

"Holy shit, Sonya. Had us worried for a minute there," Rich says as he extends a hand to help her up.

Vitra is quickly at Sonya's side as Rich lifts her onto her feet. Vitra's hands begin examining Sonya, checking her for fractures and feeling her pulse.

"So what did Enki tell you?" Vitra asks them all.

"Well, it turns out I'm like over a century old now. So that's neat," Sonya replies.

"Yeah. I'm finally as old as I feel," Rich adds with a roguish grin.

Evan is silent, his emotions clear on his face though he refuses to speak. Vitra looks at him and offers some words of comfort. "I know you're upset. I, too, was upset when I had to leave my family and friends behind. You are aware that we are your direct family? Yes? That means we did not just get born into this cave. We had lives. We had friends and family and lovers. All of them, we left behind because we knew we must to restore the order. Knowing that my loved ones were growing old and dying mere seconds after locking myself away here was too much to bear. I wept for several days, but ultimately, the well-being of the planet is more important than my own. I will be with them again once this is all over. That's why we are so hard on you three. Gaian, Ral, and I are waiting for you to succeed so that we can all be reunited with our loved ones. I understand it is selfish. We are but human."

A silence falls over the group as they are consumed by the memories of what they were forced to leave behind. The room slowly stagnates as the deafening quiet coats the room like a thick blanket.

"Were your instructions clear on what you must do next?" Vitra asks, her tone solemn from the refreshed sorrow.

"Yeah, basically," Sonya states. "Enki said that we are to meet up with the remaining groups of human resistance that are in the area. They will take each of us to our next objectives, then it will be up to us to recover our respective artifacts and somehow signal the guys who dropped us off so they can pick us up again, right?" Rich is standing next to her and shrugs in agreement.

"In a nutshell, yes. That is what you must do. However, you need to experience the world as it is now before you can truly be ready for what lies ahead of you. We have prepared a small outing. There is a town nearby, Vernonia. Are you familiar with it?" Vitra asks.

"Yeah. We drove through it on our way out here," Rich answers.

"It is a small town. You need to go back to take a look around and examine the remnants of Erra's destruction. You may encounter some of his hordes. So do not take this trip lightly. Keep your wits about you and be prepared for a hike. You are roughly ten miles away." Gaian walks over to a large wardrobe and opens it up. Inside are the three backpacks the trio had when they left Rich's truck at the beginning of their hunting trip. Gaian sets them on the table at the far end of the room. From the same location, he removes a long sword, a large double-headed axe, and two long-bladed daggers. He sets them on the table with the bags.

"Your bags are prepared. I have hand-forged weapons for you. Rich, twin daggers, made from a steel alloy that is light and flexible. I folded the steel in such a manner that allows the blade to stay sharp with minimal maintenance. At night and after you retrieve your cloak, you won't need them very much, but do not dispose of them.

"Sonya, I made a sword for you from the same material I made Rich's daggers, but it has been reinforced and blended in a way to make it more aerodynamic. I curved it and hammered in a deep blood groove, allowing for enhanced airflow. This weapon will be unnecessary once you find Ral's hilt. You can keep it with you or dispose of it. The choice is entirely yours. Evan, you have this axe."

Evan stares at Gaian, waiting for further explanation or grandiose description of how it was made, but Gaian just blankly stares back. Evan stops him as he turns to walk away.

"So that's it? Just an axe? Nothing cool? Not manufactured in a special way that cuts through shit better? Not like a superlight material? All these weapons are so plain. They don't look very fancy at all." Evan is clearly perturbed at the giant's casual dismissal.

"You do not need a 'fancy' weapon. Appearance does not make a weapon more or less deadly. Besides, YOU are the weapon. I only gave you the axe as a placebo." Gaian pauses for a moment after saying these words.

"Although if you know it is a placebo, then it will ultimately lose the desired effect a placebo is intended for. So you may as well leave it here." The giant walks away as he finishes his thought.

Evan's spirit is broken. He looks at the axe laying on the table, then looks to Gaian. He sticks his bottom lip out as he whimpers out loud.

"But…they both got special weapons and stuff. Mines' 'Just an axe'," Evan says, openly mocking Gaian's tone.

The giant turns to him and scowls. "I do not sound like that," Gaian booms.

Rich, Evan, and Sonya laugh. Ral giggles a little as well, and Vitra almost cracks a smile but turns her face to hide it. Gaian picks up the axe and throws it at the wardrobe he pulled it from. It splits the furniture in two with ease and sticks in the granite wall behind it. Gaian grabs an apple from the table then walks over to the axe and rips it free. He holds the edge that was stuck in the wall upward and drops the apple on it. It splits effortlessly in two and falls to the ground.

Evan's mouth is agape with surprise. Rich is visibly impressed, and Sonya watches from behind her fingers.

"It is not just an axe." Gaian sets it back on the table and begins packing their bags for their impending journey.

"So, Vernonia," Vitra says, abruptly changing the subject, "it's roughly ten miles from here, less if you feel up to crossing rough terrain. You will most certainly *not* want to be out at night. This area does not seem to be dense with Erra's minions. If they are here, they are hiding very well. Either way, it is important to see firsthand what you are up against. You need to experience the horrors that he is responsible for because you must know what it is you are fighting."

"Okay. When do we go?" Rich says. As he finishes affixing his sheaths to his belt, he grabs the blades off the table and twirls them in his hands, and with a flash, he slips them into his belt, holstering them in place. He folds his arms across his chest and leans against the table.

"You're trying *way* too hard, Rich." Sonya rolls her eyes as she picks up her sword, removing it from the scabbard. After a brief inspection, she slips it back in and slings it over her shoulder.

Evan picks up his axe and begrudgingly slips it into his belt. He runs a finger across the blade. Its razor-sharp edge slices his skin open without any sensation, but as fast as it opened, his body closed it again.

"How am I supposed to walk around like this? It's going to cut the shit out of me. They both got sheaths," complains Evan as he fiddles with his axe, trying to find a safe way to have it in his belt.

"Use your imagination or just carry it," Gaian offers from the far side of the cave.

"Imagination, eh?" Evan places a hand on the head of the axe, the skin on his hand turns to stone and begins to spread to the blades of his weapon. Once they are safely coated, he grunts contently to himself. "How's *that* for imagination!" he proclaims.

Gaian looks back at him, his expression formless. "That should ease your worries."

Evan shakes his head and turns to his friends. Rich nods at him then looks to Sonya. She stands up straight and returns his acknowledgment. Vitra walks up to their group.

"Are you all finally ready?" Vitra asks.

"Ready as I'm going to be, ma'am," Rich replies.

"Follow me," Vitra says as she begins walking in the direction of the cave entrance.

The trio sets out behind Vitra. Sonya is following behind her with Evan lumbering right along with them. Rich trails behind a few steps, his eyes angled downward to the cave floor as he mulls his thoughts over in his head. He is anxious to get out after spending so many days inside the cave, but for all his eagerness, there is just as much apprehension. He has no idea what the world has in store for them now or what it will even look like, but either way, he knows he has to push on.

Evan is still attempting to process that it's been over a hundred years since they were locked away with their ancestors. He's never even been away from home for more than a week before. Now it has been over a century, and his parents are long dead, but not knowing what happened to them is the worst part. Everything in life had always been so predictable for him. Occasionally, things would veer off course, but ultimately, it was very routine, which he knows made him too complacent, too relaxed. He didn't want to enter the cave at first, and now he doesn't want to leave it.

Sonya follows closely behind Vitra, her sword hand resting on the pommel of her blade. Every footstep feels like it takes an hour as they progress down the hall. She is so anxious for their excursion back to reality. It used to be that she always tried to avoid fighting and almost all confrontations. Over the course of her training, that meekness has been tempered into a steadfast determination.

As they reach the entrance, Rich sticks a hand out, trying to feel for the wall that Evan busted his nose on when they first arrived. He stumbles around with both hands blindly searching the air in front of him. His fingertips brush the wall. He places his palms on it and begins slapping it gently making sure it's actually there. Vitra shoos him aside.

"So how often do you guys go out?" Sonya asks as she leans against the cave wall.

"Gaian is the one we allow to leave the cave for the purpose of reconnaissance and resupplying. We have been here for years. Food still goes bad," Vitra says dryly.

"So why him? Why does he get to leave? Don't you guys want to get out too?" Sonya replies.

"Well, of course, we wanted to. In the earlier days before humanity started living in the area, we would all take turns venturing out for resource collection. However, if we needed a specific material that couldn't be sourced from the land herself, we would have to find a trader. That was a task left for Gaian since he can shape-shift. He could always have a fresh face. He would obtain the goods and carry them until nightfall. Once he was alone, I would use the darkness to essentially teleport him to the cave entrance." Vitra's answer came with a tone that poorly conveyed her annoyance at the questioning.

Almost as if he could sense the irritation building in Vitra, Rich interrupts with a question of his own.

"Since you're in the mood for answering questions, how are we going to get through the, uh, wall thingy you guys have in place here? The same way you guys came and went I assume?" Rich asks as he looks around the perimeter of the barrier, patting areas as though he's searching for a magic button to open it up.

"It is a simple spell that momentarily weakens the barrier in this area only, allowing for those on the inside or outside to pass through it unhindered. However, it only works from the inside and only lasts about thirty seconds." Vitra pushes her hands together, fingertips pointing upward. She whispers something under her breath and moves her clasped palms forward. As her arms reach full extension, she opens her palms and shows them to the barrier. It shimmers and glows for a moment, then turns transparent again.

"You may pass through now. I will be here waiting for your

return." Vitra lowers her hands. Rich and Sonya hurry through the barrier. Evan hesitates. He is starting to inch toward the door when Vitra barks at him.

"If the spell ends and you are part way through the door, it will atomize your physical body into nothing. Now GO!" she shouts.

Evan leaps through the wall and lands next to his friends. He looks back to Vitra in time to see her image slowly fade away behind the barrier as the spell wears off.

"Well, that's a neat trick," Rich says as he watches her fade away. "Let's get going. We need to see how much daynight we have. A ten-mile hike will take us at least two hours, that's if we stick to a fast clip."

"Did you just say 'daynight'?" whispers Evan.

"Uhhh, yeah. It is a term Vitra uses when she talks about daytime. I guess I picked it up." Rich looks away and casually brushes the sleeve of his heavy cloak. "Anyways, let's get going. Got some ground to cover."

The trio heads to the mouth of the cave. As they turn the last corner, they see the dim glow of daylight breaking through the darkness. Sonya rushes to the entrance, eager to see the sun once more. As Sonya reaches the opening, she shields her eyes from the piercing light of day, squinting as her eyes adjust. Once the blinding has subsided, she lowers her hand and stares out at the world before her.

"Are you fucking kidding me!" Rich exclaims as he walks up next to her. Evan stands in silence behind them. The scene they are beholden to so starkly contrasted from what they remember leaving behind.

The image of the once-dense green forest they retained has been replaced by a bleak gray wasteland. Only dust and hard-packed earth lay before them. Remnants of trees that have managed to stay standing dot the landscape, their bark long dead, leaving almost petrified trunks bleached white from the decay of time. Most had no branches at all, just ghostly pyres reaching up from the dirt. The mountains around them are bare rock, not a trace of life left on them. The air itself is stale and unmoving while frigid and cold, like the dead of winter. The sky is a dark gray with thick clouds that glow from the rays of the sun that struggle to break through, coating the entire land in a perpetual hazy gray hue.

After taking in their new surroundings, Rich spurs the group on.

"We have to get going, guys. I can't even tell what time it is. I don't have a watch in my pauper's robes, and it's pretty cold out here. Vitra said we *really* don't want to get caught out here at night. So let's step to it. Pretty sure we came from that way." Rich raises a hand off to his right, pointing to a small hill about three quarters of a mile away. "Let's get going."

They set off in the direction Rich indicated. Every one of them is too busy staring at the drastic change the world has gone through to bother speaking. Their footsteps send little plumes of dust swirling up from the ground. The absolute absence of life is more disturbing than the landscape itself—no birds, no squirrels or chipmunks, not even bugs. It's like the life had been drained from everything around them. The most disturbing feature of this new landscape is a silence so deep that not even their footsteps are enough noise to stop the monotone hum of the stillness around them.

After a few minutes, Evan's curiosity gets the better of him.

"What do you think happened here? Was this Erra?" Evan asks.

"I remember Enki saying something about nuclear weapons being used against Erra. This seems pretty consistent with a 'nuclear winter.' No vegetation, no animal life. Portland is just a little ways from Vernonia, so it makes sense that if they bombed it that this place could still be suffering from the fallout." Rich kicks the ground as he speaks, sending a cloud of dust shooting in front of him.

"When do you think they did it? Like how long ago?" Sonya asks as she wipes some dust from her arm.

"Couldn't tell you," Rich replies.

They push on for a while more. As they crest the hill they had been walking toward, Rich has a brief moment of jubilation.

"Guys! She's still there!" Rich shouts.

He takes off running at full steam toward a solitary obelisk standing out from the rest of the land, a large rectangle covered in thick dust. He reaches it before everyone else and grabs the side of it and opens up the door to his old truck. He digs around under the seat and pulls out an old leather bag. It was once a good quality satchel, but time took its toll and left a mummified carcass instead. He opens the flap that promptly crumbles in his hands. He pulls from it a rust encrusted chunk of metal.

"Well, shit," Rich groans.

"What was that?" Sonya asks, moving closer to see.

"It was my truck gun. An old revolver, .38 special, but now it wouldn't even be a good paperweight." He throws it into the bed of the truck. It lands hard on the hammer, hard enough for the firing pin to puncture the primer and set off the old powder inside the cartridge. The handgun explodes with a loud bang. The force of the concussion knocks the thick caked dust off the cab of the truck. Rich recoils from the shock of the negligent discharge, his ears are ringing, leaving him slightly disoriented. After a few blinks, he comes to his senses. The exposed cab is now filled with dim daylight. Evan's eye is drawn to some movement coming from the back seat.

"What the fuck is THAT!" Evan shouts.

A face can clearly be seen looking back at them, its eyes huge, round, and solid black. Its flesh is as pale as the earth around them, dry and cracked. Thin black veins slithering sporadically under its translucent, papery skin that looks almost reptilian. Where should have sat a nose is just two slits in the skin that open and close like a fish's gills. The creature moves closer to the window. Its eerie eyes are unblinking, just staring at them.

"Is that...a person?" says Sonya, her words stumbling on their way out.

"Not a fuckin' clue," Rich whispers.

"What do you think it wants, Rich?" Evan is backing away slowly, despite being roughly ten times the size of it.

"Pretty sure it wants its fucking ring back," Rich quips. He draws his dagger and steps back from the truck. Sonya and Evan also bare their weapons.

The odd creature begins to crawl out of the back seat. A long, skinny arm with a hand full of thin visually sharp claws grabbing the roof pulls the rest of it from the cab of the truck. It lands on the ground with two legs that looked like they could be interchangeable with its arms. Rich squints as he examines the creature.

"Dude, it's got, it's got fuckin' hands for feet, like literally," Rich stammers.

The creature begins to move closer to them, its nose flaps moving more excitedly. Without warning, it opens its mouth and begins howling. The sound is piercing and ominous. It throws its head back several times. The noise is almost too much for them to bear. Evan and Rich are trying to keep their ears protected from the painful sound. With a gust of wind, Sonya effortlessly closes the gap between her and the beast, cleaving its head clean from its body. Thick black blood spills from the neck stump as the cranium spins in the air. The body collapses to the earth, with the head landing on its chest.

Evan uncovers his ears, looking on in disbelief. He can't help but stare at Sonya as she holds her bloodied sword in one hand. Her chest heaving from the exhilaration of combat.

"That was so hot," Evan says under his breath.

"You're going to have to tuck that boner in your waistband. We've got a problem," Rich growls.

All around them, the ground is stirring. Long thin claws begin sliding their way out of the dirt. Rich can't even count them. There has to be at least three or four dozen emerging in a circle around the truck. They shake off the dirt and focus on the trio.

"It's a trap...," Evan says. "It's totally a trap."

The creatures enclose around them, several climbing on top of the truck from the other side. They all chitter together, looking around at one another. Then in unison, they attack.

CHAPTER 13

The attacking creatures close in quickly, leaping across the ground on all fours. Evan backpedals away from them, stumbling ass first into Rich's truck. The impact startles him enough that he loses his footing and falls backward to the dirt. He throws a hand back to break the fall, losing grip on the axe in the process. The weapon slides under the truck, its rock sheath crumbling off with the impact. Two of the creatures are looking down at him from the top of the cab as he lays on the dirt. Seeing an opportunity, they throw themselves at him. As Evan's hands reach out to stop them, he locks eyes with the closest one as it falls, his brain taking in every horrific detail. Its fangs are bared and coated with brownish-gray saliva dripping from its mouth in anticipation of feasting on its prey.

As Evan stares on frozen with fear, a shining glint of a sharpened blade enters his vision. The tip of Rich's dagger penetrates the monster just to the right of its nose, its blade quickly disappearing into the back of its skull. Black blood and drool explode from the mouth of the fiend as the hilt of Rich's dagger impacts its face with a wet crack so sharp that one of the eyes is ejected from its socket. Evan is snapped back to his senses as Rich kicks him sharply in the ribs. He scrambles to his feet. Rich has the head of the beast pinned to the ground as he rips his dagger from its face. The other monster is lying dead on the ground with a massive gash from its chest to the middle of its abdomen, entrails scattered on the ground.

Sonya has already killed four of the attacking beings. Their bodies lay around her in pieces. She is in process of dispatching her fifth and sixth as Rich leaps into action, guarding her back as more come at her from behind. Sonya severs the arm from one then slices the head of the other clean in half. The freed section of skull falls to the ground and bounces, fracturing the enclosed chunk of brain into pieces. She splits the armless attacker in half at the waist. Its lower section falls forward and lands on the skull of the former.

Evan is finally getting back on his feet, his mind in shock from the stress of battle. With one giant hand, he grips the bed of the truck and pulls himself up, his focus on his friends standing at the front of the truck. Evan stands motionless in the midst of the fray. He wants to help, but his body is numb and refuses to move on its own. As he stands there watching, four more of the hellish imps are creeping along the ground on the passenger side of the bed. One crawls its way under the truck while the other three go around the tailgate.

With a quick slash from its razor-sharp claws, the beast under the truck splits Evan's right calf open, leaving several deep lacerations and nearly cleaving the muscle in half. Evan looks down at his leg in shock. The wound is massive and already bleeding profusely. Several streams of hot crimson are pouring out and pooling at his foot. The thing that flayed him open is now emerging from under the truck. With a fit of rage, Evan swings his left leg at its head, catching it under the chin. He drives its head up into the bed. The immense pressure from his kick combined with the mass of the vehicle causes the monster's skull to pop like a water balloon filled with meat. Evan turns to the others that had circled around the truck. He grabs the truck bed and with a swift might rips it from the frame, flipping it over on top of the encroaching monsters. With the bed gone, Evan spies his axe laying under the corpse of the first creature. He reaches down and grabs the handle, pulling it straight up between the frame rails. The body comes up with it, impaled on the axe's beard. Evan rips the axe upward, tearing the body in half, sending a brief geyser of blood and hunks of intestine into the air. His attention is turning to the three monsters struggling to escape from under the bed of the truck.

The first one to its feet is cleaved in half straight down the middle, the bevel of Evan's axe burying itself into the dirt as the two halves flop to the ground. Evan pulls the axe out and moves forward, his right ankle buckles slightly under his weight. His wound is still open despite his rapid healing. He forces his skin to harden, covering his body in thick rock and closing over the wound, sealing it from further damage. The next monster out is caught in the left side of its neck, the momentum from his swing combined with the sharp edge slices it clean through to its right armpit. Evan follows with a kick to its gut, sending it flying back into the truck bed as the last one frees itself. Evan swings his axe at the beast, but it jumps back dodging his blow. He lunges at it, bringing his axe crashing down overhead. His target rolls to its right, safely avoiding the strike. The creature scurries away, circling around the truck. Evan clumsily chases after it, tripping over the dismembered bodies and rusted metal he left all over the ground. The fiend leaps onto the cab and leers at Evan, making a sour squealing noise from its nostrils, like a pig drowning in snot. The monster looks around and sees its pack has been bested and the squeals intensify. In a display of fear, its limbs retract tight against its body as it takes in the carnage.

Sonya and Rich have ended the threat on their side of the battleground. Bodies lay all around them, their clothes spattered with black blood and chunks of flesh. Rich wears a disturbing smile as he looks upon the aftermath. Sonya takes a corner of her cloak and wipes the blade clean, then eases her sword home into its sheath. The sound of the creatures' shrieking draws their attention. They both look to see a solitary fiend huddled atop Rich's old truck with Evan slipping and tripping over everything in his way.

"Would you just KILL IT ALREADY!" Rich shouts.

Evan nears the cab and takes a swing at it. The creature easily jumps to safety on the other side of the truck. Rich reaches back and winds up to throw a dagger. He looses his knife. It spins through the air on the way to its target. Just feet before impact, the beast turns, looking directly at its impending doom. The pommel of the knife slams into the eye of the monster, causing it to burst in its socket. With a final piercing shriek, it scrambles over the frame of the truck, easily avoiding Evan as he frantically flails at it like someone trying to scare off a bee. After breaking clear of Evan's onslaught, it took off running full tilt away from them, whining and wailing as it ran.

"Well, shit. I missed. Sorta." Rich scratches at his beard as he bends over to pick up his dagger. He wipes the blade on his pants and sheaths it.

"Where do you think it's running to?" Sonya asks as she walks over to Rich.

"Well, same direction we're heading, actually. Vernonia is southeast of here. That little donnybrook didn't take too long, so we have plenty of time still, but we need to get there quick, fast, and in a hurry. Vitra was very explicit about *not* being out here at night, and I feel the same way. So step to it." Rich begins walking in the direction the monster went.

Sonya walks around the old truck to Evan. His hardened skin is crumbling off as he returns to his normal appearance.

"Those things were nasty little buggers, weren't they, Sonya?" Evan says as he brushes the last of his armor off his shoulders. He turns his leg out to check his wound, expecting to see something but discovering that it had totally healed over the last few minutes.

"Yeah, they were. I don't even know what to call them. Does a word for *that* even exist?" Sonya says as she kicks the leg of a dead creature, nodding her head at it.

"Your idea is probably better than mine. All that comes to mind is like, freaks? Geeks? Satan's hobbits? I don't even know." Evan tries to wipe his axe off on the ground, but the blood is much stickier than he anticipated, leaving his axe covered in a thick paste of blood and dust.

Sonya examines the remains of the creature Evan chopped in half. As she studies it, her eyes widen as a soft recognition hits her. She turns to Evan with a mixed expression of concern and intrigue.

"Those are similar to human organs. Look, that's a liver. There's part of its heart. I mean, I'm not a rocket surgeon or anything, but those are definitely humanlike." She stares at it, trying to come up with some explanation for what she's seeing.

From a hundred or so yards away, Rich turns back to his cohorts. He throws his hands up in the air with frustration, letting his arms rest akimbo on his waist.

Evan goes to speak to Sonya, but he's cut off by a distant profanity. He looks and sees Rich flailing, urging them to hurry along. They both start off toward Rich, who it's now holding his head in his hands as he waits for them.

"How about Sleepers? Or Shriekers? Maybe Black Bloods? Nah, that's too long. Needs to be one word," Evan says as he thinks out loud.

"I honestly don't care what you call them, Evan. They are gross and awful, and I *hate* them." Sonya wraps her arms around her elbows in an attempt to comfort herself.

"How many did you kill? I got three. Pretty cool, right?" Evan boasts.

"Ummm, I wasn't really counting, but if I had to put a number on it, I'd have to guess like twenty or so? Rich got at least ten or twelve. Not really sure," Sonya replies.

Evan looks at the ground, the shame almost unbearable. The weight of his failure hangs from his neck like a ton of bricks. Sonya, as though she was sensing his thoughts, offers some comforting words.

"Don't feel bad, man. You never really were a violent guy. You didn't play sports or do anything very competitive aside from gaming. This isn't something you can just pick up. Remember my first year of softball back in, like, eighth grade? I was so nervous and clumsy. I wound up totally choking at bat and then fractured my wrist tripping over a base when I finally got a hit." Sonya looks at Evan and slugs him in the shoulder.

"Then you remember the next year, my first year of high school? I owned that field. Made it my bitch, right?" she asks him.

"Yeah. You actually got to play with the varsity team when they were short a couple of players. You were really good." Evan's voice begins to reflect his rising spirits. "I'll probably get better. Just need to find some more of those, uh, Creepers? To practice on?"

"Ehh, I don't like that either," Sonya says.

When they finally catch up to Rich, he's looking off at the next hill.

"All right, if we get to the top of that hill right there, we should be able to get a good view of the surrounding terrain. It's also the direct route. So we should just sack up and climb it," Rich says.

"Uhh, what if you don't have a sack to up?" Sonya asks sarcastically.

"Then give the nearest one a squeeze," Rich replies as he notions to Evan.

"Whatever." Sonya huffs as she walks past Rich.

"Hey, Rich, what do you think we should call those things we beat up? I was a-thinking like Creepers or Freeks or something," Evan asks as they head for the hilltop.

"Beat up…" Sonya laughs as she shakes her head. "Think we did a little more than that, buddy."

Rich chuckles at Sonya's quip, then says, "Nah. Those are lame. How about Lurkers? Cuz they kinda just lurk around underground waiting for shit."

"I like Lurkers!" Sonya shouts back to them.

"Good god, I've been trying to figure this shit out for ten minutes now, and you just shoot from the hip and nail it. Is there nothing I can do right?" Evan shakes his head as they begin to climb the hill, his frustration in full swing again.

"It's not that big of a deal, man. Hey, did you see how many of those Lurkers I killed back there? Pretty rad, huh?" Rich slaps Evan on his back as he laughs.

Sonya gets to the top of the hill before her friends, her eyes scouring the landscape ahead of them. All she can see is a vast spread of emptiness for the next several miles. Rich and Evan stop next to her and take in their grim new reality.

Nothing is left of the once-lush and fertile forest—just empty fields of gray earth. There is an occasional edifice that still stands, but most of the ones that are discernible are nothing but piles of debris. A long dry riverbed can be seen snaking its way between the hills and into the vast plains of nothing. Rich follows it along until he recognizes the layout of the old landmarks.

"Look there," Rich says as he points toward the edge of a ridgeline about three or four miles away. "We follow what used to be a river to that ridge, take it up and over, and bam. We're basically in Vernonia. I'll take the lead if you guys want me to."

Evan and Sonya look at one another, neither object as they shrug in unison.

"After you, then," Sonya says as she gestures him forward with a wave of her hand.

"Wussy…" Rich pokes her in the shoulder as he walks by.

"What happened to ladies first? I mean, in the name of equality, you really should take the lead, Sonya," Evan says as he walks next to her, a cheeky smile on his face.

"You better watch it in case I decide to *sack up*, Evan." Sonya takes one hand and slaps Evan in the crotch. He stops in his tracks and doubles over.

"Oh god, why…why?" Evan takes deep breaths, trying to work through the pain.

Rich looks back and laughs. He shakes his head and turns to the path ahead of them.

They walk for a couple of hours, keeping a good pace to make up for the lost time. Evan is in the back, Sonya walking in front of him with Rich about ten yards in front of her. His eyes are always watching ahead, keeping a lookout for more Lurkers or anything else that may be problematic. They are following along the riverbed, the last big ridge only a few hundred yards away on their right. In just a few minutes, they will be able to see what's left of the town.

As Rich reaches the foot of the hill, he looks back as he waits for his friends. He quietly studies them as they approach. He can't help but notice how ridiculous Evan's new frame is, especially when compared to his still meek personality. More impressive, though, is Sonya and her innate ability to wield a sword. She was dispatching Lurkers twice as fast as he could. Rich's instinct is to blame it on her having a better weapon than he, but part of him knows she was just simply better than him even though he would never admit it.

While his friends closed the gap, Rich lends his eyes to the rolling hillsides, examining the devastation that had befallen the forest. As his focus sweeps from left to right, then back again, he notices something that's a bit off. On a distant slope, his eyes catch sight of an odd protrusion. It feels like he should have noticed it, like it was far too obvious to be missed.

"What is it, Rich?" Sonya asks. She turns to look in the direction Rich was transfixed on.

"Nothing. Just checkin' stuff out." He looks away for a moment then steals another glance as Sonya walks past him. His eyes find the same spot on the hill, but the anomaly is gone. He scans the area, double-checking that he didn't make a mistake. He finds it again. His eyes begin to focus. His vision clears just as the large object crawls over the ridge and out of his view. Very suddenly, he feels an icy pang of fear in his chest. Considering the distance between him and whatever it was he saw on the hill, it had to have been sixteen or seventeen feet long at least. It was massive and quick.

"All right, guys, let's get over this hill and we will be able to see the town. We must be in the fall or winter because daylight is fading fast. I don't know what they expect of us, but let's hurry the fuck up and do it." Rich swallows hard, trying to keep the unease in his belly. He begins climbing upward, wanting to put as much distance between his friends and whatever it was he saw. He had no idea what that could have been, but one thing was certain—it was stalking them.

CHAPTER 14

"So the plan is for us to wait until the moment they walk through the barrier, then follow after them to oversee their excursion?" Ral says in a hushed tone. They are walking just a few yards behind Vitra and the trio as they head for the entrance to the cave.

"Yes. That is the general idea." Gaian's attempt at quiet is less than successful. Even lowered it still echoes from the walls. Fortunately, the group ahead of them is loud enough to drown his voice out.

"We have only seconds to get through the door. As soon as the last one is out, we need to be right behind them. Remember, we are not to intervene unless absolutely necessary. They are trained but not experienced. The trauma of battle can be overwhelming." Ral looks over at Gaian.

Gaian says nothing as he walks with Ral.

"I'm glad to see you're on the same page, my friend," Ral says, smiling.

Ral and Gaian stop as the other party reaches their destination. They listen intently as Rich and Evan probe Vitra about the details of the barrier and their impending journey. Vitra recites the words to open the barrier. Sonya, Rich, and Evan run through. As Evan's foot breaks the threshold, Gaian and Ral take off at a dead sprint, brushing past Vitra as she holds the barrier open. They both hit the wall at the same time and jump through to the other side.

"Gaian, did you count how many seconds before we made it through the barrier?" Ral asks as he studies the ground, looking for signs of the trio.

"Almost two full seconds. That puts us roughly thirty minutes behind them," Gaian responds.

"Good. That should give us plenty of following distance. Let's get after them."

Gaian and Ral set off at a brisk pace after the three friends.

Rich is almost on all fours as he scrambles up the hill. He does not want to stop for anything. His friends whine and complain as they climb, but he knows that they don't have the luxury of taking a break yet.

"Rich…what is the…fucking hurry…man?" Evan gasps between breaths, trailing in the rear of their party.

"Yeah. Seriously. You're runnin' us pretty hard," Sonya adds.

"Like I said, it's getting dark. We need to hurry. That's all there is to it, okay?" Rich's curt response barely hides his rattled nerves. "Just another fifty yards and we're there. Keep at it. We will take a breather then. I must have a bit of Aunty Vitra's Magical Go-Juice left in me. I don't think I've ever done this much cardio in my life." Rich laughs, attempting to lighten the mood.

Finally, they reach the top of the ridge. Rich and Sonya are a little winded. Evan collapses on the ground. His chest heaving furiously in an attempt to catch his breath. Sonya looks down on the town of Vernonia. She is surprised at how much of it is still standing. The layout of the town is fairly clear. Streets and alleys are easily distinguishable with several of the buildings intact, only missing an odd window here or there.

"So where are we supposed to go? Like just walk around town for a minute then head back?" Sonya turns to Rich as she asks. He just looks back at her and shrugs.

Evan clumsily gets his feet back under him, still doubled over as he chases his breath.

"Maybe this was all we needed to do? Just come look at it?" Evan says hopefully.

Sonya starts down the hill, heading directly toward the ghost town with Rich hot on her heels.

"Goddamn it, guys," Evan whimpers as he heads down with them.

Sonya and Rich are soon standing on the outskirts of the town's remnants, Evan hanging back just behind them. Rich cautiously examines the area, plotting how to proceed. The main road is fairly clear but too obvious with more than a few spots that could set them up for another ambush. The side streets and alleys are narrow and crowded with debris but offer a chance to sneak around possible encounters.

"I don't like this very much." Rich squats down and plays with some rocks near his feet. "There's bound to be more Lurkers in there, and our little buddy that slipped by Evan was headed this way. I just feel like we're walking into a shit show, ya know?"

"What don't you like about it?" Evan asks as he leans on his axe.

"Well, look around you. See how basically *everything* is covered in rubble? Now look at what I assume is the main drag that ran through town, wide open, barely anything on the road, almost like something cleared it out for us. Doesn't that seem a little suspicious?" Rich stands up and turns toward Evan.

"Well, when you put it that way, I guess so," Evan says quietly.

"I don't know." Sonya asks, "Maybe the military or local law enforcement did it? Like after whatever happened, happened. Maybe they cleared it out so they could get through town to help people?" The positivity in her words feels refreshing to all of them.

"I suppose that's a possibility. Maybe I'm just being paranoid after getting jumped by those damn Lurkers back at my truck. I mean, they weren't anything we couldn't handle, but in larger numbers, they could be problematic," says Rich, looking back at the ruins of the city trying to decide what to do next.

"Let's just charge right in. Isn't that the most 'Murica thing possible?" Sonya says.

"Okay. I'm sold. At least we're aware we are walking into another trap." Rich smiles as he pushes on toward the town.

As they enter the city proper, they can see signs of the people who used to live there. A few small shops are scattered around, their shells haunting and silent. Some odds and ends can be seen in windowsills even though most of the glass was missing or broken. They pass a gas station with a couple of cars sitting at the pumps that are nearly rusted into nonexistence. A portion of the canopy that sat over it had fallen into the station itself.

After only ten minutes or so, they had already made it to the edge of town and started working their way in to the residential areas. A fire station sits to their right, two of its engines still in the bays. Evan notices a sign at the far end of the fire depot's property.

"Hey, it says 'Vernonia Schools,' and below it, says, 'EVAC station.' Maybe the military did come through here. Let's go check it out. Might be some cool military gear or something," Evan says as he points down the road.

"That's not a half-bad idea, my friend. Let's go," Rich replies.

Walking through the neighborhood between them and the school, they can see most of the houses are destroyed. Sonya notices something odd and breaks from the group to take a closer look.

"What are you doin'?" Rich asks.

"I want to check something out," she replies as she heads around the back of a house as they round the corner into what used to be a backyard.

Then they see what caught her attention. Before them is a huge swath cut into the ground, about seventy yards long, with a giant machine at the end of it. It was laying mostly on its side and partially buried in the earth from its impact and the years of collecting dust. One large metal wing protrudes into the air with a large cylinder attached to the end of it. The tail of the craft was about as long as the wing. On the end sat two more of the same style cylinder, just about a quarter the size. Its cargo hatch was missing entirely, leaving a large open hole.

Sonya crept closer to it, her curiosity taking over her judgment. As she neared the rear end of the aircraft, she could hear Evan whispering intensely at her.

"Sonya! Don't!" he says, trying to be simultaneously as loud and as quiet as he can.

Sonya slowly steps closer to the downed craft, her right hand cautiously grasping her sword. After a glance back at her friends she silently slips into the gaping maw of darkness. Rich and Evan grow anxious as they approach the rear of the aircraft. Their ears strain for sounds of distress or a cry for help, but there is just silence.

Sonya's head emerges out from the back of the craft, eyes full of tears. "Guys, look at this," she says as she wipes a tear from her cheek.

Evan and Rich step inside the hull of the ship, and as their eyes begin to adjust to the low light, they are met with a horrifying scene. Lined up and down the sides of the craft are the mummified remains of at least three dozen people: men, women, and children. Their bodies are still strapped into the seats. Old, weathered clothing still wrapped around their bodies.

"Oh, for fuck sake." Rich puts a hand on his brow and wipes it down his face.

Evan is speechless as he stares at all the hollow faces. Their expressions of horror still etched into their faces, even after all these years.

"How long has it been since this happened? These corpses are completely desiccated." Rich leans in closely, examining them as best he can in the dim light.

Evan is staring at what was once a mother clutching her child. The baby's face buried in her chest, the top of its head barely visible from within the mother's clothes and arms. If it weren't for the few sprigs of red hair still poking out, Evan may not have even noticed the child's body. The mother wore a forest-green shawl with a brown sweater under it. Her body was curled around the child as tightly as possible in some last-ditch attempt to protect her baby. The mother's dark red hair is still pulled back in a hastily tied bun.

"I don't know. I don't even want to know." Evan is nearly in tears. He can't handle the scene anymore, he turns and walks out of the hull and waits outside.

"Rich, what do you think happened here? Don't bodies normally get eaten by bugs and stuff? Small predators or something? These people are all still intact," Sonya says as she picks at the sleeve of a bearded man wearing a flannel shirt.

"I, uh, I have no idea. I agree that they don't look like they have decayed, but they obviously haven't been scavenged by any animals either." Rich is quiet for a moment, considering his own words.

"Come to think of it. I haven't seen *any* creatures besides Lurkers," Rich adds.

"All right. I've had enough. Let's get out of here and take a look at the school." Sonya walks out. Rich slowly backs toward the door, his eyes still studying the bodies in the aircraft that is now a mass grave. He turns and steps through the door. Leaving them to their rest.

The trench carved out by the crashed ship leads straight from the parking lot of the school. It seemed they were in the process of taking off when whatever caused the crash happened. The party walked in silence as they approached the school. Every step taken was done with abundant caution. Sonya and Evan were expecting to see more Lurkers at any moment while Rich was still fixated on whatever it was he saw crawling across that hill just before they got to town.

The parking area and the entire school had a large chain-link fence wrapped around it with strands of barbed wire at the top, leaning away from the lot. Each panel of fencing was anchored in place by a large concrete barrier set directly on the feet of the prefabricated fence. They followed it around the right side, looking for a potential opening. They reached the main gate to find one side of it ripped clean off its hinges and laying on the ground a few yards away.

As they enter the gate, they come across a set of barriers that were meant to direct people to a large platform that fell in line with the downed craft. The path moved them by a mountainous pile of luggage and other personal belongings. Next to that was a metal table with several binders laid out on it. A couple of temporary shelters were set up behind that. Most of the fabric was loose and decayed, and only a few tattered scraps still remained attached. One of the structures held several large metal lockers and wooden crates.

"I'm gonna check that out." Evan steps over the retaining wall and walks to the storage area.

He tries the handle on one of the cabinets only to find he is locked out. His shoulders slump in defeat for a moment before he remembers his newfound strength and simply twists the handle off the cabinet. He swings it open to reveal a weapons locker fully stocked with armaments none of them have ever seen.

"Duuuuuude," Evan exclaims, his massive hands delicately pulling what looks like a rifle out of the locker. Its exterior is completely smooth, comprised of a very sturdy white polymer. It has no optics or even basic iron sights mounted to it. Just a small piece of blue-tinted glass on the top side of the weapon above the trigger and a single fiber-optic cable on the end of the barrel. He runs a hand across the body of the weapon. When his index finger grazes the top of the trigger guard, the weapon makes a tactile vibration, almost like a cell phone receiving a text. Simultaneously, the little strip of blue glass on the top of the rifle lights up. A red battery with a broken lightning bolt passing through it is displayed in the air just millimeters above it.

"Whoa! It's got a holographic HUD! And apparently, the battery is dead. Lame." Evan tries looking for a place to insert a battery, but the weaponry is far too alien to him to grasp. He sets the rifle back in the cabinet and rejoins his friends.

"What's a HUD?" Sonya asks.

"It stands for 'Heads Up Display,' and sadly, aside from some cool tech that needs to be charged, I don't see much else here." Evan walks over to the large pile of luggage and starts rummaging through it.

"For fuck's sake, man. Have some respect, those belonged to someone," Rich says as he glares at Evan, shaking his head.

"Yeah, I don't think he's going to find anything of value in there, and if he does, they won't need it." Sonya elbows Rich in the ribs.

"Yeah, I guess. I mean, these people have probably been dead for like at least what, eighty years? Still, we need to get going. Don't have the time to spend snooping through dead people's shit." Rich walks back through the gate.

Sonya sighs and walks after him, pulling on Evan's arm as she walks by. He tosses the black satchel that was in his hand to the ground in front of the pile of luggage. It bounces on the ground forcing the clasp to pop open, spilling its contents in the dust. Among the personal effects scattered across the ground is a silver-framed photo of a young red-haired woman and her infant daughter.

CHAPTER 15

Rich looks up to the sky, trying to pinpoint the sun's location, but the thick cloud cover makes it virtually impossible. It's clear that the sky is darkening, but he has no idea how much daylight they have left. He hasn't seen any reason to be concerned, and that's what bothers him the most. His gut rumbles in discontent from the constant grating on his nerves. The sensation of worry biting at the back of his neck like a white-hot poker. Nothing about this feels okay at all.

"We need to leave. It's getting late, and I'm growing increasingly more paranoid with every second. There is nothing left to see here. Just a bunch of old houses and dust." Rich spits on the ground and smears it into the dirt with the toe of his boot. The soil is so starved of moisture it is absorbed almost instantly.

"Yeah, I think so too," Sonya says. "The sky looks like it's getting darker with every passing breath. I can't imagine there being any more reason for us to be hanging around here. Gives me the creeps anyways."

Evan wanders a little ways from the group, his attention drawn to what used to be Vernonia Lake. Its shores are now cracked and dry, steeply dropping into a great pit filled with dozens of old logs. He studies the area for a few seconds when his eyes catch movement along the far side of the lake. He squints trying to focus on it, but it's hard to make out. He loses sight of it as it moves deeper into the lake bed, getting lost behind the piles of ancient timber. He strains his vision trying to watch for movement.

"Guys, I think I saw something out there." Evan tries to say it loud enough to be heard, but the words get caught in his throat.

A gaunt gray face slowly peers over a pile of lumber. One large black eye peers out at him. The other is closed tightly with dry black blood still caked around its socket. The Lurker slowly lifts itself into full view. It glares directly at Evan, showing itself in a sign of pure defiance, teeth bared, and arms spread out wide. It takes a deep breath in and lets out a series of sharp cries that sound somewhere between a shriek and a bark. They ring sharply through the air, echoing off their surroundings.

Rich and Sonya whip around to face the noise. They see Evan standing near the lake bed and rush toward him.

"Oh, for fuck's sake. It's *that* one again. Why's he hollerin' like that? Does he want me to poke his other eye out?" Rich pulls a knife and begins to move in on it.

As he comes to the edge of the lake bed, the air is filled with a sound so sinister that Rich stops dead in his tracks. A sound just like the chittering they heard when they first encountered the Lurkers only multiplied by hundreds. Its tone is so piercing that all three recoil from its magnitude.

One by one, Lurkers begin unearthing themselves. Erupting all around the one-eyed instigator and spreading out like ripples in a pond. Soon there are easily hundreds of them looking toward their comrade with a tense intrigue. With a long hate-filled shriek, it points a sharp yellow claw at them. The horde turns in unison, locking eyes on the trio who is locked firmly in place from the terror of the spectacle before them.

"Run! Fucking run now!" Rich shouts, taking off at a dead sprint. Sonya is right behind him but gains with ease. Evan is desperately pumping his tree trunk legs up and down in his attempt to keep up.

Sonya looks back at her friends. She slows herself enough to give them a chance to catch up. As she watches, a massive wave of pasty gray flesh comes pouring over the bank of the old lake. All she sees is a wall of gnashing teeth and outstretched claws. Her eyes reflect enough panic to force Rich and Evan to look back over their shoulders. Evan screams out loud at the sight, his adrenaline driving him on like a man possessed. In the blink of an eye, he is next to Rich.

"Shitshitshitshitshitshit!" is all that can be heard from the large man as he overtakes Rich. His giant legs are slamming into the ground with such ferocity that his footfalls reverberate through the ground.

Even though Rich and Evan are running faster than they ever have before, the Lurker horde is hot on their heels. Their gruesome maws agape, with long streams of saliva pouring out in anticipation of a fresh meal. Hundreds of starving black orbs watch Rich and Evan's every move with violent determination. The sounds coming from the mass of hungry Lurkers are just as horrifying. Grunts and short barks interweave with growls and occasional cries of pain give it a tune that is similar to a gargantuan stomach rolling across the ground in search of sustenance.

Rich's eyes dart back and forth frantically as he searches for any means of escape. There is no way the three of them can fend off the legion of Lurkers chasing after them in open combat. His eyes light up with a spark of inspiration.

"Guys! We aren't going to outrun them! We have to fight! We need to find a way to funnel them down! Look for a small building! Sonya, you're the fast one here! Go scout ahead!" Rich shouts between breaths.

In the blink of an eye, Sonya is gone. Rich and Evan have yet to see her in true form, and for a fleeting moment, they forgot about the horde chasing behind them. Sonya is back almost as fast as she left.

"There is an old bank with large windows, but it's made of solid brick and still standing. It's only about a quarter mile away. We can fend them off there." Sonya is gone again after sharing the information.

The advancing horde is now just feet behind them. So close that the smacking of lips and grinding of teeth can be heard. Their thick yellow talons scrape and scratch at the pavement under them as they careen toward their intended meal.

Rich and Evan cross a bridge and look ahead of them. They see Sonya jumping up and down, waving her arms hysterically.

"Front door! Front door!" Sonya yells. Then ducks inside the old brick building.

There are three large glass windows on the east side of the old bank. Aside from that, most other entry points are small enough to allow maybe two Lurkers through at a time. As Rich is sprinting alongside Evan, he notices the sky is growing much darker. Nighttime is nearing. A menacing smile spreads across Rich's face as they near the bank.

With the force of a speeding semitruck, Evan is first through the door, his massive frame slamming into the doorway and actually jarring the jamb slightly out of its seat. Rich comes through right after him. Sonya is already standing behind the counter, sword in hand. Rich leaps the counter and makes his stand next to her, daggers at the ready. Evan frantically scurries over and falls hard into the floor to Rich's left. Dropping his axe yet again.

"EVAN! Get your shit together, NOW! This is gonna get—" Rich is cut off by the smashing of glass as the first two large windows are shattered by the horde.

Their bodies pour through with the first to hit the floor getting buried by those that fell through after that. They hurl themselves at the trio. Leaping clear across the room onto the counter. Sonya and Rich begin hacking at them, limbs and hunks of flesh filling the air around them like snow in a winter blizzard. Their combined ferocity routes the enemy forces, pushing them left, toward Evan.

Evan is swiftly being outnumbered. He frantically swings his axe, attacking blindly without strategy. Even though his movements are erratic, he has managed to cut down a few but more quickly overwhelm him and take him to the floor, ripping and biting at his flesh then eagerly lapping up the blood as it gushes from his wounds. He forgoes the axe and takes to crushing them with his bare hands. Easily palming their heads and popping them like overripe tomatoes, but it is futile, each one that he dispatches is replaced by another. Each one takes its chunk of flesh before being snuffed out. Evan is fighting with all his might, but the stress of battle has left him unable to summon his powers.

Rich hears Evan crying out, his shouts ringing with pain. Evan is lying in a large pool of his own blood. His body is covered in gashes and stab wounds. He's still fighting back, but it's obvious he's losing strength. Rich dispatches a Lurker and moves to help Evan; when another leaps over the counter at Rich, he shifts to his right and evades its claws. His dagger lands firmly in its neck, severing the brain stem. As its body collapses, Sonya leaps through the air over the top of Rich, slaughtering the Lurkers that have Evan pinned down.

Her arms and blade are moving with such speed that Lurker blood is being sprayed up the wall and ceiling. The corpses begin to stack up on top of Evan, covering his body enough to shield him from further attack. As he lays on the cold floor, a quiet slowly washes over him. His massive frame relaxes, and he finds a morbid comfort from the blanket of Lurker blood oozing over his body. He can hear his friends clashing with the scores of enemies around them, but as he listens, it sounds like they are getting further and further away.

Sonya is fighting with a ferocity Rich never knew she was capable of. Lurkers are being flayed open and severed in half with such speed that the ones in the back are now having difficulty climbing over their fallen comrades. She glides to the top of the pile and continues her assault, the bodies of the dead fall back onto those trying to overcome the growing mass of carnage.

Thanks to Sonya's rampage, Rich sees his chance to begin looking for a way to get Evan out of danger. Two Lurkers come at him from the other end of the counter. He throws a dagger at the closest one, skewering it through the sternum. The second jumps left, then right, landing on the wall, and leaps at him. Rich throws a haymaker with his empty right hand and catches it midair in the forehead. It crashes hard to the ground, bouncing off the floor. He slips the dagger in his left hand directly in its heart, black blood spurting out around the blade as it parishes.

He looks up to see another wave of Lurkers climbing into the building from every conceivable entrance. His eyes dart around the room, trying to find something that can help Evan. The dull shimmer of old steel can be seen from the deep shadows behind them, the vault door is at the other end of the counter away from Evan and Sonya. If he can get in there, Evan could be set at the far wall, giving Rich and Sonya plenty of room to fight. His mind races as he tries to figure out a way to open it. He looks to the window. As more Lurkers pile through, they are barely visible against the dying light.

"FINALLY!" he shouts.

He throws his right hand toward the door, a spike of black smoke enters around the frame. With a loud clank and a groan, the locks are forced to retract, and the door swings open. His left hand reaches out to Evan, more smoke pouring from his palm and wrapping around the body of his friend. He pulls Evan's limp body from the pile of dead Lurkers, then slides it deep into the darkness of the vault. Sonya is on the counter at this point. She has been fighting them for so long without faltering. Rich knows she will begin to tire soon, which will leave her vulnerable.

As Rich rushes to the vault entrance, he turns to Sonya and shouts, "HEY, GET IN HERE NOW!"

Sonya leaps back and turns to his voice. As she does, Rich backs away into the inky blackness, disappearing from view entirely.

Sonya darts into the shadows, feeling her way to Evan's body. The fading sunlight gives her barely enough illumination to see what's coming through the door.

"Stay with Evan. Catch your breath," Rich says, his voice emanating from all around her.

There are several dozen Lurkers standing just outside, crowded around one another, hesitant to enter where they cannot see. She readies her weapon as they begin to creep into the doorway.

As the first Lurker enters the darkness, it freezes in place for a moment, then falls back into the space behind the counter. The front of its face sliced clean off, half its tongue still twitching between its remaining bits of jaw. The two Lurkers right behind it leap into the black to confront whatever attacked the first one. In a split second after entering the room, they both explode into a fine mist.

Sonya hears the same shriek they heard earlier when the one-eyed Lurker woke the horde. All those remaining in the building slowly leave, climbing back out through whatever opening was nearby. Soon the bank was empty, the air still and quiet. Sonya stands over Evan's body, weapon readied and waiting. She strains her ears, trying to pick up what's happening outside the brick walls.

The sun has fully set, leaving the sky black—no stars, no moon, just infinite night. The gray ash covering everything lends some contrast to the environment, like a dull glow from snow on a clouded winter night. They are now completely alone in the building. She hears only her own heart pounding in her ears. No movement from outside the safe. No noise at all. She slowly moves to the doorway and pokes her head out. Even in the absence of light, she can still sense her immediate surroundings.

Rich appears from nothingness next to Sonya. "What do you think they are doing?" Rich says.

Sonya jumps from the shock of him, popping up next to her. "Don't *do* that, DICK!" She smacks him in the stomach with the back of her hand. "I don't know what they are doing. They all just left. It's dark AF right now. I can't really see anything."

"Did you just *say* 'AF'? Are you twelve? Why not just say 'dark as fuck'? I mean, they are both one syllable. Doesn't take any longer to say the words," Rich says as he stares at her in bewildered awe.

"*Why is that the issue right now?*" Sonya asks in a violent whisper.

"Sorry, just caught me off guard. I can totally see outside from here. Give me a sec." As Rich finishes his sentence, his eyes turn solid black. After a few seconds, they return to normal, and he looks at Sonya.

"There's around two hundred and sixty-seven of them out there. They are all around the building, standing still and looking toward the lakebed they came out of," Rich says.

"*Around* two hundred and sixty-seven?" Sonya says as she rolls her eyes.

"Yeah. Give or take a few. Didn't want to waste too much time counting them all. I'm just glad we got a chance to catch our breath," Rich says with a sigh.

"What do you think they are waiting for?" Sonya asks him.

"I don't know, but I recall Vitra saying something about not wanting to be caught out here at night. So I'm a tad on the worried side." Rich begins pacing behind the counter, contemplating his next move.

"How's Evan doing? Is he still with us?" Rich asks.

"I, uh, I haven't checked. I was waiting for more of those effin' things to come at me," Sonya replies.

Rich sends a tendril of the night to check Evan. He can feel a pulse, but it's very faint and slow.

"He needs to get back to the cave right now. He doesn't have much time left," Rich says with a solemn tone.

"Whoa, did you feel that? The air just changed. It got…stale, almost rotten, like I'm standing in a crypt." Sonya's neck hair stands up straight. Her skin is breaking out with goose bumps.

Rich sniffs the air and waves his hand around in the space in front of him. "Weird. I don't feel anything different," he replies.

From the distance, a chilling howl is heard, deep and angry. All the Lurkers outside the bank begin excitedly chittering in unison.

"Oh, shitballs. This is not going to be fun." Rich vanishes again, leaving Sonya standing alone just outside the vault.

"Would you stop doing that? What are we going to do, Rich?" She looks around the room, trying to see where he went.

Faintly, off in the distance, a rhythmic thud can be heard drawing nearer and nearer. At first, Sonya doesn't know what to make of it, but as it approaches, it dawns on her that it's the lumbering footsteps of something huge coming directly at her.

She faces the wall with the broken windows, her sword held in front of her, ready to engage whatever may come through. As the stomping gets close, she can feel her body readying itself for battle. A fresh wave of adrenaline rushes through her veins, flooding her with reinvigoration.

With a fierce blast, the windowed bank wall is smashed open, taking a section of roof with it. Dust fills the darkened bank, burning Sonya's eyes from the soot. An ear-piercing roar shatters the night, reverberating off the walls and sending blinding pain into Sonya's head. The dust settles to the ground, allowing Sonya to see the nightmarish golem towering over her.

CHAPTER 16

The entity before Sonya would be forced to stoop inside the building were it not for the destroyed roof. Its gargantuan figure filled the entire section of the destroyed wall. If it were possible to pile meat two stories high, then breathe life into it, this would be the outcome. This pile of flesh has standard biological features—legs, arms, and a torso—but that's where the common traits ended. It had no uniform shape to it, just an amorphous blob. Its skin multicolored, almost striped but in irregular patterns. Its legs were the size of a large human. However, when compared to the rest of its being, they were comically short. It stood mostly upright with arms that stretched its entire height. The knuckles easily dragged the ground as it stood in the opening it had made, swaying gently back and forth as it processed its new surroundings.

In between the area where its arms connected to its core sat a small mound, just slightly raised up from the rest of its upper half. Once the dust had settled entirely, dozens of little black eyes of all sizes began opening up, blinking frantically as they try to clear the debris from their orbits. The upper half of the meat brick began twitching left and right, as if it was receiving different commands from multiple directions. A solitary Lurker had been left behind in the bank, pinned under some of the rubble from the wall. It crawls its way toward the hole in the wall, trying to creep behind the monster filling the void.

With a speed beyond what should have been naturally possible for a creature this size, its left arm shoots out and grabs the Lurker. The Lurker begins squealing and shrieking as the arm brings it closer to the eyes on top. The beast studies its prey for a moment, then leans back. A slit appears just under the cluster of eyes. It grows larger, and larger, stretching and elongating until the whole front of the being is nothing but a gaping maw filled with jagged chunks of bone that it uses for mastication.

Its meaty hand releases the Lurker, dropping it into its open mouth. The wailing Lurker falls, landing on the waiting shards of bone. The maw of the beast slams shut, muffling the screams of the doomed Lurker as it's ripped apart. The body of this new horror gyrates and ungulates, dissecting its latest victim. As the shrieking stops, the body also grows still, then begins to vibrate intensely, its whole body quivering, similar to a massive gelatin mold made from flesh.

With a sickening pop of breaking skin, a new set of eyes appears on the mound atop the wretched beast—two large black eyes.

"I think I'm gonna barf…," Sonya whispers to herself.

Rich steps out of the shadowy bank vault and walks over to Sonya's side. "This is probably the reason we were supposed to be back by dark, yeah?" Rich says as he pulls his hand back, gathering dark energy in his palm. With a quick swing, he sends a massive spike of the night through the middle of the creature. The spike dissipates, leaving the creature with a massive hole in its chest at least two feet wide.

It raises one hand to the hole in its front side, probing itself with a couple of fingers, then slipping its entire fist into the cavity. With a sickening wet *slorrrp* sound, its fist pops back out. The hole slowly shrinks, returning to its normal state in mere seconds. The beast tries to stuff another finger where the hole used to be, but it was gone. "Clearly, it ain't very smart, eh, Sonya?" Rich whispers, gently poking Sonya with his elbow.

She did not respond. Her eyes fixed squarely on the threat before them. It stopped playing with itself and is now seemingly focused directly on her. "Rich, we gotta get the heck out of here," says Sonya, grabbing his arm and squeezing it tightly.

As if spurred by her words, the beast charges. Its meaty long arms swing wildly as it crosses the gap between them. Sonya dashes to her left, and Rich vanishes into the night as the beast smashes through the wall behind them and into the neighboring shop.

"Rich! We got to lure it away from Evan!" Sonya shouts. She shoots out of the bank with a gust of wind while Rich uses the dark to peer outside. He sees the remaining Lurkers watching from a safe distance as the creature rages inside the building.

The monster thrashes about violently, leveling the small shop attached to the bank. Its long arms destroy anything in the way. It charges into the street with its massive fists still flailing in a blind rage. It slows as the realization sets in that there is nothing being smashed with its swings. The eyes flutter once again, searching for a new target.

With a burst of wind, Sonya is standing before it, sword in hand and hanging at her side. Her eyes are burning with righteous fury as she slowly grasps the sword with both hands and brings the blade up to shoulder level. The point of the sword pushed forward and ready. She unleashes a growl that surges into a guttural scream. With a torrential gust of wind, she throws herself at the fiend. She dashes around its feet, slashing and stabbing as she runs. She delivers a devastating final blow, cleaving the left leg of her target almost in two. The creature loses its balance and falls to the ground with a thunderous crash. It tries to stand again but falls back to the ground.

Sonya moves in on her prey, readying herself to deliver a killing blow. As she nears it, she senses a peculiar sound, like a grating of stone on wet wood. Her eyes find the source of the noise. The monster's leg has reattached itself entirely. She is surprised by the lack of blood. With such a massive wound, she would only assume it would be bleeding. Her focus snaps back to the top end of the beast in time to catch a huge fist in the chest.

Her body skips across the ground and slams face-first into the old bank. Her forehead splits open from the impact, revealing the skull. Blood pours from the wound. Her eyes quiver in their sockets as she drifts into unconsciousness.

In her moment of vulnerability, a handful of Lurkers close in on her, their nasal slits huffing and snorting as they cautiously examine their next meal. They begin picking and nibbling at her unconscious body, savoring the flavor of their meal. As they do, dark crimson smoke curls around their feet and slowly encircles them.

Dozens of black pikes covered in sharp hooks shoot out of the ground, shredding the Lurkers into pieces with chunks of their flesh hanging from the hardened night like macabre tree decorations. The pikes retract, leaving a salad of meat on the ground around the comatose Sonya.

The night around Sonya grows denser, examining her with concentrated tendrils of night. Every little cut and scrape it comes across is filled with a solidified darkness, sealing the wound. Focusing on her forehead, tiny little hooks of darkness grab either side of her wound and draw it closed. The hooks penetrate through her skin and connect together, forming little hoops of the night to keep the skin drawn tight.

Rich emerges from the bank to see Sonya's body lying on the ground, the darkness around her watching as he walks out of the building. Rich kneels to check her pulse. She is alive, just knocked out. He turns her head and looks at the closed gash on her brow, noticing the makeshift sutures.

"Did you do this?" Rich asks the night surrounding her.

A single curl of smoke points itself in his direction and shakes its tip up and down.

"Guess that's a yes. Thank you. I have to deal with these guys now. Can you keep her safe?" Rich asks the little tendril.

It nods once more, then the tendril retracts back into the mass around Sonya.

Rich stands and examines the situation outside of the bank. He sees the large creature slowly getting back on its feet. Around him are Lurkers too numerous to count. The big monster is standing once more. It spins around and looks at him, slamming its fists into the ground with rage. It opens its mouth wide in a shrill, wet squeal. Bits of flesh and gobs of liquid left over from the Lurker come flying out of its mouth. It pounds the ground again and begins running at Rich and Sonya.

A flash of hate overcomes Rich as a massive pillar of night shoots out of the ground in front of the beast, catching it directly in center mass. It flies back and lands in the ruins of a building across the street, crushing several Lurkers in the process. Rich throws his hands up above his head and razor-sharp blades of the night shoot up through the monster. It screams with pain as they rip through it. The mad beast thrashes on the ground trying to escape its confinements. It swings an arm and shatters a blade into shrapnel. The shards pepper a group of Lurkers that were standing nearby, slicing and stabbing into them, killing a handful instantly and causing the rest to writhe on the ground as they bleed out.

The beast continues to shatter the blades pinning them down, grabbing them and snapping them off then throwing them away or smashing them to pieces. It rolls off the remaining shards and stands up, its wounds already closing. It charges at Rich again. He tries throwing another pillar at it in desperation. The beast anticipates his move and smashes it out of the air, crushing it to bits with its might. Rich hesitates, surprised by his adversary's reaction.

The beast is on him in an instant. It leaps into the air, fists clenched above it and ready to strike. They swing down at Rich as the monster falls back to earth. Rich's senses come back in time for him to drop into darkness. The fists of the beast crash down where he stood, just yards away from Sonya's still motionless body. The beast lifts its hands and looks under them, expecting to see its intended victim crushed on the ground. When it sees nothing is there, it slams a fist into the dirt again and screams.

Rich apparates across the street, holding a long spear of night in each hand. He throws them at the monster to draw its attention away from his friends. It spins around and rushes him, using its arms to propel it along as it closes the distance between them. Rich vanishes again, reappearing on the roof of a nearby structure. He begins hurling spears of night at it, one after another. One finds its home in the mound on top of the creature, piercing an eye. With a scornful howl, it desperately tries to rip the spear from itself.

Rich sees he has found a weakness and begins to exploit it. He targets the beast's mass of eyes with every throw. He manages to land a couple of blows to its optical hub. With an unsettling display of intelligence, the monster covers its weak link with one hand and charges at the building Rich is standing upon. It slams into the edifice with full force. The roof Rich stands upon shakes and shimmies, then collapses under his feet. As the section he stands on gives way, it drops him into the void inside the building.

Rich doesn't have time to react. He falls into the old building and lands hard on a pile of rubble and shelving. A large chunk of wood has pierced his flank, hot blood spilling out and quickly cooling in the night air. Without pause, the beast throws itself through the wall of the shop and begins blindly, slamming its fist down indiscriminately while the other hand still covers its eyes. Rich tries to regain his footing, but his wound is enough to cause his legs to buckle under him as he tries to stand. The beast's wild pummeling grows dangerously close to Rich's place on the floor. He collects himself enough to disappear into darkness.

He apparates by the bank, his body weak from the wound he sustained in the fall. He can hear the creature continuing to destroy the inside of the shop. Desperation coils around his chest, and he can feel the pangs of fear growing in his stomach as he struggles to conceive an idea to get himself and his two wounded friends out of harm's way. From the corner of his eye, he sees a group of Lurkers is approaching Sonya, their hunger overruling their fear.

The protective shadow does its job. As they near it, several spikes shoot out, penetrating the skull of all the Lurkers. They fall in place, lifeless. Rich feels something moving behind him and turns to see three Lurkers creeping up. He throws daggers of night at two of them, the third leaps over its friends and lands on top of Rich, sinking its rancid teeth into his shoulder. He grabs a dagger from his waist and stabs it through the ear. Its body goes stiff, arching its back sharply. It gurgles, choking on its own blood as it pours out of its mouth. Soaking Rich's chest and face.

Rich throws the Lurker off him and scans for any others nearby. He then turns his attention back to the main threat that has now emerged from the destroyed shop. It has taken its hand away from its eye pile and is looking for Rich. It locks on him from across the street and charges him again. Rich throws forward a closed fist then spreads his fingers wide. As the beast runs at him, the ground under its right leg disappears. The monster falls into the void Rich had created. He closes his hand, and the hole shrinks around its leg, trapping it in place. With his other hand, he manifests a massive hammer of darkness just above the beast.

With a mighty crack, he strikes it directly on top of its torso. Its arms go limp for a moment, then reach up to cover itself from attack. Rich begins swinging the hammer like mad, striking it anywhere he can. He is giving everything he has to this assault because he knows it may be their last chance. Fatigue from the blood loss catches up to him. His hammer hangs over the monster for just a second, enough time for it to reach out and grab it. Rich tries again to swing, but he can't overpower the beast. It now has both hands on its weapon, easily overwhelming his control. His focus shifted to the power struggle; he neglects to maintain a grip on the creature's leg.

The beast, loose once more, throws the hammer to the side and rushes at Rich. He begins casting huge spheres of darkness at it. They bounce off the beast, slowing it down, but not stopping it. It lifts one massive arm over its head and brings it down on Rich. He throws his hands up, forming a wall of night to shield him from the blow. The impact hits with such a terrible force that the shock wave knocks the air from Rich's lungs. He struggles to hold the wall in place. It is the only thing keeping him, and his friends, alive. To his left and right, he sees Lurkers slowly encroaching on him. He looks back to check on Sonya. His shadowy friend is doing its job still, but he doesn't know how long it will stick around if he dies. Rich notices a handful of Lurkers making their way into the bank, going after Evan.

He is pinned down by the constant barrage of attacks from the monster that's on top of him, and he can feel his body succumbing to fatigue. Fear grips him again, settling over him like a wet rug, making his movements feel sluggish and weighted. His blood runs cold with the realization that this is where he will end.

As he falters, a soft tremor grows under him. Not obvious at first, it was drowned out by the pounding of fists against his shield. It grows more intense with each second. The Lurkers begin to look around in concern, save for a hand full of them that are approaching him from all around, eager to help in his demise. He can feel the vibration in his back, like something is burrowing up from under him.

As he looks on, a gust of wind stronger than anything he's ever felt severs the heads of the encroaching Lurkers clean from their bodies. The monster on top of him howls with pain and clutches at its eyes again. Ral stands next to him, hand extended.

"WE MUST MOVE NOW!" Ral shouts.

Rich grabs his hand as the rumble coming from below intensifies to an earthquake. With an explosion of liquid rock, Gaian erupts forth from the middle of the street, his body coated in a full suit of armor fashioned from the magma that now surrounds him.

"Ral, take him and the others to safety," Gaian booms, a note of exhilaration can be heard in his voice. "I will hold this abomination at bay."

CHAPTER 17

Gaian stands tall among the evil before them. Lurkers attack from all directions, but their attempts are futile. Gaian's red-hot armor is more than enough to deter them. They slash and stab at him only to pull back burning stumps and scalded flesh. He doesn't even bother to defend against them as he strides toward the giant beast that had devastated the trio of friends.

The raging fiend calms as the pain from Ral's surprise attack subsides. It spins around to face its attacker, finding only Gaian staring up at it. The beast rushes at its new target, throwing its right arm behind it then slinging it through the air in a massive sidearm sweep. Gaian does not move to avoid it. He shows no signs of concern for the impending attack at all.

As the arm nears, Gaian brings his left arm up, tucking his hand behind his head and shielding his face with his elbow. The monster's arm makes contact with Gaian but stops dead in its path of travel. The old pavement around Gaian's feet warps and shifts from the force of the impact being diverted into the ground. With a vicious fury, Gaian throws a single punch at the arm of the creature. In an explosion of fire and molten rock, the beast's limb is blown off midforearm. It screams in pain and howls with rage as its flesh smolders at the end of its now stubby appendage. Gaian quickly follows his first attack with another. He swings his left leg around behind him, catching the warped pavement with his heel, using the inertia to increase his power. His core turns counterclockwise loading up his hips for a kick. His right leg draws up close to his body. He throws it out sideways as his hips snap to catch up to his torso. His right foot makes contact in the midsection of his foe and blasts a hole straight through it. The beast falls to the ground, thrashing. Gaian moves to the side of the creature. He extends a hand out and fills with magma that pours up from the ground. In but a moment, Gaian is holding a mammoth axe made of solidified lava. With a single swing, he severs a leg off the monster. In a final attempt to defend itself, the monster raises its remaining hand up, slamming a meaty fist down on Gaian who causally catches it with his free hand and hacks it off with his axe. Its convulsions continue as Gaian hacks it to pieces, chopping it apart bit by bit as writhes and howls on the ground.

Soon there is nothing left but smoldering chunks scattered across the ground. Gaian throws his axe down, crushing it under heel, and walks away from the beast in search of Ral and their disciples. As his axe cools, it crumbles into rubble, but all around it, the bits and pieces of the fallen monstrosity are slowly coming back together, reshaping themselves into something else, something new. A long lean torso begins to form on the ground. A set of strong legs emerge from its rear, followed by a front pair. The body rolls and flops on the ground as it pieces itself together. The last bit of it assembles itself into a neck and head sporting a long snout full of jagged bone teeth. The mound of eyes takes its place where the head and neck meet. Its new body resembles a dog if it had been skinned alive then boiled in engine oil.

Gaian can hear the shuffling of flesh on the ground behind him. He turns to see the hunks of meat have reassembled themselves into a new form. He groans with discontent and walks toward the renewed creature. He pulls back a fist and takes a swing, but the beast leaps out of the way, dodging his attack. Gaian falls back into a warrior stance, his hands up and ready to strike. Feet staggered and poised for movement. The beast's new form is significantly quicker than its last. It leaps around Gaian, attempting to circle behind him. Gaian holds his ground, anticipating its next move. With one quick lunge, it reaches for his back. Gaian snaps his upper body to his left, delivering a spinning back fist to the side of the creature's head, violently detaching its lower mandible.

As the monster recoils from the shock of Gaian's blow, it leaves an opening. Gaian grabs it by the neck, his right arm reaching over its left side while his left arm goes under. He slams his foot into the foreleg of the beast, forcing it down to the pavement. Gaian arches his back and drives his hips forward with every ounce of might he can muster. The beast's head is removed from its shoulders with a sharp snap and a burning hiss from his armor, its body drops to the ground and begins flailing about. The head, being without a lower jaw, is now totally useless. Gaian calmly walks a few steps from its body and sets it on the ground. The eyes of the beast are darting and blinking frantically, searching for some possible redemption. Gaian raises a heavy fist in the air and slams it into the earth. All around him, the pavement begins to melt as boiling magma bubbles up to the surface. Gaian looks at his fallen foe, and with a gentle nudge of his foot, he sends the head into the liquid rock. It cracks and hisses as it burns in the lava, its flesh blistering then turning black. In just a few brief seconds, the entire head of the beast was rendered into ash, no trace of it left save for the bits floating in the air.

Gaian looks back at the body to see it lifeless on the ground, but just for good measure, he grabs it by a leg and drags it to the lava pool. He crams its body halfway in the magma and walks off as it is consumed, meeting the same fate as the head. The watching Lurkers are silent. Hundreds of black eyes glare at the giant as their champion's corpse burns to ash. Gaian reaches down into the lava near his feet and grabs two fistfuls of liquid rock, quickly cooling it into obsidian. He pulls back and draws from the pit two long strands of braided slag that end in razor-sharp hooks made from lava glass. Gaian flicks and snaps his whips, making them crack and spark as they scorch the night, leaving a strong smell of hot ozone hanging in the stagnate air.

Ral gusts up next to Gaian. "I have secured our progeny. They will be safe for now. Remind me to ask Rich how he made the night defend Sonya in such a way. I am quite intrigued. It was defensive at first but relaxed when I spoke to it and allowed me to take Sonya away," Ral says as he draws his sword.

"Good. Let's clear out the remaining filth and take them back to the cave," Gaian says as weighs the encroaching Lurkers.

Ral whirls his sword around his body and tosses it in the air. He extends his hand and catches it, pointing its tip at the surrounding

Lurkers. He and Gaian stand at the ready, weapons in hand as they wait for them to attack.

The remaining horde charges at the two men. Ral begins laughing as they rush in, the joy of violence lighting up his eyes. With a burst of wind, he dives into them, cleaving them in half and cutting them down with the ease of a scythe through wheat, each swing hacking through multiple Lurkers. Ral gracefully dances through the crowd, twisting and dodging slashes and lunges as he skewers and slices them apart. His blade emits a ghostly shine in the darkness, the black blood coating it dampening its glow. Ral smiles broadly as his enemies fall like leaves in an autumn storm.

Gaian walks calmly toward the stampeding Lurkers. His whips sizzle as he flicks and snaps them against the pavement. The first wave to come in range is met with a torrent of strikes. Their flesh cleaved to the bone, their limbs ripped from their body, every strike landed more lethal than the last. Gaian begins to slam his feet into the ground, forcing the earth to quake and causing nearby Lurkers to lose their footing. He swings his whips up and starts to spin them overhead, the rushing air making them blaze white hot. The downed Lurkers get back to their feet in time to be split in half by the searing hot lashes of his whips. He cuts through the horde, smiling as they topple over and writhe in pain from the searing strikes.

Gaian has slain scores of Lurkers. Smoldering bodies litter the ground around him so dense that he can hardly take a step without crushing their remains underfoot. Gaian drops his whips. As they hit the ground, the obsidian handles shatter into shards, and the lava braids cool and solidify into a stone cord. A lone Lurker crawls out from beneath one of its dead comrades. Gaian sees it attempting an escape and catches it by the back of its neck. He lifts it off the ground and looks it in its eyes. He studies its body for a moment as it struggles to not scald itself on his armor. Gaian slams his free hand palm down on top of its head, splattering its cranium and the contents within all over himself. The Lurker matter sizzles and cooks as the magma armor burns it away. Gaian throws the body away from him, disgust evident on his face as he searches for more stragglers.

Across the battlefield, he sees Ral gently thrusting his blade into the hearts of Lurkers who were still lively.

"Is that all of them?" Gaian asks Ral.

"I do believe so. Awful little beings, aren't they? So foul and vile. Easy to kill, though. It's a shame. I was hoping for more of a challenge from our last fight," Ral replies as he flicks his sword down, trying to clean it of blood.

"Even the large one was less than satisfactory. I feel I have been denied true glory." The giant sulks over to Ral, his armor cooling into glass and falling from his body. "We must check on the three."

Ral leads him to where he had hidden the trio, perched safely on a rooftop just down the road from the battle. With a stiff breeze, Ral is on top of the building. Gaian looks up after him and takes a step. As his foot comes to a stop, the ground rushes up to meet him, each footfall met by another earthen step as he climbs his way up. Once Gaian reaches the roof, he sees the three wounded friends lying side by side and quickly assess them. Evan is completely motionless, his body cold and limp. He is covered in deep wounds, his clothes soaked in blood. Sonya's breathing is shallow but constant. There is a large gash on her forehead, extensive bruising on her ribs. She may have further internal injuries that will need to be addressed. Rich is conscious, leaning against the low wall of the roof. He is covered in his own blood and clearly weak from his injuries. Gaian approaches him.

"I do believe you were explicitly told to not be out after dark," Gaian says with a sneer.

"No need to scold me. It wasn't exactly intentional," Rich says, his words interrupted by a series of ragged coughs. A bit of blood dribbles down his lip onto his chin. "We were about to turn back when those fuckin' Lurkers swarmed us. Then the big'gun showed up and really ruined our fun."

"Lurkers? Is that what you call them? Seems appropriate," Ral mutters with a shrug as he attends to Evan.

"You are all in very bad shape. We must get you back immediately. Ral, please take Sonya. I will carry Evan and Rich." Gaian hefts Evan's limp frame onto one shoulder. He offers a hand down to Rich.

Rich reaches out, the giant grabs him by his arm and slings him over the other.

Ral has Sonya draped over his shoulders already. He holds on to her limbs with one arm and gathers her sword and Evan's axe with the other.

"I am ready when you are, old friend." Ral nods at Gaian.

Gaian grunts in response then steps to the edge of the roof. With a small hop, he falls to the ground, his massive legs catching him and his two passengers with ease. Without hesitation, he starts running back in the direction of the cave, Ral easily keeping pace right behind him. They run flat out, focusing all their effort on crossing as much ground as possible. They have lost too much precious time already.

From the nearby hilltops, something is watching, waiting for the right time to make its move.

Gaian and Ral near the cave, their lungs burn from the cold night air. Their limbs are sore and begging for relief, but they have not slowed. They speed for the entrance, Ral backing off to allow Gaian to enter first. They turn the corner into the entryway and see Vitra standing on the other side. Gaian bursts through the barrier and flies past Vitra.

"Gaian! Take them to the main chamber!" she shouts after him.

Ral is next through the barrier. Vitra barks the same command at him.

Once they were both inside, she released her hold maintaining the opening and disappears into darkness.

Gaian bursts through the door into the main hall. Vitra is already standing at her medicine cabinet preparing various tinctures and balms. Gaian lays Evan on the table. His body totally listless and seemingly devoid of life.

"Gaian, is Rich still conscious?" Vitra asks.

"I am unsure," Gaian booms.

"I'm hangin' in there," Rich replies.

"Good. Once I heal you I'm going to beat you to death. I told you *not* to be out past nightfall! Do you think me a fool? Are my words spoken for my own pleasure? Gaian, throw him in that chair."

Vitra shouts at him as Gaian sets him down. She aggressively stuffs his wounds full of healing compounds.

"Okay! I get it. I stayed out too late, and now I'm in trouble. For fuck sake, it's not like I *intended* to get gang-raped by like three hundred of those Lurkers," Rich snaps at her.

Ral shows up with Sonya. Vitra motions for him to set her down next to Rich.

"Lurkers? What manner of fiend is that? If there were so many, they must have been small. How can you let such things harm you all so badly? Have you learned nothing?" Vitra is visibly shaking.

Vitra force-feeds Rich another one of her mysterious concoctions then moves on to Sonya. She starts by closing up her smaller wounds, rubbing slaves and balms into them. She examines the large wound in her head and pauses.

"Rich, did you put these sutures in her? These are solidified night," Vitra asks, her glare intensifying.

"Uhhh, not exactly," Rich stammers.

"*Would you care to enlighten me?*" Vitra's tone sharpens significantly, causing the candles to flicker and die down.

"I, uh, was fighting this big pile of meat, ya see. Sonya was banged up and not really operational anymore. Then that same little bit of shadow that kept catching my water glass showed up, and I asked it to take care of her. So it did. I assume it also was responsible for sewing her head wound shut." Rich is looking up at the ceiling as he recalls the events to her.

Vitra is quiet. She is processing the information just given. The concept of a sentient element is not foreign to her, but it's nothing she had ever experienced firsthand.

Rich sits up straight with a shocking realization.

"Hey! Why aren't you working on Evan? He hasn't moved in fucking hours!" Rich's voice is filled with worry.

Vitra pauses for a moment, then turns and looks Rich dead in the eye.

"Well, I'm not in any rush to heal him because he's already dead." Vitra's words are emotionless and cold as the night air they just escaped from.

A chill sweeps over Rich as he looks toward the body. He stares, hoping to see some sign of life, looking for the rise and fall of a breath, but there's nothing. The familiar pang of fear rises deep in his chest again. His breath grows more shallow and rapid as the realization sets in.

"Rich, be calm. He is with Enki now. You have no reason to worry," booms Gaian.

"Vitra, isn't there anything that we can do? What about that shit you gave me when I bled out?" Rich's eyes widen with fear as his desperation grows.

"Rich, calm down. He is *with* Enki. I have plenty of time to fix his wounds. I needed to attend to you and Sonya first because you are still among the living. All we can do now is wait." Vitra's words strike into the hearts of everyone in the room.

Rich sits silently in his chair. Staring at the corpse of his fallen friend, streams of hot tears cascade from his eyes. He lies back in his chair, covering his face with his hands in an attempt to stifle his weeping.

CHAPTER 18

Evan's eyes slowly open as he wakes from his trauma-induced slumber. His vision blurry, he tries to blink away the haze, but it doesn't help. He looks around the room as he tries to deduce where he is. He catches sight of a familiar single torch glowing on the wall next to a hallway. His hand drags the ground as pushes himself up from the floor. He inhales deeply, letting it out in a slow exhale to calm his nerves as the realization sets in. He's back in the chamber they first arrived in when they were sent to talk with Enki.

"Ohhh, man… I feel like I got hit with a truck." Evan rubs his face, trying to brush away the fatigue. Through the blinking, he catches sight of something odd. As he opens his eyes, before him are two skinny pale arms.

"Whoa, what happened? I'm stick-Evan again. I had just gotten used to being the extraordinary bulk," Evan says to himself with a chuckle. He had finally started feeling comfortable with his prior self, so much so that being thin again seems more strange than it did to be big in the first place. He pats himself down as he quickly inspects himself.

Come sit with me, Evan.

Enki's voice gently resonates inside Evan's head. He looks down the hallway toward Enki's chamber. Aside from the single torch near the entrance, there was no light around him. Evan hesitates at the edge of the darkness, curiously eyeing the torch. He grabs the handle and gives it a tug, but it is fixed firmly in place. He sets off down the hall, the light of the single torch soon fades behind him. The hall is so dark it forces Evan to reach out in front of him as he cautiously stumbles through the black. He bumps into something unyielding and leans into it as he continues down the hall. He sticks his left hand out in front of him, waving it around like a blind man's cane.

"Where is that damn door," whispers Evan.

Evan stumbles along in the dark for what felt like an eternity. Finally, his left hand slams into a solid object. He fumbles around the door, searching for a handle. His fingers latch on to something protruding from the door. With a soft grunt, he yanks it open and cautiously peers inside. There sits Enki, cross-legged in the same position Evan remembers him—only his shape appears diminished and slightly transparent.

Please sit.

Evan creeps over to him and sits down. He waits in silence, waiting for Enki to speak to him again. Soon, the silence becomes uncomfortable. Evan tries to get Enki's attention by waving a hand near his face.

I am still here. I'm just very busy maintaining concentration.

"Concentrating on what?" Evan asks, his curiosity overtaking him.

I am getting ready to send you back to your body. It's going to require a great deal of energy, but I have reached a point where I can stop for now. I'm sure you're wondering why you're here, yes?

"Well, yeah. I mean, last I remember, I was getting dragged into this bank vault, and then I wake up here. What happened in between is just blank. I must have been knocked out pretty good." Evan is trying to gauge Enki's reaction, but he is completely devoid of expression.

You are here because you died, Evan. You bled to death in that bank vault. I was able to intercept your life force on its way to Erra.

If Evan's ethereal form had a functioning heart, it would have skipped a beat. He shakes his head, trying to gather his words, wanting to ask a thousand questions, but he can't get a single one out. He wants to cry, but he only feels it building up inside him, the pressure begins to boil over into a seething rage. Evan's hands clench into fists. He slams them into the ground in front of him, letting out a deep groan.

"What if I can't do this? What if I'm not cut out for this shit? Huh? What if I'm on my own and don't have anyone to hold my fuckin' hand while I continuously screw shit up left and right? I can't do this, man. This just isn't me. I'm not some superhero like Gaian wants me to be. I'm no one, never have been. Never will be. All I know how to do is let people down, Rich and Sonya, my long-dead parents, but hey, at least they didn't live to see me fuck up saving the goddamn planet." Evan's frustration is palpable at this point. His hands flatten out on the ground as he vents his feelings to Enki.

Evan, there is nothing I can say to you that will make you into the person you need to be. It is a decision that only you can make. I am aware of the conversations you have had with Gaian. I know that he pushes you very hard, but that is because he believes in you. Not just because you are part of our last hope, but because he sees within you the potential for greatness. You lack confidence, and nothing can be done to give it to you. You must find it on your own. You have the abilities, you have the strength, you need but open the door and let it out.

Enki is silent again. His form is frozen in place as though he was a paused recording. Evan ponders his words for a moment, allowing them to digest. As Enki's form reanimates, his hand extends to Evan.

Take my hand. I have something to show you.

Evan glares at Enki's outstretched arm hesitantly, unsure of how to feel about this offer, his soul already a whirlpool of mixed emotions. He reaches for Enki's hand but hesitates, apprehensive of what may happen next. Enki, not having the time to waste, snatches Evan's wrist, locking eyes with him.

Evan's body accelerates sharply, hurtling through an existential void until it comes to a halt just as violent as its beginning. Evan is now standing in total darkness so thick he can't even make out his hands in front of his face. The eerie groan of a heavy door turning on its hinges fills the room, and Evan snaps around to face it. A slim beam of light breaks up the black. It grows wider, gradually revealing a figure silhouetted by the daylight pouring in.

Evan's eyes adjust to the flood of light. Before him is a small hunched figure partially leaning on an old walking stick. He's an elderly man with a long wispy beard and hair up top to match and a face that resembled old cracked leather. Despite his haggard appearance, he wore a kind smile full of a strangely comforting joy. Evan feels a small amount of relief in his chest, as though he can breathe a little easier now. The old man pats his leg as he takes a breath to speak.

"Come 'ere, boy. Come on. Let's go for a walkabout, eh?" the weathered man says as he looks right through Evan to the back of the room.

Evan turns to see what he was calling to, expecting some kind of dog to come rushing out of the shadows. He catches glimpse of matted pale red hair, with skin so white it bordered on translucent. Long spindly arms and legs propelled the hunched entity across the floor in a mad flurry. It quickly ran into the legs of the old man and began nuzzling his upper thigh.

"There, there, my pet. I know I was gone for too long. Daddy had much work to do, but now I'm back to spend some quality time with you!" The old man reaches down and pets his little friend behind the ear.

As he watches with a curiosity most morbid, Evan notices that the pale red hair hangs long and shaggy around a very human ear. He is frozen in place as he studies this being that emerged from the shadows. It's a man, an emaciated one. Long arms and legs ending in hands and feet, so heavily calloused that they are cracked and stained from dried blood. They are attached to a torso that is little more than just ghost-white skin pulled taut over bones that had been broken then improperly set. It was totally nude save for a simple loincloth hanging from its waist.

"Go get your collar and we will go for a walk!" the old man says excitedly as he points back into the darkness from where his pet came.

As the disturbingly human figure turns back to honor its master's command, Evan gets a clear look at its face. The shock of what he sees hits him in the chest like a cannonball. He is staring at *himself*. His own image rushes at him. Evan's body freezes as he struggles to comprehend what he's seeing. He falls backward to the ground as this other Evan rushes past himself. The visage passes cleanly through his own body as though he were mere vapor. It gleefully returns from the darkness with a sturdy leather collar in its teeth. Evan stares up from the ground, overcome with repulsion.

The old man gently takes the collar from Evan's other self and places it around its neck, stroking him on the head as he slips a leather strap through an iron ring on the collar to form a leash.

"Come now, Evan. Let's go see your friends," the old man lovingly says to his companion as they walk out of the room.

Go with them.

Enki's voice sounds clear in Evan's ear. He looks around the room, expecting to see him standing nearby, but he is alone.

You are not in danger here. This is a projection of what may come to pass, but be prepared for what you are about to see. This will not be easy on you. This is the future that is in store should you fail to stop him. Now follow Erra. See what has become of you and your friends.

Evan hurries out the door, his eyes squint as they adjust to the sunlight. He can make out figures in the daylight, what at first appears to be large men walking around with massive weapons on their backs and hips. As he begins to see clearly, he finds that what he's staring at are hardly men at all.

The nearest one stands an easy seven feet tall, just as broad and massive as Evan was after his transformation. Its skin is a patchwork of different types of flesh. There are several shades of human skin, animal fur, and even reptilian scales covering its body. Muscles bunch together on its back as it walks, resembling a burlap sack stuffed with pythons. Massive legs slam its feet into the ground as it stomps by. One scarred hand rests on the hilt of a roughly smithed piece of steel; the other points at a pile of supplies near an empty doorway. With a deep bark, it commands several others in the vicinity to attend to them.

"*You three*, move these crates down to the larder." The underlings snap to attention. They sprint to the boxes and begin hauling them off as instructed. The voice of the commander is unnaturally rough, like shards of iron being ground against one another.

He turns to watch his subordinates work, allowing Evan to catch glimpse of his face. Its features are human in structure but more similar to the Lurkers. Two large eyes track the work going on around it, its nose just two slits with more pronounced flaps. A full head of long black hair hangs across its brow, the strands matted and filthy. It sports an equally grimy beard littered with chunks of meat and liquids of an undeterminable nature, its mouth very flat and wide with irregular teeth jutting out here and there, preventing its lips from sealing. A thick brown drool oozes from its lower jaw and rolls onto its beard.

Evan forces himself to look away from whatever rancid hell stands before him and chases after Erra, passing at least a dozen more as he follows behind. They wander past all sorts of soldiers busy with various tasks, Erra occasionally waves to them, offering pleasant greetings. His pet Evan scurries along the ground beside him, sniffing and fondling whatever catches its fancy as it gleefully walks at Erra's side. Soon his pet tugs at its leash and whimpers as it turns in circles.

"Oh, my sweet, do you need to potty?" Erra says as he reaches down and strokes his Evan's chin.

The pet Evan nods vigorously as its eyes water from the stress of holding its bowels. Erra quickly removes its loincloth so it may relieve itself. His Evan sniffs the ground for a second, then lifts its leg so it may urinate on a nearby crate. As Evan watches himself find the perfect position to piss in, he gets an eyeful of his potential self's genitalia or, rather, lack thereof. His crotch is smooth, no scrotum or phallus to be seen, just a bit of scar tissue and an imperceptible urethral opening that only became evident when a hot stream of urine came spraying out from it.

Once Erra's pet had finished its business, he places the loincloth around its waist again.

"Let's go now. We mustn't leave your friends waiting too long," Erra says with a smile. "Let's go see Sonya! How about that?"

Evan's future self begins to hop and jostle around in joy.

"All right then, my pet. Let us go." Erra continues down his path, both Evans trailing behind him.

In just a few moments, they arrive at a door with a line of Erra's soldiers standing outside of it, all waiting somewhat impatiently for their turn to enter the room. Erra steps in front of the next in line and looks at him, the soldier immediately bows his head and steps away from the entrance. Erra opens the door, gesturing for his pet to enter, then disappears inside right behind him. The door quietly closes but is thrust open a second later as another of Erra's minions comes bursting out, hastily trying to pull its pants up over a massive erection.

Evan is disgusted and wants to look away, but the image is already in his head. He cannot unsee the inhuman phallus that was attached to that monster. Evan is no veterinarian, but he would have put his money on what he saw being more at place attached to a horse than a man.

The door is still open. As he stands outside the doorway, Evan contemplates whether or not he can move through inanimate objects the way his other self moved through him a few minutes ago, but given that he is standing on the ground, he chooses to not chance it and rushes the door, sliding through the opening just as Erra closed it shut.

Inside the room are several candles and a pile of incense meant to mask the stench of bodily fluids, but the festering stink of putre-fied flesh is easily picked out over the smell of the incense. In the middle of the room is a platform, maybe three feet off the ground. Long heavy chains run up the sides at each corner, one of the chains rattles as whatever is attached to it shifts in place. Evan looks to see what caused the motion. He sees a single leg covered in rough, dry skin. Scratches and cuts crisscross its surface. The shackle affixed to the ankle has worn on the skin so long that the flesh around it is swollen and blackened with dried blood and seeps a milky-green purulent fluid. Evan's gaze follows the leg up the torso. The body is clearly female, a black female. Her sex is raw and bleeding as seminal fluid leaks from within her.

With a shaky effort, the head of the woman lifts up to see what has caused the pause in her abuse. Evan looks into the vacant expres-sion and immediately recognizes the hazel iris staring at Erra.

"Oh my fucking god. No. *Noooo. Sonya!* What the fuck are they doing to *you!*" Evan falls to his knees as he learns the severity of Sonya's living hell.

He punches the floor over and over again as his rage builds within him. Deep in his chest, he feels an odd sensation, a tightness unlike his usual anxiety. It pulls at the fabric of his soul and fills him with hate. He screams and curses and cries out for Erra to release his friend, but all his efforts are in vain. He can only watch helplessly as Sonya's torment continues.

"Aren't you a mess? You should really clean yourself up. You have been having far too much fun with my legion. It's truly disgusting." Erra plugs his nose as he looks Sonya over. "Here, let Evan help you. Come on, boy!"

Erra points a crooked old finger at Sonya's femininity and tugs on Evan's leash. His pet rears up, placing its hands on the edge of the table. He looks back at his master for final approval.

"Go on. Have at it. She needs your help," Erra says as he motions toward Sonya.

His pet Evan begins eagerly lapping at whatever fluids it can find. It greedily consumes, enjoying itself profusely while Sonya lies her head back on the platform and sobs. She tries to cry out, but only a harsh squeak escapes her mouth.

"I sure am glad I cut out your vocal cords. The screaming was always so, so unnecessary. Who is going to hear you? Who actually *cares*? Eh?" Erra laughs at Sonya's face as tears pour down her cheeks. Her mouth contorted in a silent snarl full of pain.

Evan closes his eyes as he tries to force the sounds out of his head, but all he can hear is the wet slather of a tongue on flesh and Erra's soft chortle in the background.

The door opens up as one of Erra's soldiers impatiently pokes hits head in to see what is happening.

"Wait, your turn. Damn you!" Erra shouts.

Evan sees his chance to get out and frantically falls over himself as he runs to the door. He ghosts through the soldier standing in the doorway and falls to the ground, his nervous system screaming at him to vomit, but he cannot. He doubles over and heaves painfully for several minutes until he hears Erra scolding the soldier who interrupted him.

"You damned fool. Did you not see me when I walked in there? Are you that desperate for release that you're willing to disturb *me* during *my* time with *my* playthings that I am benevolent enough to allow you to use freely?" Erra's stare is ice cold. His mask of pleasantry cast off, revealing his more preferred nature.

The soldier is frozen in place, struck dumb by the response to his impudence. Erra lifts a wrinkled finger and points it at the chest of the soldier before him. With a panicked expression, the soldier just stares as the finger closes in and gently prods him in the chest. A sharp snap can be heard, like the arc of electricity, followed by an audible crackling. Flames erupt from the point of contact, rapidly engulfing the hapless soldier. It bellows and wails as it burns alive, rolling and twisting on the ground, reaching out to his comrades for help. His skin and muscle are quickly immolated, rapidly exposing his skeleton and organs. Soon, all soft tissue has been consumed, leaving nothing but bones and ash in its place.

Erra looks to the second in line. "Clean this up immediately," he commands. The soldier falls to the ground, removing its own shirt to be used as a means to collect the remains of its peer.

Erra walks on, his mood so soured that those who see him coming move away urgently. He tugs sharply on Evan's leash. As they walk, his patience is clearly worn thin. He is nearly dragging his Evan along behind him, and by the time they reach their next destination, Erra's pet was bleeding in several places. With a soft whimper, his Evan protests the treatment.

"Shut your *damned* mouth, you ungrateful cur!" Erra scowls as the poisoned words leave his throat. He backhands his Evan squarely in the mouth, busting his lip and sending blood spurting onto the floor.

After a stern glare, Erra turns toward the door he had stopped in front of and twists the handle. As the door opens, he lifts his free arm up and covers his eyes. A beam of unnaturally bright light comes bursting through the crack. His pet Evan winces and tries to pull away from the light. Erra walks into the doorway, tugging Evan along with him. He turns and fumbles for the doorknob with closed eyes.

As Erra opens the door, Evan cringes as he tries to block the blinding illumination. He squints and tries to shade his eyes with his hand. He sees Erra moving through the door. Quickly, he scrabbles up next to him and slides his way in. Erra pulls the door shut and begins walking down a long hallway. Evan tries to follow them, but he can barely see where Erra and his pet are heading. He just listens for the shuffling of feet and the soft pads of skin on the stone floor and does his best to stay behind it. As he progresses down the hall, the overpowering light normalizes and slowly reveals more of his surroundings.

The hall is made entirely of a bright white material, smooth, hard, and oddly reflective, with no apparent seams or cracks. After taking in the room for a moment, Evan noticed that the hall was not reflective, but it was actually the source of the light. The entire structure of the hall is glowing from some internal magic. He turns back to their point of origin, but it is impossibly bright and too much to look at. He glances up ahead, eyeing Erra and his pet, wondering what awaits him at the end of this hall as Erra's foot catches the back of his own heel and he stumbles slightly, causing his Evan to jump in freight.

"You dumb animal. You're afraid of your own shadow." Erra scoffs with a yank of his Evan's leash.

"This guy's such a dick," Evan says with a sigh as he follows behind him. Erra's words replay in his head, the sinister tone juxtaposed with the first impressions of him. He was almost likable then, but now that his true colors are more visible, Evan feels nothing but hatred for him.

The snap of a whip can be heard up ahead, accompanied by the groans of a man in pain. Evan's senses ignite like a wildfire as his body reacts to the sounds of pain. As they get closer, the scent of blood starts off faint but steadily grows more powerful until it permeates his senses.

As they reach the end of the corridor, a single entryway stands ahead of them, the room beyond glowing with a faint red hue that makes the entrance contrast sharply with the white walls preceding it. The crack of the whip is much louder now it makes Evan cringe with every lash. Erra hurriedly walks through the portal and into the room. Evan hears another sharp snap of a whip, but this time, there is no moan.

As Evan catches up to Erra and his pet, he sees them standing next to another soldier holding a whip made of thick leather braids with several barbed pieces of metal laced into the end of it.

"How disappointing. Did you break him already? You know how I like to be here to watch when he passes. If it weren't for this filthy beast having to stop and spray its waste all over my fortress, we would have made it." Erra kicks his pet in the ribs out of spite. His Evan falls to the ground from the force and struggles to get back to its feet.

The soldier hangs up his whip on the wall behind him next to a plethora of other instruments of violence—some obvious to their purpose, others much more obscure and concerning. He apologizes to Erra and steps back to the wall hands behind his back, head facing forward.

In the middle of the room is a chain hanging from the ceiling with broad leather straps at the end fastened to the wrists of a limp carcass dangling just off the ground. The entire being is covered in its own blood. Thick brown hair is matted to the scalp with bright white strips of cranium breaking up the pattern. The back is flayed wide open with layers of muscle dangling off. Large patches of his ribs are clearly visible from across the room. The floor is littered with bits of flesh soaking in a pool of blood that covers nearly the entire floor. Red footprints litter the perimeter of the blood puddle from the soldier walking back and forth from the victim to the morbid menagerie of instruments in front of him.

Erra carefully steps through the blood to the front of the dangling body, choosing his footsteps cautiously. Even with his immense power and affinity for evil, time still clearly held a grip on his physical form. As he approaches the front of the man, he raises his right hand and places his palm directly on the center of his chest. A pale-blue light begins to emanate from his arm as the wounds adorning the flensed corpse begin to seal. Cuts close and removed tissue regrows. The dried blood absorbs into the skin, returning some of the hues that had drained away.

With a violent inhalation, the body is reanimated. It hangs still for a moment as if to process being resurrected, then it speaks.

"You sick fuck, just let me *die already*!" the man shouts.

Evan instantly recognizes the voice. It's Rich.

"Day after day, after day, after day. Don't you get tired of this? You *won*. There is *nothing* left! What's the fuckin' point? Why even keep me here? Kill me. Take my power. Take the darkness. It's yours. I don't want it anymore. Kill me! *Come on! Do it! Do it now! Kill me!*" Tears stream down Rich's face as he screams and pleads with Erra.

"You foolish boy. Why would I willingly give up a wonderful toy such as yourself? You have given me years of entertainment. I don't imagine I'll get bored of you for at least another decade." Erra smiles coldly in Rich's face as he watches his spirit begin to break once more. "Even then, I will likely just leave you here and allow you to starve to death. Then after a day or so, I shall come revive you again, just to let you die in isolation once more! Isn't that wonderful?"

Rich screams so hard he retches, hot bile spews from his mouth and dribbles down his chin. He wails and moans like a wild animal, his mind eroding from the pain-induced madness creeping in on him. Erra looks to the lone guard and extends an empty palm. With a swift motion, he places a large dagger in Erra's empty hand. Erra deftly slices open Rich's belly and reaches inside. With a burst of blood and shrieks of pain, Erra pulls out Rich's liver. He then places a hand on his belly again and heals the fresh wound.

Erra looks down to his Evan and throws the organ at the ground in front of his pet.

"Go on then. I'm sure you're famished. I haven't fed you a proper meal in days." Erra looks on as his Evan begins to voraciously gnaw and chew on Rich's liver. A twisted smile cracks the placid expression over his face whilst his pet consumes the flesh offered to it.

"You, take it slower. I want to watch him die next time I visit. If you fail me, it will be you in those shackles. Am I understood?" Erra stares down his nose at the guard as he leaves, his pet scampering along right behind him with a partially eaten liver hanging from its teeth. Had his Evan come with a tail, it would have been wagging.

"You may continue. Just try to use some patience this time." Erra's voice is resonating from deeper down the shining hall as he makes his way to the exit.

As they leave, Evan just stares at his friend, his mind incapable of processing everything that he has seen. He doesn't know if he should follow Erra more or stay and try to help Rich. His mind snaps back to Sonya and the sickening treatment she is receiving. He begins to hyperventilate as his chest contracts. His instincts are screaming at him to act, demanding that he step up and save his friends. He feels the same seething hatred burning inside him that he did when he saw what had befallen Sonya. The pain in his chest turns to an intense heat that radiates through his whole body. His jaw clenches tight, the muscles in his neck feel like they are about to rip away from the bone.

Unable to contain this immense rage within him any longer, he throws his head back and releases a scream rife with hate. His hands squeeze into fists, his entire body tenses up as he explodes with emotion. Once the wave has passed his body collapses, his mind numb from the toll this entire vision has placed upon him.

Do you see now? You are the linchpin. If they do not have you at their side, this is what is awaiting them.

As Enki's words fill Evan's head, he is overtaken by a wave of relaxation. Gradually, the world he is standing in fades away. The lights dim, and the walls turn black. The guard and his weaponry disappear. Rich's softly sobbing form is the last thing to vanish from Evan's vision. He closes his eyes as he slips away into a sleeplike state, his body feels like it's wrapped in a soft blanket. It feels almost like he's floating for a moment then gently he is placed on the ground. He opens his eyes again to find Enki sitting across him, but the room they had met in is gone. There is nothing left but blackness and silence. It's just the two of them adrift in this boundless void.

You cannot fail, Evan. You cannot fail. The fate of us all is in the hands of you fragile three. Even now, I am about to expel what energy I have left to return you to your body. I know that I will not be returning to my family. Erra is going to snatch me up as I pass from this realm to the next, and I will become his. He will gain the ability to manipulate creation itself, and it will only make him more dangerous. The task ahead of you is by no means easy, but it is not impossible either. You must make the choice. You must choose to overcome your own fears. If you do not, we are all lost.

Now go. Go back to your body and your friends. When you open your eyes, see the joy on their faces at your return to them. Remember what you saw here with me and know that their lives are in your hands.

With that, Enki's image shimmered and vanished. Evan could not see or hear anything at all. He feels his being slip into a cold pool of nothingness, its presence threatening to smother his existence out. Evan wants to struggle. He wants to fight back against it, but he is overcome with a desire to just accept it.

Not yet. Not here.

Enki's voice reaches out to him, and the encroaching cold is repelled. He snaps back to his senses and tries to call out to Enki, but nothing escapes his mouth.

Goodbye, Evan.

Evan is launched through space, his body under constant undulating acceleration. His head feels like it's being crushed and exploded simultaneously. With a violent intensity matching his initiation, his body stops as though smashed into the side of a mountain.

His nerves are engulfed with pain. He tries to scream, but nothing comes out of him. He tries to thrash and flail about, but he can't move. All he can do is soak in his suffering. He feels a huge thud deep in his chest, then another right after it. The pounding keeps hitting him over and over again at a steady pace. He feels his lungs burn as they fill with air then spasm. His ears begin to ring so loud he fears he may go deaf, but through the painful tones he can pick out someone yelling.

"WAKE UP! DAMN YOU! WAKE UP!"

It was a woman's voice. He wonders if he knows her or not. Something about it is so familiar. It's Vitra. Why is she yelling at him?

"I'm going to have to inject him with darkness. I don't think his body is responding. We have to get his blood pumping, or else, the serum won't work," Vitra says.

Evan wonders what's going on. Who did they give this serum to?

Suddenly, his chest is filled with pain so cold that it takes his breath away. Through the pain, he can feel a gentle beat in his chest. The pounding stops. He feels another beat, this one stronger than the last. It's his heart. His heart is beating.

His body jolts from whatever medicine is coursing through his system. He feels his physical form restarting. His heart races. His chest heaves as his body cries for oxygen. Slowly, Evan's eyes open. He sees Vitra, Ral, and Gaian standing over him. He tries to sit up.

"Wait, don't do that yet, Evan. You need to rela—" Vitra was unable to finish her sentence before Evan began vomiting profusely all over himself and the table he was lying on.

CHAPTER 19

In an instant, Sonya and Rich rush over to Evan. Sonya wraps her arms around his giant neck and squeezes him tight.

"Sonya, I'm covered in puke," Evan says with a raspy voice.

"I know. It's gross, but I'm too happy to care right now," says Sonya between sobs.

Rich pats him on the shoulder. "How you feelin', man? You were dead for quite some time," he says, struggling to hide the tears in his eyes.

"So what did Enki have to say?" Vitra stands before Evan, contempt for his failure clearly evident on her face.

"He, uh, made it very clear to me that I need to be better. We had a long discussion, and I… I will not fail again." He manages to squeak the last few words out before being overtaken by emotion from the memories of what he had been shown. He can't even look at his friends without having painful flashes of their grisly fates replay in his mind.

"I don't remember what happened to me. I know we were holed up in that bank, then the Lurkers attacked, and after that, nothing." Evan dries his eyes and looks at his friends for clarification.

"Well…," Sonya begins, "after you, I guess, died. We got attacked by this giant pile of, uh, meat? It burst through the wall of the bank and started tearing the place up. Then it plowed through another wall so we ran outside to lure it away from you. I cut it up pretty good but got knocked out. I don't know what happened after that." Sonya looks over to Rich as she finishes retelling what happened.

"Yeah, she got put down pretty hard. I jumped in after that, but I couldn't really figure out a way to kill it. I think I only managed to piss it off real good. I was about to get smashed when Ral and Gaian showed up and saved my butt and Sonya's and your dead ass. They made really quick work of it and, like, a couple of hundred Lurkers." Rich returns Sonya's look and then glances at Evan.

The sad giant doesn't say a word as tears run down his cheeks and drip off his chin, a giant palm raises up to wipe away the falling sorrow.

"So did you guys name it? The meat monster that nearly killed us all?" Evan asks with a sly grin.

"No. We really haven't talked about it yet. Didn't feel it was relevant given the current situation," Rich replies.

Sonya begins to speak but gets cut off by Evan.

"Meat-zerker," Evan blurts. "How's that?"

"That's…actually not too bad. Given how it just kinda plowed through everything," Sonya says, her agreement makes Evan's smile beam.

"Fuckin' Meat-zerker," Rich says with a nod.

Ral, Gaian, and Vitra stare at one another as they share a very confused gaze. The weight of the situation has been washed away entirely by some idle chatter as the friends begin to actually laugh and joke about the injuries they received during the fight.

Vitra is growing unusually tense. "All right! You must gather your wits. We need to get ready for the next step in the process. Your journey has yet to even begin, and you've already wasted a great deal of time. You have an appointment that must be kept."

With a palpable sense of urgency, Vitra sets their hunting packs on the table, along with their weapons that had been collected during the aftermath of their first real fight. "Inside, you will find two fresh changes of clothes, like what you wear now, a heavy cloak and nine tonics. Three for energy. They are best used once you've exhausted yourself from strenuous physical activity. Their effects last about eight hours or so. Three for recovery. Take them right before you rest. They will heal most minor and moderate wounds, but it takes time. Two for increased speed. These greatly increase your reaction time. Your brain will process information roughly fifteen times faster than normal, significantly aiding you in combat. The last one is for emergencies only. It should only be used if you have been mortally wounded. Its effects are enormous and very painful. Do not use this unless you are about to die." Vitra shifts her eyes at Evan and glares at him. She pushes each pack toward its intended body along with their weapons.

When Evan reaches for his pack, Vitra's grip remains firm on it.

"Evan, Enki was a dear friend to us. He was our safety net for when you three encountered much more significant…problems… outside this cave. Knowing that he has already given himself to that monster is positively infuriating. You now have *no* second chances. If you fail, it will mean the doom of us all." Vitra's eyes are dark and cold as she stares daggers at Evan.

The tension in the room is thick as Vitra removes her hands from the bag. Evan gently pulls it toward himself, not daring to make eye contact with Vitra. He quietly places his axe in his belt and throws the pack over one shoulder. He sits down on the corner of a chair and rests an arm on his knee as he stares at the floor.

"Everyone, get your gear in order. You must be leaving soon. We have exactly twenty-three minutes and eleven seconds before you must be out and on your way. Ral, please help them with whatever they may need." Vitra heads out of the room, pausing briefly near Gaian to hand him a folded piece of paper. He opens it, glances at it, and nods at her, then quickly leaves with her.

Rich noticed the surreptitious exchange between Vitra and Gaian. His thoughts wander, but he keeps them to himself. He grabs his pack from the table and slings it behind him. He feeds his arms through the straps and clips the belt around his waist. The weight of the pack reminds him of when they first set off from his old truck. He was so happy to have them with him, then it was a much-needed distraction from the daily grind of his painful existence. For a moment, he closes his eyes and imagines he was back there, just him and his two friends.

"Okay, so where are we going, and who are we meeting there?" Rich asks Ral as he cinches his pack around his chest.

"The man you will be meeting is Captain Cephus Johnstone of the Allied Human Resistance. The rally point you must get to is located west of here, roughly twenty miles away in some fairly diffi-cult terrain. You are heading for what's known as Saddle Mountain. The mountain is U-shaped with a large draw on the eastern side that forms a small valley at the foot of the mountain. You are to meet him there, in the mouth of that valley. He will take you to the AHR's last remaining airship." Ral's explanation lacked his normal flair.

"Airship? Like a dirigible?" asks Rich.

"You will soon find out, Rich," Ral replies, his words still oddly placid.

Evan stands up from his chair. "What are you guys going to do while we're gone? Are we going to meet back here once we have what we need?" Evan asks as he carefully reaches for his axe. He touches it with one massive finger, and a thick casing of hard clay quickly consumes the axe head.

"We will remain here. There are a few preparations we must see to before, well, just some things that need wrapping up here in the cave. That's all." Ral fills one of three small satchels with enough food and water for their short journey. Then moves on to the next.

Rich looks at Evan, his eyes widen and brows raise as he tries to imply some kind of inflection through expression at the significance of Ral's sudden change in demeanor.

Sonya approaches from the other side of Ral and looks at her friends.

"Are you guys okay? Seems kinda weird over here," she asks as she steps near them. "Ral, you look like someone took the wind out of your sails. Ha, see what I did there?"

"Yes, my dear. That was quite clever." Ral flashes her a smile, but his eyes are far more somber. Ral closes up the last bag and hands one to each of them. He smiles again and nods, then rushes off in the same direction as Gaian and Vitra had earlier.

"What the fuck was that?" Rich exclaims under his breath. "These people are acting janky as hell right now."

"I noticed too. A few minutes ago, I saw Vitra hand Gaian a letter, and he scrambled off like his life depended on it. I don't know what's happening right now, but they don't seem like they want us to know about it," Sonya says as her eyes shift back and forth between Evan and Rich.

Shortly after she finished her sentence, all three came walking back into the hall. Gaian was first, followed by Ral with Vitra trailing shortly behind him. All three of them line up across the room, each of them standing across their progeny. Vitra steps forward and addresses them with a very formal tone.

"You three have excelled beyond our original preconceived notions of what you would be capable of. You took to your training with shocking alacrity. You have done nothing but surprise us with your dogged persistence to achieve greatness. Even in the face of rather formidable enemies, you did not hesitate. You may have stumbled, you may have fell, but you showed no fear in the face of an enemy you could have never conceived." Vitra pauses for a moment and glares at Evan, then continues her speech.

"The time has come for you to set out on the next step in your journey. The Allied Human Resistance has spent the last three decades searching for your items of power at our request, and I'm glad to say that they have found them. Their exact locations will be divulged to you once you meet them and are briefed on the current situation. You are to head to Saddle Mountain. It is approximately twenty miles away due west by northwest from here. Considering the terrain, you will take most of a full day to get there. As soon as your feet hit the dust outside this cave, you will have exactly thirty-six hours to reach the valley on the east side of the mountain. Noon of the second day, Cephus will arrive to take you to their airship, the Salvation." Vitra pauses for questions, but the group is silent. She starts to speak again, but Rich cuts her off.

"So what are you guys going to do once we leave the cave? Ral hasn't stopped moping around, and you were being all sneaky with your note to Gaian. So what's the plan?" Rich blurts defiantly.

Vitra's expression goes blank with surprise. Ral only stares at Vitra, waiting for her reaction. Gaian is still, his composure totally unchanged by Rich's revelation. Vitra is quick to recover and offers an explanation.

"We are tasked with restoring balance to the natural world once we finished with your training. I'm sure you noticed the significant lack of vegetation, yes? This is a result of not just nuclear winter, but Erra's hunger to consume all life and make it his own. He is not satisfied to just rule the planet. He wants to be a god and reshape everything into his own design. It is your job to stop him. It is our job to heal the land. Does this satisfy you?" Vitra calmly looks into Rich's eyes as he absorbs the information.

"How are you going to go about that exactly? Maybe there is something we could do to help?" Rich asks.

"No," Vitra's answer comes abrupt and short.

"We do not have the luxury of time. You have a very slim window of opportunity to work with," Gaian booms at them.

"I do not want to send you all away. It has been quite nice having the company, but I promise you that we will be able to handle *our* task with relative ease," Ral adds.

"Well, all right then," Rich says, defeated.

A heavy blanket of melancholy settles over the room. Rich, Evan, and Sonya feel a weight in their hearts that they cannot explain. Vitra looks at them, and for a brief moment, she feels her eyes begin to water. She hastily turns her back to them so she can wipe it away, masking her actions by rummaging through her potions cabinet.

"I guess if you guys got everything under control, we should probably head out then," Rich says as he toes the leg of a nearby chair.

"Yes. There are about thirty seconds left before you needed to leave anyways. Gather your supplies," Vitra says with her back still to the group.

The trio readies their gear for the journey ahead. Ral grabs a lit torch and stands near the opening to the cave exit. Vitra has regained her composure enough to lead the party and takes her place in front of Ral. Gaian is standing mountain like on the other side of the large table, his eyes focused squarely on Evan. Vitra walks down the hall, and Ral follows immediately behind her—Evan, Sonya, and Rich right behind them. Gaian remains stationary. The friends rush along the dark hall, barely keeping pace with Vitra and Ral who are walking at a pace so fast that Rich has to jog to keep up. They reach the end of the passage and are standing before the barrier separating them from the outside. Rich is lightly panting, his breath echoing in the silence of the hallway.

"Are we ready? They must pass through in just a few moments," Vitra says to Ral.

"Wait one moment please," Gaian booms from the darkness. Evan nearly leaps out of his skin from the shock. They had all assumed he had stayed back in the main hall.

Gaian walks up to Evan and stands squarely in front of him. He takes a deep breath and in and slowly exhales.

"I am not good at sharing my emotions. I find them unnecessary. I do want you to know something." Gaian takes a lengthy pause. Vitra coughs gently to encourage him to hurry up. "When I gave you your axe and you reacted poorly, it upset me because I had made that with the intention of giving it to the one who would be a part of the group that destroyed Erra. I find you to be less than what I had hoped for, but I do believe you are capable of completing the task laid before you."

Gaian goes silent. He extends his massive open hand out. Evan reaches out and clasps his hand with Gaian's. The giants exchange an intense glare over an epic handshake.

"Destroy them all in the name of the Creator," Gaian booms.

"You bet your giant black ass I will," Evan replies.

The silence after their exchange is broken by gentle sobbing. Everyone turns to look at the source to find Ral gently wiping away his tears.

"I have known that man for millennia, and that is the most emotion I have ever seen from him." Ral gasps as he takes a deep breath.

"The time is upon us. I will open the barrier. You three must leave as soon as I give the word." Vitra's hands are already clasped before she finishes speaking, her intelligible words blending into the same strange tongue that she had been using for incantations. She pushes her hands toward the barrier, and it shimmers like it had the last time they were sent out into the nightmarish wasteland that used to be their home state.

"You must go now. Rich, your compass is in your pack. Head west by northwest from the entrance. Remind them why they fear the dark." Vitra's last words to Rich are colder than the abysmal void in which they first met Enki. A chill runs down his spine as her steely gaze burrows deep into his core. Rich's only reply to Vitra is a curt nod. Vitra smiles as Rich passes by. She knows her progeny is more fearsome than she ever imagined him to be. Rich quickly leaps through the barrier and disappears from view.

Sonya is up next. She hugs Ral tightly and gives him a kiss on each cheek. He smiles warmly and returns her affection, placing his lips squarely on her forehead.

"You remind me so much of my eldest. She was just as spirited and loving as you. She also had a mean streak that would make most men run for their lives!" Ral smiles at Sonya, taking one last long look at her. He hugs her tightly, then pushes her away. "Go on, my child. You have much work to do and not enough time to do it." Sonya's tears fall freely from her eyes. She waves goodbye to them all and steps through the barrier.

Evan is last. He steps forward to the cusp of the entrance and looks at Vitra. He turns back and begins to address the remaining party.

"I know I fucked up. I froze when things got real. Enki showed me some seriously horrifying shit, and I realize exactly how important I am to the group. This can't be done if it's just the two of them." Evan's words hang dryly in the air. No one responds to him. Vitra is focused on holding the barrier open. Gaian just stares blankly at him. Ral is the first to break the silence.

"Evan, we are not mad. We are just scared. Your success or failure has a direct impact on us. I believe in you. I know you will find Gaian's—well, your amulet—and I know that you will make us proud." Ral reaches out to shake Evan's hand.

Evan gladly takes Ral's hand and gives it a hearty shake. A small smile of relief breaks his grim expression. Gaian takes one large step forward and gives him an approving grunt with a nod. Vitra just looks at him, her eyes swelling with tears.

"You must not fail, Evan. Please, I don't want everything we fought and worked for to be defiled by that monster. Now go. Don't let the hell Enki showed you come to pass." Vitra's voice is trembling from carrying the weight of her words. This is the most vulnerable she has been since they arrived there.

"I swear to you that I will not fail. Gaian, I will make you proud."

With Evan's final goodbyes made, he shambles through the barrier. Vitra's hands are shaking violently as she maintains the spell to hold the door open. Once he is safely through, she collapses on the floor and begins wailing in grief. Ral places a hand on her shoulder in an attempt to comfort her. Gaian approaches from his side and picks her up as though she were a child. He gently cradles her against his chest and looks at Ral.

"It is time," Gaian says, his voice still deep and foreboding but missing its usual boom.

Ral nods solemnly and begins heading back into the cave. Gaian follows behind him as Vitra sobs heavy tears down his massive chest. Her once-strong-and-sleek frame is now a crumpled wreck in the giant's arms. Gaian gently strokes her back with one hand, his show of sympathy betraying his stoic nature.

Sonya stands next to Rich just inside the mouth of the cave. She looks around at the now-arid interior, examining the sharp contrast of what she remembered it looking like not very long ago. Rich is leaning against the wall, looking to his feet. In the early morning darkness of the world they had left behind, little tendrils of night swirl and dance in the darkened cave entrance.

"Why are you doing that?" Sonya asks.

"I'm not," Rich replies flatly. "Remember when I bled out during my training? Well, ever since then, I've had this little thing following me around."

Rich points to the ground a few feet from his position and barks his order at it. "Go," he says.

The shade immediately leaves his feet and zips over to where he was pointing. It shudders as it settles onto the ground and continues to twist and wriggle in place.

"That's really weird," Sonya whispers under her breath.

"Yeah. But that little fella saved your life when the Meat-zerker knocked your ass out. Shit, I think it killed more Lurkers than I did." Rich scoffs and snaps his fingers. The little cloud of night flurries its way back to his shadow and softly caresses his feet as a dog pleased to be back with its master.

"Neat tricks, but can it make a decent martini?" Evan laughs as he walks up behind Sonya and Rich. His face wears a smile, but his eyes are distant.

"Martini? Thought you were a cosmo fan?" Rich snaps around and gives Evan a shot in the ribs.

Evan winces out of instinct despite feeling nothing.

"It's tasty. You don't have to drink just to black out, you know." Evan slugs Rich in the gut, doubling him over and knocking the wind out of him. "Oops. Sorry, man. Not 100 percent used to being back in this meat suit I guess."

"Nohh wohhries." Rich gasps as he tries to suck air and talk at the same time.

"Okay, boys. You need to play nice, or I will have to separate you," Sonya says as she rolls her eyes. "Since we're all here, we should probably be getting a move on, yes?"

"You're right. We don't have very long. Vitra said that we have exactly thirty-six hours 'once our feet hit the dust.' Was that all of us or just the first of us? I was first through, and I think I waited like forty-five minutes or so before Sonya came through. Then it was at least that long again before you came out, Evan. So I reckon that we're close to two hours behind Vitra's schedule. Wish she would have told me how she managed to keep such a good time. Wish she would have told me a lot of things before sending us out." Rich looks out at the surrounding hills as his words echo gently off the walls of the cave.

Sonya checks her laces and backpack, ensuring everything is ready for travel. "If we're that far behind, then we should get going. We need to make sure we meet this 'Cephus' guy on time. If we miss our ride, it will be an awfully short trip."

"Yeah, you're not wrong. Let's head out," Rich says.

The group moves out of the cave entrance. Their thoughts split between what's ahead of them and what they left behind. Vitra and Ral were incredibly vague about how they were going to accomplish their final task. Sonya swallows hard against the lump in her throat. It was evident that there was something they weren't sharing. Something troubling that had them all walking on eggshells right before they parted ways.

Sonya bounces a couple of times, trying to shake off the negativity. She knows that Ral can handle whatever it is. Most of her dilemma is just anxiety from leaving the only thing close to a home they have left. She forces a smile to keep her spirits up. Things may be irreversibly different, but she still has her friends.

Gaian gently sets Vitra on the ground inside a white circle surrounded by similar markings to those used when they sent Sonya, Rich, and Evan to Enki. Her circle is a part of a larger diagram with two other identical circles placed equidistant from the center image. Gaian places a large piece of crystal on the central glyph. Ral takes his position and eases himself down to the floor within the lines. He looks over to Vitra, her face still wet with tears. Long black hair matted to her cheek and jaw on the side that rested against Gaian. Gaian places a smaller crystal on the ground in front of Vitra and Ral then takes his place to complete the arrangement. He sets his own crystal on the floor and looks at his old friends.

"Now is the time. Are we ready to begin?" Gaian asks.

"I am ready," Ral replies.

They both look to Vitra. She does not speak, just nods her head quietly at first but then swallows her fear and speaks to them.

"I am ready as well. Let's get on with it," Vitra says. "I love you both so much. Thank you for all that you have given me."

"I love you as well, Vitra. It has been an honor to be stuck in this cave with you," Ral says, flashing half a smile across his uneasy face.

Vitra looks to Gaian. He simply nods and grunts deeply. She smiles, drinking them in.

All three of them begin to disrobe. They shed their clothing and cast it aside, exposing their bare flesh to the cold chill of the cave around them. Gaian extends a hand to both of them. They accept and join hands themselves. As soon as they are all connected, the crystals in front of them begin to glow with a warm yellow light. Gaian starts humming a single steady tone. Ral joins in. Vitra looks at them one last time, her eyes still full with tears as she picks up the tone. As the humming grows, the reverberation of their song off the cave walls intensifies with each second. Their voices come together as one harmonious hymn. The central crystal glows brightly, filling the room with blinding light. The crystals in front of them slowly glow brighter to match.

In unison, they look down at the glowing rocks before them. Three large beams of energy spring out of the central crystal, striking the other three and immediately redirecting into their eyes. The humming rumbles the cave and the earth around it. With a thunderous clap, the spherical barrier surrounding the cave implodes. Its immense energy is absorbed by the central crystal. The outside air rushes into the old cave, filling it with a cold gust of wind. The light from the larger crystal dies—the three smaller ones do as well. The humming has stopped.

Vitra, Ral, and Gaian sit motionless on the floor. A gentle rustling breaks the quiet. Their skin darkens and cracks, turning rough like tree bark. Gaian's is thick and striated with deep splits between the angular ridges. Ral's is similar but grows more curved and flowing with a lighter complexion. Vitra's skin fades to a rough ghostly gray with dark stripes forming at the splits. As their skin transforms the cracks deepen in places, exposing their flesh underneath, but instead of blood, they secrete sap from their wounds. With tremendous force, thick roots erupt from their mouths—dark brown from Gaian, deep red from Ral, thin and gray from Vitra. They entangle everything in their path, crashing down the hall, ripping torches off their mounts, and smothering them. They bash their way through the door to the kitchen, destroying the furniture—smashing plates, crushing pots, blunting knives, and bending forks. The roots continue their rampage, finding their way to the cave entrance. The early evening light shines down on the exterior of the cave mouth. The stampede bursts forth into the light. The small amount of sunlight penetrating the clouds is enough to whip the cavalcade into a frenzy—each branch into hundreds more and each of those does the same. The advancing roots tearing up the earth, spreading like wildfire and covering the entire valley in minutes. The ground immediately around the laid roots grows damp with moisture. Small sprigs of grass shoot up from the moist earth. Little white flowers gently push their way through the rough bark of the network of roots.

Back in the cave, everything has stopped. No sound can be heard. The air is calm and fresh. In the room from where it all emerged sit three earthen sentinels. Their figures voided the vitality they sacrificed to restore life to the valley. All three of them are bound together in solidarity. Their place as wardens of the earth carved into eternity.

CHAPTER 20

The trio has been walking for what feels like hours, climbing hill after hill as they make their way to meet the pilot. They are pushing their way forward at a decent pace, trying to maintain a balance of speed and efficiency. Ahead of them lies what promises to be the worst of the terrain.

The trio marches on in silence. Worried expressions and furrowed brows follow along with them. Sonya brings up the rear. Every so often, she glances back in the direction they came, scanning the hills behind them, expecting to see Vitra, Ral, and Gaian catching up to them. Sonya sniffs hard against a runny nose and tries to mask any sadness with a cough. Rich turns his head slightly to glance back at her from the front.

"Hey, Rich, how close do you think we are?" Sonya asks, trying to take her mind off more gloomy thoughts.

"Oh, I don't know," Rich says. He pulls his sleeve back and glances at his watch. "Looks like it's been a couple of hours since we left. Not sure how far we have gone, though. We got plenty of daylight left, so we should be there by nightfall. I'm not totally sure why they had us leave so early though. Seems kind of unnecessary." Rich is rambling a little. A clear sign to the rest of them that something is bothering him, and he's trying to distract himself from it.

"So what are we going to do when we get there?" groans Evan. "Just hang out? Maybe discuss our feelings? Have some snacks and talk about the days when things didn't suck ass? I'm starving, and if they gave me what they gave you, that will not be enough," he says as he reaches into his bag and looks longingly at his rations.

"How about you just shut your mouth and eat something then?" Rich barks.

"How am I supposed to shut my mouth then eat something? That's illogical. I have to open my mouth to put something in it." Evan's sass is as voluminous as his physical being.

"I'm going to put something in your mouth here real quick if you don't—" Rich's words were cut short by a tremendous rumble in the earth, followed immediately by a deep clap of what sounded like thunder rushing at them from the rear.

The trio stops and looks back in the direction the sound came from. Off in the distance, they see a plume of dust and soot rising in the air. All three watch as the cloud rises higher and higher into the atmosphere. The ground tremors slightly from the aftershock, then all is quiet.

"That came from the valley. What the fuck happened?" Evan puts his hands on the back of his thick neck and tries to calm his breath as panic washes over him.

"We-we need to go back!" Sonya stammers as she begins heading back down the hill.

"Sonya, no. We need to go. We can't afford to waste the time backtracking all that way!" Rich grabs her by the backpack in an effort to stop her. She pulls her arms out of the pack and stubbornly continues heading back to the cave. "SONYA! RAL WANTS YOU TO KEEP GOING. You know they were going to do something shitty. We all knew it. Hell, I could feel it. I had this deep dread inside me when we left that cave, and don't tell me those goodbyes they gave us didn't feel like it was the last one."

Sonya's head hangs low as the tears falling from her eyes land softly in the soot at her feet. The air around her swirls and spins, whipping around her in several tiny cyclones. They spin faster. The wind becomes sharp and biting. Rich puts his hand up to shield his eyes. Evan turns his back to it and tries to call out to Sonya, but before he can get words out, she is gone. Her pack lays in the dirt, with nothing left of her but a trail of dust streaming over the hills they had spent the last few hours trekking over.

"Well, shit!" Rich exclaims. "I kinda expected that. Should we wait for her, or should we keep going?"

"Bro, with the speed at which she is moving, it probably won't be long. I could use a break anyway." Evan sits down on the ground and opens his pack. He pulls out a chunk of some brownish-orange pastry and takes a bite. "Wow. This ain't bad. Kinda expected it to taste like, well, almost everything else they made us eat or drink." Evan munches on his snacks, momentarily unconcerned with Sonya's sudden disappearance.

The sky over the valley was glowing brighter than normal. Rich peers off into the distance, watching the dust rise from Sonya racing across the landscape. With a grunt of annoyance, he sits down next to Evan and opens his pack, retrieving the vittles from therein. He takes a bite and then hums contentedly.

"Wow, you weren't kidding. This ain't bad at all. Should have got the recipe before we left. Maybe we should send Sonya back again?" Rich says through a mouthful of partially chewed food.

Evan side-eyes Rich and then starts laughing, his massive head tilted back as he bellows at the sky. Rich begins to chuckle. It grows in power until he's laughing just as hard as his old friend. As they calm themselves, Rich looks over to Evan.

"What was so funny exactly? I didn't even make a joke," Rich asks, his ears burning slightly with embarrassment.

The ginger giant didn't say a word. He just opened his mouth and bared his teeth. All of them were stained a very dark brown from whatever was in the food. Rich just smiles as he shakes his head.

Sonya slams to a halt on the hill, overlooking the valley. The jet stream behind her blasts on, whipping her hair forward as dust and debris hurtle past. Her eyes dart across the field as she tries to process what exactly she is seeing. The entire floor of the valley and the sur-rounding hillsides are covered in a thick layer of brown, green, and white. Sunlight breaks through the clouds, casting spots of golden light sporadically. The smell of flowers and moist soil wafts up the hillside, filling her nostrils with a scent she never thought to know again.

With a gust, she is down on the valley floor. She carefully steps over roots and flowers. The resurrected beauty of the world around her is overcoming. Her eyes weep with joy and relief as the overbearing darkness of the world is lifted from her shoulders. Her hands reach down and graze the knee-high grass growing up from around the thick brown roots that cover the ground. Little white flowers shine brightly in the sun while they dance and twist in the gentle wind.

Sonya heads for the cave entrance. She stops just short of where the barrier should be, her hands waving as she walks forward in her search. The barrier is gone. Her steps hastened by wind, she blows through the halls searching for Ral and the others. Roots line her path, showing her the way to their source. In a span of a breath, she is standing in what was once the same chamber they gathered in to first visit Enki. In the center of the room, softly illuminated by the still glowing crystals, she sees the remains of their mentors, and everything becomes painfully clear.

Sonya kneels next to Gaian. Even in the dim light of the cave, his shape is still ominous and foreboding. She sees that he is covered in a thick scale of rough bark. To the right is Ral. His strong and noble form distinguishes him from Vitra's wispy frame. Sonya drapes herself around his shoulders and sobs heavily. Her weeping drips onto the shoulder of Ral's remains. His thick brown skin absorbs her tears. As Sonya cries, a soft cracking emanates from under the bark. The noise grows louder, catching Sonya's attention. She pulls away from Ral and looks on with cautious intrigue, unsure of what may come next.

With the innocent apprehension of a chick hatching from an egg, a single green stem begins to push through the husk of Ral's chest. It extends out and unfurls. A single bud presents itself to Sonya. She reaches for it. As her skin brushes against the protective casing of the new bloom, a soft breeze strokes her cheek. A warm feeling of happiness blankets her body. She can feel that Ral is with her. As she makes contact, its rough green casing folds back and exposes vibrant red petals with bright yellow stamen. The stamen glows softly, lighting Sonya's face and illuminating a heartfelt smile.

"I understand now," she whispers to the flower.

*****

193

Rich is lying in the rock and ash staring up at the gray sky. The break from the trek is welcomed but disconcerting. Sonya had only been gone for ten minutes or so at this point. "Man, she better hurry up. I want to get there sooner than later." He sits up and sees Evan holding his empty food satchel in one hand. His large head looking down at it.

"I'm so hungry I think I'm going to die." Evan's stomach growls in protest. He sighs and throws the food bag to the ground. As the bag hits the ash with a *floof*, a small scrap of parchment with a hand-written note slips out. Evan reaches down and picks it up. He reads it out loud. "Evan, eat half a bar and take one drink of water. Signed by Vitra. Well, why didn't they mention this previously?" Evan rolls his eyes and reaches for his water bladder. As he puts it to his lips, Rich calls out to him.

"Hey, wait a minute," he says to Evan, freezing the giant in place momentarily. "How many bars did you eat? I had four in my bag and only ate like a quarter of one. Hand me that water for a sec." Rich grabs the water from Evan and takes a mouthful. As soon as it hits his stomach, the food in his belly expands abruptly. Rich looks down to see his gut bloat from the swelling food.

"I ate six. What did the water do?" Evan asks with a twinge of concern in his voice.

"It made me really full really fast," Rich warns him. "You should have read the directions first. Surprised you didn't eat them too." Rich laughs as his friend ponders his new quandary.

With measured caution, Evan gently puts the bladder to his mouth and pulls a drink from it. As soon as he swallows, his gut begins to bulge and lurch. It expands and grows until he looks like he could be pregnant. He moans and groans as he rolls around in the dust. His body reacts to the situation in the only way it can. Evan begins vomiting up his stomach contents. He rolls on to all fours and continues to profusely void his gullet. The regurgitated snack starts to pile up around his elbows.

"It won't"—*blooorrfggghh*—"stop coming"—*hhrroollphh*—"out of me!" Evan can barely get the words out between streams of chunky vomit.

Rich is laughing hysterically at his friend's suffering, his laughter echoing off the hills around them—so loud and clear in the cold air that the creature stalking them easily pinpoints their location.

Sonya's return is just as swift as her departure. With a burst of wind, she is standing before her friends again. The force of the stream following her catches Evan's pile of vomit and sends it hurtling through the air directly at Rich. With considerable force, the upheaved bile strikes Rich in the chest and face. His laughter is immediately halted. All are silent as the sudden chain of events is processed by the three friends.

"Oh my god, what is that smell? Is that *puke*?" Sonya covers her face to stifle a gag.

"Dude, you're covered in my barf." Evan bares a grin that grows to match Rich's own level of discontent.

"I suppose I deserve this." Rich sighs as he scrapes himself clean of Evan's vomit.

"Boys are so gross. I couldn't even leave you alone for ten minutes without you guys literally covering each other in barf. And why is there so much of it?" Sonya stands before them with her hands on her hips and a very disappointed look on her face, casting them both a stern glare one might expect from an angry mother.

"It's a long story. Read the note in your food sack before you eat," Rich says as he slaps a handful of sick onto the ground next to him.

After cleaning themselves up while dealing with Sonya lecturing them both for being so irresponsible, they set out again. The terrain grew more rugged as they marched on. They crossed several hills so steep they were forced to climb in sections. Eventually, the terrain leveled out and their progress grew easier. Soon they are within sight of their destination, but the sun is nearly set. Evan, giving in to his own curiosity, asks Sonya about the cave.

"So what did you see back at the cave?" Evan blurts out.

"Well," Sonya begins, "there are a ton of new plants and flowers coming out of the cave. Grass too, all over the valley," she says, refusing to volunteer any more information.

"Really? That's it? Sure there isn't anything else you want to tell us about?" probes Rich, his irritation prominent in his words.

"Yeah, Sonya. You know exactly what I was asking. What happened to them? Are they okay?" Evan adds.

"They, uh…" Sonya chokes on her words, the guilt of intentionally lying to her friends makes her face burn. "They weren't there. They were just gone. I went into the cave, and the barrier had vanished. The whole place was empty." She swallows hard against the lump in her throat.

Neither Rich nor Evan press the subject further. The level of discomfort between the group was blatant. They just continue on in silence, no one daring to ask any questions.

The trio has only a mile or two left before they reach their goal. Rich encourages them to pick up the pace so they can establish camp and get some rest before they get picked up the following midday. They push on hard. Rich and Evan huff and puff as their wind gets tested. Sonya, however, easily glides along the ground. She floats back and forth in front of Evan, smiling at him as he breaks sweat. Evan scowls at her while trying to keep his breath in rhythm.

Seeing how close they are instills a fresh vigor in Rich. He quickens his pace as the target grows near. When they get closer, the silhouette of Saddle Mountain can be seen standing tall against the dimming horizon, its form taking command against the twilight of the coming night.

"It's going to be dark soon," Rich mutters to himself, his words sound simultaneously concerned and comforted by the approaching darkness.

"Well, I don't think there will be another Meat-zerker all the way out here," Evan says. "Besides, I heard you kicked its ass."

"Right. Maybe for a minute. It quickly put me in my place. I mean, I'm pretty good compared to when I started, but maybe not good enough…yet." Rich smiles and slugs Evan in the arm. "I think Sonya is the real star of the show, though. She has really outpaced the both of us, literally." Rich finishes his sentence just as Sonya lazily glides by like she's ice skating.

"What were you boys just saying about me? Feel free to continue," Sonya says with a cheeky grin.

"Evan…," Rich whispers, "trip her with a stick or somethin'."

"I heard that, *Dick*," she replies. "Hey, you boys want to see me do a double backflip?" Without waiting for an answer, Sonya bends over, looking back at them from between her legs, then proceeds to flip them off with both hands.

"Rich, how big you want that stick to be?" Evan says as Sonya glides away.

The mountain stands before them now, looming so high above that the top is lost in darkness and clouds. Rich takes note of the landscape. There is a large open plain all around the east side of the mountain. Two large opposing ridgelines create a massive draw in between them. That draw runs down the side of the mountain and forms a tight valley, maybe a hundred yards wide and steeply climbing to the west—a reasonably defensible position should anything happen to be following them.

"Ahhhh, shit," Rich grumbles under his breath.

"What's wrong?" Sonya asks.

"When we were heading into Vernonia, I thought I saw something on a hillside behind us. It was only a flicker of movement, and I didn't see it very clearly, but I know I saw something, something large and fast." Rich's tone has flattened, his ominous recollection leaves him visibly paranoid as he studies the hills and ridges around them.

"You felt that you should share this *now* and not, I don't know, when the shit happened?" Evan huffs at Rich as he hastily scans his surroundings, his massive head whipping around fast enough that you could almost feel the breeze from it.

"I didn't know what it was at that point. Then after we got attacked, I just assumed it was the Meat-zerker stalking us on our way into town, but I don't know for sure. I kinda forgot about it amid getting my ass handed to me by a giant pile of hamburger." Rich's words lacked his usual zest.

"Guess we should keep our eyes open then," Sonya says quietly.

Their focus is split between any possible places for ambush along the way. Cautiously, they enter the mouth of the valley. Its walls stretch higher than they seemed on approach. The sun has set, leaving them standing in the surreal afterglow of their ashen landscape. Rich gathers whatever chunks of wood he can find.

"All right, we need to gather as much burnable material as we can. It's going to get cold fast, and I don't think these burlap sacks are going to do much to stave off hypothermia," Rich says.

Sonya and Evan join in gathering wood. Rich picks out a spot on the south side of the valley and begins building a fire. Evan walks up to him and drops an arm full of small branches and sticks. He leaves to search for more kindling, but Rich stops him.

"Hey, can't you like, grow some wood or something? That would make it a lot easier. We have these abilities, might as well use them for more practical purposes," Rich asks. He is kneeling on the ground, vigorously drilling a stick into a broader piece of wood in an effort to create enough friction to start a fire.

"I think I have a better idea." Evan kneels next to Rich and closes his eyes. A soft rumble starts to reverberate out from where Rich is building a fire. The ash slowly gives way to earth and stone. The rocks begin to crack and spark as they squeeze together. The sparks turn into steam and heat, and a dull glow can be seen from the center. Evan's eyes are closed as he focuses effort to manipulate his element in a new way. With a loud hiss, the atmosphere around the rock sizzles as the temperatures increase drastically. The pile of rocks twitch and grind into themselves until the pressure and friction are great enough to make them liquify into a small puddle of molten lava.

"There. That should help," Evan says with a clear aura of self-satisfaction.

Rich is momentarily shocked by what he saw. He recovers and quickly starts tossing the kindling he had nearby onto the mound of liquid rock.

"Evan, that was pretty fuckin' cool." Rich stares into the fire as it crackles to life. He tosses some larger logs into the growing fire.

Evan smiles and rocks back on his heels. "It almost feels like I gained a new appendage, I guess? This reminds me of learning to ride a bike. At first, you don't think you'll ever get it figured out, but then it just kinda 'clicks,' ya know?" As Evan speaks, a small column of rock raises out of the dirt. It crumbles back to the ground and turns to dust. "I have noticed that it's easier for me to form rocks than it is roots. Maybe it has something to do with the environment?"

"I can see that. With me, it's more like an extension of my sense of touch. I can *feel* with the darkness. I close my eyes and kinda just let it touch me all over." Rich crosses his legs and tilts his head back, then begins rubbing his nipples in a clockwise motion. "Ohhhh, I can feel something. *Wait.* It's going the other way." He tilts his head forward and switches to a counterclockwise direction.

"You're sick in the head," Sonya says while she sits down in the ash. She turns to Evan and pouts. "Evan, can you please make me a chair or something? I don't want to sit in the dust."

"I don't know, *can I?*" Evan pouts back at her.

Sonya moves to throw a pebble at him but is thrown off-balance as a small granite stool raises out of the ground right under her butt. She laughs and throws the pebble anyways. Rich laughs under his breath then stands up and walks away from the fire. The night comes with a quiet serenity that Rich is not used to, but it's welcoming and oddly comforting, like he is back where he belongs.

As Rich meanders around the outskirts of the camp, he reaches back and scratches at the encroaching mania gnawing away at the nape of his neck. He is constantly looking out for any signs of movement. Whatever that thing was, it's still out there, and the uncomfortable feeling in his gut assured him that it was going to show up again. Rich slowly works his way back to the fire. Evan had erected a stone seat for him as well. He pats him on the back as he passes by.

"All right. We should take turns keeping watch. I'll go first. One-hour shifts. Which one of you wants to go next?" Rich says as he eases himself down on the chair Evan had made for him.

"I will," Sonya says as she half raises a hand.

"Good. After barfing my brains out and then having to haul my very heavy ass around, I'm beat!" Evan lies down on the ground next to the fire and sprawls out. He folds his hands under his head and sucks in a deep breath.

"Okay, you guys get some rest. I'll keep an eye out for now." Rich tosses a couple of smaller logs on the fire. He rearranges the coals a bit to help it last longer, then stands back up to start his shift.

Rich examines his darkened surroundings. He decides on a strategic location and climbs the southern ridge that forms one side of the valley. Once he's satisfied with his vantage, he sits on the ground and crosses his legs. Here he is enveloped in night and can focus his senses much more sharply. A small wisp of blackness raises up from the ground around him.

"There you are. I was wondering when you were going to show up again. Can you stay near our friends and just keep an eye on them? I'm not exactly sure if you can see or not, but just do whatever you can to be alert. I'm going to sit here and send some lines out. See if I can't get a bite." The eager cloud of night shudders in response and glides down the hill toward the fire. It settles down in the shadow of a stone chair and fades from sight.

Rich begins to weave his net. Tendrils of dark crimson slither away from his position. They cross over and under one another as they form a large web, extending out from him for hundreds of feet. Once Rich is satisfied, he closes his eyes and centers his consciousness. He has no intention of waking either of his friends. He has a sick feeling that they are going to need their rest.

CHAPTER 21

Rich has sat for hours, his cohorts slumbering blissfully as he dutifully watched over them. Not a single grain of dust had been disturbed all night long. Everything had remained unpleasantly quiet. Even his little pet had not returned since its first appearance. The night sky was lightening far to the east. Soon his web of night would be burned away by the coming dawn. Rich's body desperately aches for rest, but his consciousness will not allow it. A manifested sense of doom still bites and chews at the back of his neck. He thought it nothing more than his nerves keeping him on edge in this new dystopia that they inherited, but the dread of concern is too overwhelming.

As the dawn slowly breaks over the distant horizon, Rich rises from his place among the rocky outcropping and makes his way down the hill to his companions. He is careful to not disturb them from their slumber. He looks down at his watch. They only have six hours until their ride arrives. His tired eyes wander the immediate horizon for any final signs of movement as he shambles toward the still-smoldering fire. His stone chair sits empty. The low burning flames cast a cozy orange glow on it, inviting him to have a seat and rest until their transport arrives.

The breaking dawn rises over the mountains behind him. He can feel the darkness retreating from him. It scurries off into whatever shady crevices it can find. He sits next to the fire and takes a breath. He unbuckles his belt holding his daggers and lays it next to his chair. Evan's enormous feet are laying just to his right. Rich lashes out and slaps the bottoms of Evan's shoes to rouse him from his slumber.

"Hey, man, time to wake up. Morning has arrived. I decided to be a gentleman and let you guys sleep all night long." Rich shakes

Evan's feet once more. The ginger giant snorts as he shivers back to consciousness.

"Night went by without a hitch, man. I'm going to get some shut-eye before our white knight arrives on his golden chariot." Rich leans back in his stone chair and folds his arms. "Hey, buddy, can you grow me a footstool real fast?" Rich chides, but Evan doesn't respond.

"Hello, are you awake yet?" Rich waves a hand overhead, trying to get Evan's attention. His shadow waves back and forth over Evan's face in the process. Rich wears his normal smirk on his face as he continues to attempt to pester his friend. Evan does not react. He just stares past Rich.

"What the fuck, man. Hello!" Rich waves more frantically as he gets more irritated, his shadow flailing across Evan's unblinking eyes.

As he waves his arm, he notices the lack of motion from his shadow. His focus shifts, and he stops moving. His own shadow has grown into one three times his own size. It stretches over and envelopes almost the whole camp. Rich slowly lowers his hand. Evan's expression is now one of fear. He is frozen in place. Rich turns his head slightly over his left shoulder only to see a blur of motion as something hurtles through the air at him.

Rich is sent flying over the fire and lands several yards on the other side of it. His teeth bite into his tongue as his skull bounces off the ground. Blood fills his mouth and bursts forth onto his face and chin. His eyes flutter in their orbit as his brain is jarred from the impact. His vision fades in and out, but his eyes struggle to focus on the threat that now stands among them.

Evan is paralyzed from fear. His eyes are fixed on the visceral nightmare standing at the edge of their camp. Powerful arms nearly drag the ground as it calmly steps closer. With one hand, it reaches down and grabs Evan by the ankle, lifting him up in the air. Evan swings back and forth as he is raised up to eye level with the monster. With just inches between them, Evan can all too clearly make out the rancid details of the new attacker.

The whole being was larger than Evan, perhaps even larger than Gaian. The upper body and head were distinctly human, but the mouth, nose, and jaws had been replaced by that of a bear. Its eyes were solid yellow with black slits staring intently at Evan as he hangs helplessly. Thick strands of saliva hang from its teeth as its jaws open. Evan can feel its hot breath on his neck and face. The stench is that of legend. Evan has never smelled anything as putrid and pungent in his entire life. His gag reflex is tripped, but he manages to choke it back. One hand slaps over his mouth as he makes audible retches.

Evan is dropped to the ground, landing on his neck and shoulders. He flops onto his back without flinching, his eyes still fixated on the intruder in their camp. He can see the entirety of it now. The core and head are the only human parts. Its arms are long, thick, and covered with dark black fur. Muscles bulge so hard against the pelt that it's split in several places revealing red meat that throbbed and writhed below with hands balled into fists the size of Evan's skull. The appendages meet the body at a seam that is poorly patched together. Despite being infused with Erra's wickedness the two skins would not mend, each rejecting the other. Cloudy serous fluid weeps from the approximation, staining the fur and skin on either side of it with a dark yellow crust.

At the waist were human hips and legs, but the normality stopped at the knee. The rest of the way down was the lower portion of a tiger's hind leg but three times as muscular as they should have been. The sutures connecting them to the upper leg were much cleaner than the shoulder. Sharp claws impatiently knead the earth underfoot while the paws shift back and forth as the rest of the being considers its situation.

The maw begins to move as words rough as sandpaper escape past the jagged teeth. "*This* is what Enki recruited? Two scrawny humans and a large infant? The darker one isn't even awake yet!"

"Hohly shit. It tahlks," mumbles Rich from where he landed. He's sitting upright now, his words slurred by a swollen tongue.

"Talk? I do much, much more than talk, Richard. I am specifically created to end the lives of the three of you. If you behave yourselves and don't waste my time, I will make it quick, as a courtesy," the large hybrid being says.

"Okay," Rich says quickly.

"What?" the being replies.

"I said okay, kill me. Just make it fast," Rich says as he stares through the beastman.

"This is, is this some kind of trap? Are you toying with me?" The confidence drains from its eyes as it struggles to process thoughts into words.

"Do they not have sarcasm in the future? Is that a skill that was lost when the world went to shit?" Rich says to Evan, who is too terrified to notice he is being spoken to. "All right, handsome, that's more sarcasm. You know my name. I assume you know his, but what's yours?"

"I do not have one, but I have many titles. We are referred to as The Nameless Ones. I am The Terrifier. The Ender of Men. The—" the being is cut off by Rich.

"You can add pontificate to the list of shit you do. Maybe something involving boring people to death as well. You should know that we aren't just normal folks. We have some pretty unique powers. Evan can control the very earth you stand on. I manipulate darkness to my will, and Sonya, well, she's really, *really* fast." Rich points to where her body was laying.

The Nameless One turns to find that Sonya's bedding is empty. He looks back at Rich and smiles. His bear snout curls its lips and bears long off-white fangs. "I had hoped it would go this way. I must prove myself to The Father." With an upward wave of its huge arm, the fire in the middle of the camp erupts into a massive pillar of white-hot flame shooting stories high in the air.

The heat is so intense Rich has to scramble across the ground to escape it. The stench of scorched wool fills his nose and mouth. He turns to look at the fire once outside the radiant heat. The column is gently rocking back and forth. The tip of the flame engorges as it takes on a shape. First eyes and a long wide jaw form, the jaw opens to reveal two long fangs and forked tongue. Large flares of fire fan out from just behind the head. Rich is on his feet now, at the base of a flaming cobra that is staring directly at him.

"I am known by one other title, human! The cremator of flesh!" The Nameless One lifts his hands in the air and casts them forward. The pillar of flame rears up and then crashes down at Rich.

Rich's instinct is to disappear into darkness, but between the rising sun and the fire snake, there is no shadow to leap into. He dashes left, trying to outrun his doom as it swiftly hurtles toward him. His legs are still weak from the blow to the head, and he stumbles to the ground landing hard on his chest. He rolls over to see the eyes of the serpent swell as it crashes down on him. The heat grows intense and scalds his face. The air is too hot to even breathe. He crawls backward, desperately trying to escape the flame.

With a torrential wind that brings a cloud of soot and ash, Sonya appears next to Rich, slowing only enough to scoop him up before vanishing again. The cloud of dirt is thick with particulates. The fire begins to wither from the lack of oxygen, shrinking down abruptly to nothing more than glowing embers.

"Impressive! It seems your time spent training with those cowards wasn't wasted after all. You've learned some, but I doubt it will be enough. You've spent just over a month training whereas I have been honing my skills for almost a decade! Nothing but rigorous training all day long for my entire existence just so I could come hunt you down!" The Nameless One walks to the fire and reaches his hand into the glowing embers. Flames spread over it and climb to his wrist. He rips his limb from the embers, pulling with it a massive sword. The hilt is a ghostly blue that grows more vibrant as it is revealed from the fire, ending in an orange tip. "Now show yourself so that we may end this!" he shouts as he swings the blade deftly through the thick haze of floating ash.

Sonya sets Rich down just outside the camp on the far side of a large rock. She turns her gaze toward the glowing cloud where their nameless foe waits for her. Sword in hand, she steps toward it. Rich grabs her wrist before she can leave, she turns to look at him.

"Sony, fuck 'im up," Rich whispers as he flashes her a rough smile.

Sonya flashes her teeth as she grins back at her friend. The thrill of battle coursing through her veins. She speeds away, zigzagging through the haze as she approaches the fire wielder. She sees his sword glowing in the cloud and focuses in on it. Ral's words during training flashback to her mind.

Speed and distraction. Strike like lightning. Never in the same place twice!

Sonya dashes past and lands a blow to its shoulder. She can feel the resistance of flesh against steel through the handle of her sword. The Nameless One howls with rage and spins around to attack, but by the time, his weapon hit the earth she was already yards away. Sonya is already arcing around to make another pass, this time on the front of him. Her blade finds its target and gashes him deeply in the outer thigh. He flails with anger and begins lashing about wildly. His sword splits the air as it sparks and cracks against the ground and rocks.

The Nameless One is driven further into rage. He stomps his way to the nearly extinguished fire, raises the fire sword overhead, and spins it around and around. The flame of the sword begins to streak through the air, creating a cyclone of fire that grows quickly. With a single violent burst, it erupts outwards, blowing away all the ash that was hanging in the air. He stands still in the center of the campground. The air around him clear and devoid of all obstruction. Sonya notices that Evan is missing from the scene.

"Enough of your deceit. Face me." The Nameless One's demeanor is steady and calm. His eyes are closed, his sword hangs low at his side.

Sonya approaches with measured caution. Her weapon at the ready. She raises her sword into a defensive posture. The hilt down to her right with the sword across her body. The flat of the blade angled slightly toward her opponent.

"I'm ready," Sonya states, her words cast in steady confidence.

The Nameless One does not reply. In the blink of an eye, he is airborne, leaping forth from the ground like a bird taking flight. Sonya watches him as he crashes down on her, flaming sword held high above his head. With raw brute force, he swings the weapon down. Just before he makes landfall, Sonya dashes left, using her mobility to her advantage. With a blast of fire, The Nameless One impacts the earth, the dirt under him melting from the heat. The impact from his attack sends a shock wave through her body that catches her by surprise, but she does not lose balance. Sonya sees the pause in his attack and launches her own. She thrusts her blade into his flank but misses her mark. With agility and grace that seems bizarre for his massive shape, The Nameless One leaps over his own sword, twirling his body in midair and away from her strike. He lands on his feet and gives his blade a flourish as Sonya recovers from her attack.

She presses forward unrelentingly. Her sword flies through the air in arcs so swift that they are nearly invisible. The Nameless One is still able to parry almost every attack. Sonya can feel her anger growing as she struggles to land a blow. She increases her speed and continues to rain down upon him. A few of her strikes begin to find their mark. She can see deep cuts opening up on his chest and arms from her unyielding advance. The Nameless One grabs the hilt of his weapon with both hands, and with a swiftness that nearly matches her own, he splits his single weapon in two. His twin swords dance and flash as he catches her attacks. He menacingly grins at Sonya then changes the direction of the battle. He pushes hard at her and begins his own assault. His strikes come at her quickly with surgical precision, gaining in speed with every strike. As Sonya struggles to find a strategy, she can hear Ral from the back of her mind again.

The eyes betray us. We look where we intend to strike.

Hearing this refreshes her spirit. She watches the pupils of her foe. They are just barely moving, but it's enough to use against him! She rebuilds her defense as he presses his attack. His weapons are no longer getting the better of her. His pattern is becoming much more evident. She measures her timing and looks for an opportunity to strike back. The Nameless One raises his elbow just enough to create an opening and Sonya takes it. She dashes into him, pulling her blade close to her body so that she may gash his torso open. She nears her target and prepares to swing when his massive knee comes crashing up into her diaphragm and sends her flying backward. She lands on her rear and tumbles across the ground but she follows through with the momentum and regains her feet.

"You are far too predictable, girl. How do you hope to beat me?" The Nameless One slams both weapons together, reforming into one massive great sword, then charges at her. His blade hisses through the air as it strikes down on Sonya again and again.

She parries his attacks with a consistent rhythm, timing her movement with his own. He presses hard and forces her to take a step back. As soon as her right foot lifts off the ground, her foe drops to a knee and kicks her left leg out from under her. Sonya falls backward toward the earth, but just before making contact, she catches herself on a cushion of air and slides away several feet before righting herself. She responds to his attack with one of her own. She dashes left and right moving so quick that her form is but a blur. She moves in on her target and lunges blade held high at him. The Nameless One casually lifts his arm to block her sword but is left wanting as Sonya's image disappears at the last moment. She reappears behind him and plunges her weapon through the outside of his thigh. She can feel the spine of the blade scraping along his femur as she drives her weapon home. Before she can retract, she is caught in the side with a burning pommel.

She is struck hard in the flank. The pain is intense as her ribs snap from the blow. The ache turns to burning as the fire of his weapon begins to sear her flesh. Her instincts make her leap away from the danger, but from haste, her weapon is left lodged in the leg of her enemy. Her eyes glaze over with regret as the severity of her mistake registers in her mind. The Nameless One laughs at her as he gingerly removes the blade from his leg as one might pluck a thorn from their finger. The same thick black blood that flows within the Lurkers seeps from either end of his wound.

"This is so pathetic! I was almost expecting you to put up a decent fight, *almost*! You were the one I had thought to be the worthiest out of all three, but sadly, you are just a disappointment." The Nameless One mocks her as he steps closer, fire blade in one hand and Sonya's in the other. "I'm going to kill you with your own weapon. How does that sound, eh?"

He is standing over her with her own sword pointing down at her chest. He steps on her leg, pinning her down. The weapon is slowly raised over his head as he prepares to strike, the smile growing ever wider on his face. Teeth bared and eyes gleaming with excitement he thrusts the blade down at her. The steel crashes down. Sonya closes her eyes against the impending strike. As The Nameless One moves in for his kill, a plume of dust clouds the air between Sonya and her assailant. The Nameless One is sent cartwheeling into the background, landing hard on the dirt some feet away. Standing over Sonya is a foreboding monolith cast in stone, its fists raised in defense of its friend.

Out of instinctual reaction, Evan had hidden his body right after The Nameless One conjured its flaming serpent. His entire form was swallowed and embraced by the earth herself. He laid mere inches under the dirt as Sonya clashed with their new foe. It wasn't until he heard Sonya's demise drawing near that he was compelled to act. His love for his friend outweighing his own cowardice, he burst back into the fight. He caught The Nameless One hard in the chest with a granite-coated fist.

The stone had shattered from the impact. Evan's bare fist is slowly encased in new material as he stands guard over his friend. The Nameless One rises to his feet. His face reflects a deep rage so intense that flames begin to leap from the ground he stands on. They continue to burn higher until his entire body is engulfed. The heat emanating from his body melts the earth around him, rendering it into shiny molten glass. The fur on his arms and legs burns away as his skin cracks from the heat, exposing the muscle below.

"FINALLY DECIDED TO MEET YOUR DOOM, DID YOU?" The Nameless One rushes at Evan, fire trailing from him.

Evan yells as he hurls himself at his enemy, his feet slamming the ground as he accelerates at his foe. The two giants meet with a thunderous collision. The combination of rock and fire meeting violently lets out a crack so loud Sonya is forced to cover her ears. Evan is by far the smaller of the two, but his size is irrelevant. He fights with unbridled hatred. His only desire is to destroy the thing that is intended to hurt Sonya. The Nameless One swings its sword down on Evan, but the fire has no effect on his hardened outer layer. With a flash of light, the sword explodes into wisps of flame that vanish into the air. As his foe hesitates from the shock of losing his weapon, Evan launches a volley of massive punches aimed at its torso. His fists land like cannonballs into the flesh of their target.

The Nameless One wraps its huge arms around Evan and squeezes him tight, pinning his arms against his sides. Evan's granite skin starts to crack from the pressure. He can feel his body about to break as stars fill his eyes. He can't breathe. He can't even move. He tries to think and tries to figure out some way to escape. His hands are trapped between the two of them. Evan desperately attempts to turn his wrist around. He can feel the stomach of The Nameless One on the palm of his hand. He uses his last drops of remaining strength to coat his fingers in razor-sharp granite, then sinks all five of his digits into the tissue of his aggressor.

The air is filled with a terrible yowl as Evan rips a fistful of meat from the side of The Nameless One. He shrieks with anger and throws Evan behind him. He lifts a hand and focuses a ball of flame into the palm then slams it into his gaping wound. The pain is so intense that he drops to his knees. Evan does not give him a moment of respite. He leaps onto the back of The Nameless One, wraps his legs around his waist, and begins hammering a stony fist into the back of its skull. With every hit, flesh is peeled back, exposing shiny white cranium. A salvo of elbows repeatedly slams into Evan's left side, weakening his hold on his opponent. The Nameless One catches Evan's right hand and swings him over its shoulder onto the dirt in front of him. A charred tiger paw lands on Evan's neck and begins digging its claws into the stone as his right arm is being twisted away from his body.

Evan grabs the claw on his throat and shifts it enough to slide out from under it, launching himself forward and to the right, freeing up the hold placed on his shoulder allowing Evan to get one foot under himself. The Nameless One maintains control of Evan's wrist, however. He swings a leg over Evan's arm and rolls under it, placing his legs on Evan's chest and leveraging his mass to flip Evan onto his back. Once they are in the dirt, Evan's elbow is forced backward against his opponent's knee. The Nameless One wrenches backward with all its might, trying to snap Evan's arm in half. Evan frantically tries to pry himself loose from the hold, but The Nameless One is just too large to manipulate.

Evan's chest clenches tight in fear as he loses control of his emo tions. He can feel the claws of his foe digging into him. His granite armor weakens as his focus fades. The chilled fangs of fear plunge into his chest once again. He looks off to the side and sees Sonya still lying on the ground, holding her chest and side. She locks eyes with him and reflected in her gaze is the same fear that is burrowing into his heart. He knows that as soon as he loses this fight that she will be next to die. As The Nameless One overpowers him, terror snaps at the nape of Evan's neck.

From behind his rock where Sonya had left him, Rich has regained his strength enough to stand. He looks toward the battleground and sees Sonya lying on the ground, writhing in pain while she clutches her side. He shifts his gaze to the two gigantic combatants locked in an intense battle. He sees Evan attempt to roll out from under the foot of The Nameless One only to be flipped hard onto his back as his arm is wrapped up and pinned against the body of his enemy. Rich can see Evan is in trouble. His hands drop to his hips hoping to find his daggers but instead grasp nothing but cloth. He frantically tries to recall where he had left them. His eyes dart to the chair he was in before getting slung across the camp. There they are, still wrapped in the belt as he left them. Rich sprints toward them, leaping over Sonya and sliding on his knees across the dirt as he snatches them up. He rips them from their sheaths and tosses their belt down as he launches himself recklessly to the aid of his friend. Both of his daggers slam down into the chest of The Nameless One. He buries them hilt deep into meat and drags them toward himself as the flames engulfing his target catch his own clothes on fire.

The Nameless One frees a hand and casually swats Rich away as though he were but an irritating bug. He plucks the daggers from his chest and tosses them away from Rich.

"Just you wait, darkcaster. I'm going to break your limbs and make you watch as I have my way with the negress!" The Nameless One spits on the ground as he points it at Rich.

Evan can't see what transpired, but he knows that Rich came to his defense. He feels that the grip on his arm has faltered and takes the chance to make his move. Evan slams his free hand into the earth and draws from it a long spike of solid rock. He slams the tip into the knee of The Nameless One and twists it back and forth, its jagged edges grinding meat and bone as turns. The pain comes as such a surprise that the grip on Evan's wrist is loosened just for a moment, a moment that Evan was hoping for. He rips his hand free and wraps both arms around the legs on his chest then rolls away, forcing The Nameless One onto his stomach with Evan lying on top of his lower back. Evan focuses on the leg he wounded and grabs it just below the knee. A sickening crack fills the air as Evan twists the limb free from its joint.

The Nameless One lets slip a very human cry and tries to flee from Evan but only succeeds in fully severing its dislocated leg. He crawls away on all three remaining appendages but doesn't make it far. Evan takes one large step and flings himself into the air above his victim. A large row of sharp spikes grows from the knuckles of Evan's fists as he falls to the ground, landing a massive blow into the spine of The Nameless One. The remaining intact leg goes limp as the nerves that supply it with signal are destroyed and with it goes the fire that once covered his body.

With unrelenting force, Evan pushes his attack. He begins savagely pummeling anything that gets in the way. His boulder encased hands slam into the meaty parts of his foe, splitting flesh and cracking bone with every meteoric impact. The Nameless One rolls onto its back in an attempt to defend itself, but its efforts are futile. Fists rain down and strike like lightning as the storm within Evan rages on out of control. One heavy blow catches the left elbow of The Nameless One, pulverizing the joint, the rest of the arm falls limp.

Evan seizes the damaged arm and looses it from its place. Black blood sprays across his face as he throws the limb away. The Nameless One grabs at Evan with his functioning arm, but it is easily cast aside. Huge fists slam down, hit after hit after hit caves in the bear maw attached to the face of The Nameless One. Blood and spittle spew from the rapidly forming cavity. The functioning arm no longer defends the body—it lays still on the earth next to its owner. Evan pauses for a moment and assess his enemy. The Nameless One is motionless on the ground. The only movement is the slow raising and lowering of his chest as he breathes.

Evan rises to his feet. He places his left hand on the forehead of The Nameless One and grips it tightly, raising it off the ground and sitting the body upright. The remaining granite covering his body begins to converge on his right hand. It scrapes and grinds over itself as it takes shape. Soon a wide blade presses firmly into the throat of The Nameless One, just below his chin. His eyes open and look at Evan. Through the gory mess slip his last words.

"You think you ended me? You're only sending me right back to his arms! Fools! You can't stop us. We are infinite. I will soon be the one looking down on you as I—" His sentence was left hanging in the air as Evan ran his blade through his neck. The eyes of The Nameless One stay fixed on Evan until he wrenches his sword hand upward, catapulting the severed head of his enemy into the air. It lands in the dirt and rolls to a stop near Rich, who is desperately trying to slap out the smoldering embers sticking to his clothes.

Evan is immediately by Sonya's side. He holds her in his arms, cradling her head with one massive hand. She winces in pain as he moves her, but the grimace turns to a smile as her eyes open up.

"Hey…you kicked…his butt…" Sonya struggles with her words, the damaged ribs taking her breath away.

"It's okay. Don't talk. You're all beat up, Sony. You really held your own against him! I was shocked to see you move like that. Well, I couldn't actually see you for most of it since I was hiding underground." Evan chuckles nervously as he holds her against his chest.

Rich hobbles over toward them and hands her one of Vitra's potions. "Sounds like we should have a toast, eh? Here, Sony. Take one of mine." Rich scrapes the wax off the top and pulls the cork. A strong scent of wildflowers and pitch fills the air around them.

Sonya gently grips the small bottle in her fingertips and downs it with ease. "This one isn't half bad. Kinda sweet and smoky," she says as the flavor lingers on her tongue. "Didn't Vitra say we should sleep when we take this one? Cuz I feel like I need a nap after all that." Sonya's index finger points toward the corpse of The Nameless One and spins little circles in the air.

"Want me to lay you down?" Evan asks.

"No. I'm fine right here," Sonya replies as she nestles her head into her friend.

Rich decides to walk away and busy himself elsewhere as the other two recover from their ordeal. He searches out the packs and all their weapons and organizes everything together along one side of the fire. He casts an eye back toward his friends as he goes, but all he can see is Evan's bulk with Sonya's feet poking out from under his right arm. A prideful smile emerges from his face. He never imagined Evan to be capable of such selfless aggression, but in reality, none of them are the same as they once were.

Once he finishes with his sweep of the camp, he takes a seat next to the dying embers of the fire. Fatigue is on him almost as soon as he hits the bench. His body is tapped out, and his spirit is burning lower than the fire in front of him. He doesn't want to rest, but his body isn't giving him the option. He slides from his chair and attempts to crawl over to the packs to retrieve one of Vitra's potions, but his body fails him, giving in to the exhaustion. He falls asleep in the dust as the last of his adrenaline leaves his system.

Sonya is awakened by the forcing of wind across her face. Her eyes flutter as she comes to. She inhales deeply but flinches, expecting to feel the stab of pain from her injury, but surprisingly, she is only slightly tender now. She takes a moment to collect herself and let her senses find their bearings. The wind that woke her is intensifying and a dull hum can be heard echoing in the small valley. The dust and ash around them whirl about. She wrestles herself loose from Evan's arms and stands up. Her motion is disturbing enough to rouse him from his slumber.

"Sonya, what's going on?" he asks as the sleep wears off.

"Something's coming. The wind is going crazy!" With her words comes an intense flurry of soot and dust.

The low tone is growing from a far-off drone to a full roar coming down on them from the sky. Sonya covers her eyes as she attempts to seek out the source of the sound. The clouds above them twist and spiral like mad as a shape begins to manifest from them.

A long gray fuselage with forward-pushing angular wings begins to emerge from the clouds. Two large turbines chop and swirl the air as the craft lowers itself down on the trio. Two more small engines are attached to the tail of the craft. Evan is on his feet next to Sonya, both covering their ears as the monotone roar from the engines overtakes them. Rich is still passed out on the ground totally unresponsive to the events happening around them. The craft touches down a safe distance from their camp. Sonya immediately recognizes what's before her. This ship is the same as the one they saw in Vernonia, just fully operational.

The engines spin down and bring the roar to a fraction of what it was. The side of the craft pops out and then slides toward the tail. Three steps drop from under the body, reaching down to the dirt. From the dark interior of the ship comes the shape of a man. Broad shoulders and a sharp V taper torso make up the silhouette. He has stocky legs and a long rust-red beard. The man's boots clunk down on the ship's step ladder, pausing at the last one. His muscular arm holds the wall of his craft as he leans out from it. In a gruff accent that's a step away from Scottish, he shouts to them.

"Well, wat the fook are you sohrry bastards loohkin'at? Get yer arses on the boaht! Huhray oop!" the man exclaims.

Evan looks to Sonya for advice, but she is already moving. She grabs all the packs and weapons from the ground. "Grab Rich and come on!" she shouts back to him.

Evan's feet move faster than his brain tells them to, and he trips over himself briefly before correcting his stride. With one hand, he scoops Rich off the ground while chasing after Sonya. He reaches the hatch of the craft and carefully climbs in, holding Rich like a football in one arm. Sonya is already in one of the many seats that line the inside of the ship, their goods set on the ground next to her. Evan looks at the available seating and quickly realizes that none of it will accommodate him. He sets Rich in a chair then secures the restraints around him. Rich snores loudly as his head falls to his chest. The surly pilot is hammering and cursing at the instrument panel as he prepares for takeoff.

"Gawd damn pihle of geriatric crahp! Bloody things' older than me gran that tahught me how to fly it! Yoo'all had behtter get buh-ckled in. 'Is'll nay be an easy trip!" The pilot looks back at them and smiles. "M'name is Cephus Johnstone! Tis'a damned fihne pleasure to mahke yoor acquahintances! Now please hold the'fook on!" Cephus pauses as he gets a look at Evan. "Eh'yoo, big boy, I rehckon yoo'r fook'd. Hold on tight!"

Evan shoots Sonya a very uneasy look as he reaches out for whatever he can to brace himself on. The sound that blasts from the engines is as concerning as it is deafening, but they do begin to rise off the ground, and soon they are airborne. The engines on the sides of the craft tilt forward to propel them through the air. The gauges and lights above Cephus flicker and flash like a Christmas tree. Alarms and buzzers are going off as they ascend into the clouds.

"Excuse me, Cephus, what do all those alarms mean? Is that dangerous?" Evan asks.

"The only dangherous thing on this boaht is *me*. Now kindly shut the fook up so I cahn concentrahte!" Cephus replies, his gruff accent only adding to the severity of his tone.

Evan looks back to Sonya. She shakes her head as she tightens the straps on her seat. Evan double-checks that Rich is secure then grabs a cargo net hanging from the ceiling and wraps it around his fist several times while clinging to a large structural beam with the other.

"Ooo-kay! Here we go!" Cephus shouts over the roar of the engines. The spool of the turbines becomes so intense that Evan can feel it reverberating through him.

The dilapidated ship blasts its way through the cloud bank at an almost vertical departure angle. The trios gear slides toward the rear of the ship. Sonya tries to grab it at the last moment, but it slips out of her grasp. It all slams into the tail of the craft with a bang. Sonya recoils with horror. She knows that something had to have been broken from that impact. The craft careens higher and higher into the air. The few portholes in the fuselage abruptly change from thick gray to a bright blue. They have breached the clouds that hang over the earth and are now soaring flatly above them. The windows in the cockpit give Evan a clear view of the gorgeous display—dark gray clouds just below them with clear blue skies as far as he can see. The sun is shining brightly just to their left as they gracefully soar over the clouds. An intercom clicks on so their pilot can make his announcement.

"Laddies and lasses, I am yoor captain today, one Cephus Jophnstone! If yoo look to yer port side, tha'means left fer'all ye land lubbers, yoo cahn see the suhn. Frohm the bow of the vessel. yoo should be'ahble to see the AHR Salvation! She'll be yoor new home for the nehxt little while!" Cephus clicks off the speaker and picks up a radio mic. He speaks into it, but his words can't be made out over the drone of the engines. Evan looks on with a sense of intrigue as the massive aerial structure fills up the ever-approaching horizon.

A pair of red eyes look on from their shadowy corner in the rear of the craft, shifting about the cabin as they examine the occupants. The eyes gaze out past the pilot toward the floating fortress in front of them, their gaze briefly hardening into a fierce stare before closing as they silently fade away.

Hundreds of miles away, Erra opens his eyes and smiles, his gentle laughter growing more menacing as it echoes through the halls. He has been waiting a very long time to meet his extended family. He rises from his place, gathering his cloak and walking stick in one hand as he heads for the door. He passes by two of his grotesque personal guard posted outside the room, keeping watch over their master as he conducted his business.

"What a lovely day. Let us begin preparations. We have work to do if we wish to welcome our new friends properly," Erra says as he walks by.

"Right away, my lord," the soldier replies, hurrying off ahead of Erra.

Shortly thereafter, a deep bugle can be heard resonating through the corridors and courtyards of Erra's domain. Outside the walls, the deafening stampede of an entire army rushing to their posts quickly drones out the sound of the bugle. Erra's smile is still proudly displayed on his face as he makes his way down the hall. He hums a tune as he gleefully saunters onward, his thoughts immediately focused on the next tasks at hand. "This is so exciting. I can't wait to welcome them home," he whispers, throwing his cloak over his shoulder. "What a lovely day indeed."

ABOUT THE AUTHOR

Ryan Sisco was born in Tillamook, Oregon. The majority of his youth was spent terrorizing the Oregon Coast. In a bid to seek his destiny, Ryan left the soggy town of Tillamook to find riches and romance. After several failed attempts at the former, he gave up entirely and married a beautiful woman with a degree and the uncanny ability to tolerate him. He now shares his wife's home with four children, three dogs, and one parakeet.

www.ingramcontent.com/pod-product-compliance
Lightning Source LLC
Chambersburg PA
CBHW021546310726
48972CB00003B/700